# NEVER
## TRY TO
# CATCH
### A
# FALLING
# KNIFE

# NEVER
## TRY TO
# CATCH
## A
# FALLING
# KNIFE

*A Lizzie Crane Mystery*

## Skye Alexander

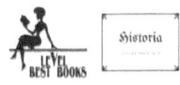

First published by Level Best Books/Historia 2021

Copyright © 2021 by Skye Alexander

This novel is entirely a work of fiction. The names, characters and incidents portrayed in it are the work of the author's imagination. Any resemblance to actual persons, living or dead, events or localities is entirely coincidental.

Skye Alexander asserts the moral right to be identified as the author of this work.

First edition

ISBN: 978-1-68512-020-7

Cover art by Level Best Designs

This book was professionally typeset on Reedsy.
Find out more at reedsy.com

*To my writing students, who help me stay focused on my purpose: to write well and inspire others to do the same. May you enjoy the process and be fearless in expressing your truth.*

# Endoresements for Never Try to Catch a Falling Knife

"A delightful mix of mystery, romance, and the Roaring Twenties set against the background of the idle rich of coastal New England during Prohibition. In actress and singer Lizzie Crane, Alexander has created a refreshing heroine, whose charm and keen understanding of human nature make her an amateur sleuth to watch. Highly recommended." —Paula Munier, *USA Today* bestselling author of the Mercy Carr series

In *Never Try to Catch a Falling Knife*, the first Lizzie Crane mystery, Skye Alexander entertains with this intriguing Prohibition-era story set among the wealthy on the Massachusetts coast. Entertainer Lizzie Crane is a forthright amateur sleuth with dreams of snagging a rich man–but only on her own terms. Alexander brings the period to life with a twisting tale of murder and desperation that will satisfy any fan of historical mystery. —Edith Maxwell, Agatha-winning author of the Quaker Midwife Mysteries

"Alexander's protagonist, Lizzie Crane, is a ball of fire. You'll love her talent, her courage, and her clothes, as she takes on the gentry to solve a murder they'd rather stayed hidden." —Kate Flora, award-winning author of *A World of Deceit*

"An intricate tale of murder in the rarefied world of Boston's North Shore elite." —Susan Oleksiw, author of *Below the Tree Line*

# Chapter One

August 1925, Ipswich, Massachusetts

*"I always had the idea that money must be a pretty good thing."*

*— O'Henry, While the Auto Waits*

On a sheet-draped table, Henry Ives lay as still as the corpse he was pretending to be. Melody bent over him, the morning sun shining on her golden curls as she removed a chalice from his hand.

" 'What's here?' " she asked. " 'A cup, closed in my true love's hand? Poison, I see, hath been his timeless end.' "

From the last row of stone benches, Lizzie called to her, "Louder, Melody. Can't hear you back here."

While she paced the outermost edges of the Wingate estate's outdoor amphitheater, Lizzie imagined how the stage would look at night, shrouded by darkness, with only a lantern under the table to give the supposed crypt an eerie glow. Her head still throbbed from too many martinis last night, but at least her stomach had finally calmed down. She'd skipped breakfast, and now looked forward to lunch.

As Melody began again, two women and an adolescent girl strolled across the lush green lawn from the Winslows' mansion toward the stage. The older woman wore a low-waisted frock of pale gray silk and shielded herself from the sun with a matching parasol. The younger one, taller and plumper, lagged a few paces behind, while the girl, dressed in a blue sailor costume, darted ahead. When they reached the stage the three stopped and looked up at the actors.

Lizzie maneuvered between the benches toward the trio. Her long-time friend and colleague emerged from the rear of the stage and hurried down the steps to greet them.

"Good morning, ladies." He removed his cap and bowed, revealing the bald spot she knew he was sensitive about. "I'm Sidney Somerset of The Troubadours from New York City. Do I have the pleasure of meeting our hostess, Mrs. Zachary Winslow?"

"Good morning, Mr. Somerset. Yes, I'm Catherine Winslow and these are my daughters, Florence and Virginia. Welcome to Wingate."

"Thank you for inviting us to your home to mark your daughter's engagement. This is a great honor. May I ask, is this the betrothed young lady for whom my colleagues and I will be performing?"

Mrs. Winslow turned to the elder of her daughters. "Yes, Florence is engaged to marry the Russian Count Nikolay Mihail Leonid Ivanovich. It is my hope that together we can provide an enjoyable celebration for her and her fiancé this coming week."

Lizzie scurried up beside him and Sidney introduced her. "This lovely lady is my esteemed colleague, actress and chanteuse Elizabeth Crane."

Although the diminutive Mrs. Winslow's blond head barely reached Lizzie's shoulder, the woman's erect carriage and proprietary air made her seem larger than she was. Her aristocratic face registered disapproval as she appraised Lizzie's trousers.

"How do you do?" she asked.

"Quite well, thank you," Lizzie answered. "I'm pleased to make your acquaintance, Mrs. Winslow. And your daughters'. Like my colleague, I wish to thank you for giving us the opportunity to perform for your family and guests this week. I assure you that we'll do our utmost to make this a most enjoyable experience for everyone."

"I trust you've settled in comfortably?"

"Yes, indeed," Sidney answered. "We appreciate your hospitality."

The girl tugged at her mother's sleeve. "Mummy, we're going to see the play, aren't we?"

"Don't interrupt, Ginny."

"We're practicing a scene from *Romeo and Juliet*," Sidney said. "Would you and your daughters care to watch?"

"Yes, we would," Mrs. Winslow said.

Throughout the introductions, Melody and Henry had remained mute and practically motionless on stage. As the Winslow females seated themselves on the front bench, Henry sat up, swung his long legs over the edge of the table, and turned to face the trio. The older daughter, Florence, gasped.

"Playing Juliet is Melody Fitzgerald, aptly named for the enchantingly melodious music she coaxes from her flute," Sidney said as Melody curtsied. "And Henry Ives, who's also a magnificent saxophonist, is our Romeo."

Lizzie noticed Catherine Winslow stiffen. Florence clamped her hand over her mouth as if to stifle a cry, but young Ginny clapped her hands in anticipation.

"Places. Melody, begin again, please," Lizzie directed.

Henry lay back down on the table.

" 'What's here?' " Melody said. " 'A cup, closed in my true love's hand?

Poison, I see, hath been his timeless end:

O churl! drunk all, and left no friendly drop

To help me after? I will kiss thy lips;

Haply some poison yet doth hang on them,

To make die with a restorative.' "

Melody leaned down and kissed Henry lightly on the lips. Florence Winslow, Lizzie noticed, dropped her gaze to her lap.

" 'Thy lips are warm,' " Melody continued.

From off-stage, Sidney called, " 'Lead, boy: which way?' "

" 'Yea, noise? Then I'll be brief. O happy dagger!' "

Melody picked up a trick dagger, which from a distance looked ominously real, and pointed it at her heart. Its rubber blade was designed to slide back into the hilt when pressed against her chest, giving the appearance of sinking into her body.

" 'This is thy sheath,' " she cried, pretending to plunge the knife into her heart. " 'There rust, and let me die.' "

As Melody slumped over Henry's inert form, Ginny clapped her hands again, delighted. Florence continued to stare at her lap.

Catherine Winslow stood up abruptly. "This will never do."

Lizzie and Sidney stared at her blankly, unsure what she meant. Lizzie spoke first. "I beg your pardon?"

"This is entirely too morbid."

"It's one of Shakespeare's most memorable love scenes," Lizzie explained. "It'll have your guests crying crocodile tears."

Mrs. Winslow smoothed her impeccably tailored frock and narrowed her eyes. "I don't want my guests crying. I want them to be happy."

"Mummy, it's so dramatic," Ginny said.

"Nonsense. It's violent and vulgar."

"It's *Shakespeare*," Lizzie insisted.

"Find something more suitable to perform. Something humorous," Mrs. Winslow stated firmly. "Girls."

She turned away sharply, ending the discussion. Florence and Ginny stood obediently and followed their mother across the lawn. Flabbergasted, Lizzie watched them retreat.

"You can get up, Melody," she told her young colleague, who still lay draped across Henry's prone body.

"Jeepers creepers. What do you make of that?" Sidney asked.

Lizzie ran a hand through her dark, fashionably bobbed hair, trying to make light of Mrs. Winslow's unexpected disparagement. "Looks like our hostess has her knickers in a twist."

"That act's the centerpiece of our opening night. What are we going to do now?" he said, exasperated.

"Money doesn't guarantee taste," she shrugged, attempting to appear calm. She didn't want her colleagues to see that Mrs. Winslow's reaction had rattled her. Although Sidney handled the group's bookings and financial matters, Lizzie managed the details of every performance, down to the last dance step and dab of rouge. It was up to her to find a way around this stumbling block. "The lady wants something humorous. She's paying the tab, so we'll give her what she wants. Anybody have any ideas?"

Sidney lit a cigarette in the silver holder that Lizzie considered a trifle too pretentious. "Hmm, something short and sweet and funny..." He snapped his fingers. "How about *Porcelain and Pink*? It might be good to do something by F. Scott Fitzgerald, considering *The Great Gatsby*'s just come out and it's such a smash."

Lizzie laughed. "If I didn't know better, Sidney, I'd think you just wanted to see me naked in the bathtub."

"My dear, every man in the audience will positively *swoon* imagining you naked in the bathtub."

"Where are we going to get a bathtub?"

Sidney grinned mischievously. "That shouldn't be a problem. I'm sure your 'relative' Richard Crane, the plumbing king, will loan us one."

\* \* \*

When Thomas Appleby, the head cook's son, showed up at the outdoor theater bearing a lunch hamper, the four Troubadours were seated in a circle on the stage, hammering out an impromptu schedule for the coming week.

"Our first performance is tomorrow evening," Lizzie reminded them. "That means we can only include acts we know well enough to do in our sleep."

"And only light, humorous bits, according to our illustrious hostess," Sidney pointed out.

"I vote to include more musical numbers," Melody suggested.

Sidney rolled his eyes. "Ever since you ladies got the vote you think that's the way to resolve every matter."

"I vote to break for lunch," Henry said.

The table from *Romeo and Juliet*'s vetoed crypt scene still sat center stage. Sidney directed young Thomas to unpack the wicker picnic basket he'd brought on it. The gangly youth set out a whole roasted chicken, a ceramic

5

pot of Boston baked beans, a loaf of fresh brown bread, an array of salad greens from the estate gardens, and a pineapple upside-down cake. Lizzie watched Sidney dig into the basket hoping to find a bottle stashed at the bottom, but he came up empty-handed.

"Ah, Thomas, m'lad, you've brought us a sumptuous feast." Sidney ruffled the boy's hair. "My compliments to your mother."

Thomas blushed. "Sir, you people are all the talk at the big house."

"Is that so?" Lizzie asked. "What are they saying?"

"That a lady stabbed herself with a knife, and it upset Mrs. Winslow. The missus is quite beside herself."

Laughing, Lizzie said, "Thomas, Thomas. It's all theater. Stage illusion. Make believe." She waved Melody over and stood behind the blond actress with her hands on her young friend's shoulders. "See, here she is. The lady in question, very much alive and well. Now you can go back and tell everyone that it's all copacetic."

Thomas shifted his weight self-consciously from one huge foot to the other. He looked as if he'd seen a ghost. Confused, he finally said to Melody, "I'm glad you're not dead, ma'am."

Melody giggled. "So am I."

"Say, Thomas, would you like to come and watch a rehearsal, you know, before the real performance?" Sidney asked.

The boy's eyes brightened. "Oh, yes, sir, I mean, if it's not too much trouble. And if my mom lets me. I'm wild for the theater."

"Come by a little early with tomorrow's lunch, and you can watch us," Sidney suggested.

"Yes, sir." Thomas started down the steps that curved from the stage to the verdant lawn.

"Thomas," Melody called after the boy, who looked to be only a few years her junior. "I was wondering...where did your mother get pineapples for the cake? I thought they grew in Hawaii, but that's a million miles away."

Thomas stared at the young woman who'd escaped death. "I think she got them from a tin, ma'am."

Lizzie collected dishes and cutlery from the kitchen of a building near the stage known as "the gentlemen's quarters." She still felt a bit envious that Henry and Sidney got to stay in this rambling clapboard structure—designed to house the Winslows' single male guests a respectable distance from the young women in the mansion—while she and Melody had to make due with a tiny bedchamber in the maids' quarters.

The two men brought out four chairs and the performers sat down to lunch. Sidney loaded his plate with food, as if he thought this might be his last meal. *No wonder he's developing that belly,* Lizzie surmised. Melody helped herself to a little bit of everything and Lizzie did the same, hoping her stomach had sufficiently recovered by now from last night's indulgence. Henry politely held back until the women had taken all they wanted, before serving himself.

"I do believe you're right, Melody," Lizzie said.

"About what?"

"About adding more musical numbers. Sid, do you think we could move the piano in your quarters out here onto the stage so that you and Melody can do some songs together? It might be fun if you played a few duets."

Sidney paused in the midst of eating a chicken leg. "I don't see why not. We'll solicit Thomas's help. If he can enlist a few other lads, we could probably relocate half of Wingate."

"Hmm, that's not a bad idea…" Lizzie grinned, mentally reviewing the Winslow mansion's lavish furnishings and imagining some of them in her Greenwich Village apartment. "But don't go corrupting the lad, he's barely out of diapers."

They spent the rest of the afternoon rehearsing songs from the Gershwin brothers, Louis Armstrong, and a host of other musicians. Lizzie wanted to sing Ben Bernie's "Sweet Georgia Brown," but Sidney thought it contained sexual innuendoes that Mrs. Winslow might find objectionable.

Waving off his objections, Lizzie said, "She'll never understand the lyrics, but anyone who does will be pos-i-tive-ly entranced."

"Especially if Henry backs you up on his horn," he agreed. "And you wear your low-cut black gown with nothing underneath."

Lizzie raised an eyebrow. *"Really,* Sidney."

"Use it before you lose it, Bearcat," he said with a wink. "You want to win the heart of one of these wealthy gents while we're here, don't you?"

"Right-o. Thanks for the reminder." On a piece of paper she jotted *Find a Sugar Daddy*. "Okay, got it on the docket." But as she tucked the note in her pocket and started humming Marion Harris's "A Good Man Is Hard to Find" she knew she wanted more than just a rich man to take care of her. She longed to be loved. *I suppose that's what all of us really want.*

By the end of the day, they'd revised their original agenda and agreed on an upbeat weeklong program that emphasized music and dance, interspersed with one-act comedic plays. They even convinced Thomas to appropriate and paint a claw-foot bathtub from the stables, where it had lately been used as a watering trough for the horses, and Lizzie agreed to do Fitzgerald's infamous "nude" scene later in the week.

"I'm keeping my bathing costume on, though," she stated adamantly.

"Of course, Bearcat," Sidney said. "It's the idea that entices, not the reality."

# Chapter Two

*"What fun it had been, having an admirer even for that little while. No wonder people liked admirers. They seemed, in some strange way, to make one come alive."*

*— Elizabeth von Arnim, The Enchanted April*

After dinner, Lizzie strolled through a rose garden near the terrace that stretched along the rear of the Winslows' mansion. Both antiques and hybrids bloomed in a riot of colors. She ran her fingertips over their velvety petals. *I wish I had rosebushes in my apartment in New York,* she sighed. *Maybe I could grow one on the fire escape?*

Next, she passed a bronze fountain twice her height depicting a naked nymph riding on the back of a dolphin. As she made her way along a grassy promenade as wide as Fifth Avenue that led from the mansion to the sea, she encountered numerous marble statues of gods and goddesses. *Are they guarding the property or standing on the sidelines watching the show?* she mused. She stopped in front of a likeness of Aphrodite, nude to the waist.

"Wondering whether it's worth taking off the rest of your gown?" Lizzie asked the statue. "My advice is, make the man give you the deed to the property first." She giggled as she touched the tip of the goddess's stone breast. "My bubs are nicer than yours. Maybe I'll get him to give *me* the deed instead."

When she reached the stretch of white sand that edged the estate's private cove, she saw a sailboat anchored offshore. A tall young man with windblown hair and suntanned arms was pulling a rowboat onto the beach. His white trousers, rolled up to his knees, revealed muscular calves. Intent on his task, he didn't notice her watching him until he'd dragged the dingy a safe distance from the water and turned it upside down on the sand.

"Ahoy, sailor," she called.

"Oh, hello there."

He straightened and strode toward her barefoot, carrying his shoes in one hand and a paddle in the other. She noticed the bottoms of his trousers were wet, his nose was sunburned, and his light brown hair was streaked with gold.

When he'd come close enough for her to see his jade-green eyes, he asked, "May I help you?"

Lizzie tossed her head and smiled. "Do I appear to be in need of help?"

He laughed and let his eyes roam leisurely from her face to her feet and back up again, unabashedly appraising her. A warm tingling started in her thighs and rose to her belly.

"No, in fact, you appear to be in swell shape." The man laughed again, fine lines winking at the outer corners of his eyes, and Lizzie thought, *he's younger than he looks.*

"I'm Peter Winslow," he said. "May I have the honor of knowing the name of the lady who awaits me?"

"What makes you think I'm waiting for you, Mr. Winslow?"

"Why else would you be here alone on my private beach at the end of the day?"

"Taking in this splendid view, of course." Lizzie stepped forward and extended her hand. "I'm Lizzie Crane from New York City. Your mother hired my colleagues and me to perform for her guests this week to celebrate your sister's engagement."

"Ah yes, I seem to remember hearing your name. Any relation to the Richard Cranes?"

Lizzie imagined Sidney laughing. He often teased her when she pretended to have ties to the industrialist and plumbing magnate who'd built an Italianate mansion a few miles from Wingate—only to have it torn down last year because his wife didn't like it.

"Distantly," she said. *No harm letting him think that, even if there's not the remotest possibility.*

Peter Winslow dropped his shoes and the paddle on the sand, and took her hand. He lifted it to his lips and kissed her fingers. "Welcome to Wingate, Miss Crane."

"My, my…"

Releasing her hand, he asked, "So, you've met Mother?"

"Yes, and your two sisters."

He glanced at the loose-fitting trousers she'd bought in the men's section of Macy's and altered to fit her narrow waist and curved hips. "What did she say about your attire?"

"She didn't have to say anything, her disdain was written on her face. In fact, I'm afraid we've gotten off to rather a bad start. Your mother disapproved of one of the plays we'd planned to give. *Romeo and Juliet.* She considered it too violent."

"Mother disapproves of a great many things. But she's kind to horses and dogs, and she's utterly devoted to our family."

Lizzie glanced over his shoulder at the sloop gently bobbing on the water and asked, "Is that your sailboat?"

"Yes. She's a beauty, isn't she? I named her *Rhiannon* after the Celtic goddess of the wind. Wait 'til you see her with her sheets up. Say, would you like to go for a sail around the bay?"

"Oh, ab-so-lute-ly. I've never been on a sailboat."

"Well, then, we must correct that oversight posthaste."

He grinned, and Lizzie admired his fine, white teeth. *The mark of a rich man,* she thought, remembering the blackened nubs and gapped smiles of the people in the Bronx neighborhood where she'd grown up.

"However, at the moment, Miss Crane, I regret that I must say adieu and leave you to enjoy the sunset. My family and my supper await. The salt air makes one ravenously hungry. Have you eaten?"

11

She nodded. "The head cook has kept my friends and me well-fed since we arrived yesterday, thank you."

"Mrs. Appleby. Good woman." He retrieved his shoes and paddle. "I'll be off then. Don't forget about the sailing."

"I won't, Mr. Winslow. Good evening."

She watched Peter Winslow amble toward the mansion using his paddle as a walking stick, his form gradually blending into the deepening shadows. The tingling in her belly subsided, but her mind whirred with possibilities.

Slowly, the sun sank toward the horizon and finally disappeared into the sea. As the vermillion sky turned steely blue, Lizzie left the beach and headed for the gentleman's quarters to tell Sidney about Peter Winslow. Before she even raised her hand to knock, he opened the door and she realized he'd been observing her.

"I just met the young 'lord of the manor', " she said, brushing past him into the sitting room of the gentlemen guests' quarters.

"Yes, I noticed."

"Were you spying on me?" She pointed to a pair of binoculars on a side table. From here one could see both the beach and the Winslows' mansion. "What a nosy parker you are, Sidney."

He winked at her in a brotherly manner. "Somebody has to watch out for you, Bearcat."

Lizzie glanced at several bottles arrayed on a wet bar situated between the parlor and a gaming room. Despite Prohibition, the liquor sat out in plain view. "Well, are you going to offer me a drink-ski?"

"I was just on the brink-ski. It turns out our quarters are stocked with gin, bourbon, and even a sonnet from the Portuguese. What's your pleasure?"

"Gin, please. Icy cold. Can you baptize it with a hint of vermouth?" She sank into the comforting embrace of a leather sofa and plumped up the pillows.

"Indeed I can." He mixed their drinks, then joined her on the sofa. "Now do tell, what's the young Mr. Winslow like?"

Lizzie sipped her martini leisurely, making him wait. Finally, she said, "You saw him, of course. A pleasing package. Gorgeous as a Greek god.

Well-spoken. Charming too. Fancies himself a cake-eater, I'd say. Well, with all that money and looks, why wouldn't he have all the ladies he wants? But here's the best part—he invited me to go sailing with him. Isn't that the bee's knees?"

"You always were a fast worker, Lizzie."

She narrowed her smoky eyes. A proprietary tone crept into her voice. "Don't get any ideas—he's not your type."

Sidney laughed and lit a cigarette. "They're all my type. Alas, I'm not usually theirs."

The front door swung open and Henry Ives strolled in, his handsome face flushed and his dark hair ruffled by the sea breeze. A few long-legged strides took him across the room to the wet bar. He poured himself a glass of gin and plunked in a couple ice cubes.

"Well, hello to you too, Henry," Lizzie said.

He settled himself in a chair beside the empty fireplace, near enough to converse, but not enough to invite closeness. She waited for him to finish a few sips of his drink and unwind. But after a couple minutes, when he still hadn't spoken to his colleagues, she pressed on.

"I met Peter Winslow today, and saw his boat *Rhiannon* as he calls it." She watched Henry's face for a flicker of interest but observed none. "I believe you said you'd met him and his sister Florence while sailing."

"I did."

"Well, here's the thing, Henry. I need some advice. Peter's invited me to go sailing with him. Other than the Coney Island Ferry, I've never been on a boat. What should I expect? What do high society ladies wear aboard ship?"

He smiled slowly, as if musing about a private joke, and then shook his head. "I can't help you there. My father was a Gloucester fisherman. My grandfather and great-grandfather as well." He paused for her to comprehend the class distinction. "We didn't have time for *recreational* sailing."

"Then how did you come to befriend Florence and Peter Winslow?"

Henry tossed back a good-sized gulp of gin. He rubbed his chin, crossed his long legs, and slumped down in his seat. He appeared to study his shoes—*nicely crafted*, Lizzie noted, *perhaps in one of Zachary Winslow's own mills.*

Just when she had decided he was dodging her question, Henry answered, "I was hired to supply fish and such for a party in Magnolia, south of Gloucester. By accident—or maybe fate—Flo was there when I arrived. We struck up a conversation. She was sweet and shy and not stuffy like the rest of those high society dolls. I liked her immediately. And she liked me."

"What happened?" Lizzie wanted to know. "Did you win her over with your horn?"

Sidney sniggered at her double entendre.

"How bold you are," Henry snapped, but she thought he seemed sad. "That's enough for now."

# Chapter Three

*"One emotion after another crept into her face like objects into a slowly developing picture."*

— *F. Scott Fitzgerald, The Great Gatsby*

After leaving the gentlemen's quarters, Lizzie strolled down to the cove again instead of going back to the stuffy third-floor room she shared with Melody in the servants' quarters of the mansion. Despite the late hour, she didn't feel the least bit sleepy. Her thoughts raced like a hamster in a treadmill—perhaps a walk on the beach would calm her.

The upcoming week of festivities was The Troubadours' most important engagement ever, and she kept tumbling the details over and over in her mind. Ordinarily, they played speakeasies and private parties around New York. Henry's connections to the Winslows, however, had landed them this lucrative opportunity to meet people in high places and take a giant step up in the entertainment world. Although she tried to present an unflappable image, inside she felt giddy with excitement. *Who knows where all this might lead?*

As she reached the cove, her thoughts turned to Peter Winslow: his tousled honey-gold hair, his shapely calves, the easy self-confidence that came with a lifetime of privilege. Stars twinkled overhead. A cool breeze caressed her skin. She unbuckled her shoes and dug her toes into the still-warm sand. Just offshore, she spotted *Rhiannon* rocking peacefully on the moonlit waves, and hoped Peter had been serious about taking her sailing.

How lovely it would be to spend your days leisurely skimming across the sea, free as a bird, with the sun on your shoulders and the salty air in your nostrils. She'd known little leisure and freedom in her lifetime. As a child, Lizzie had helped her mother wash and iron other people's laundry and swept the floor of the barbershop where her father cut hair. At fifteen she'd dropped out of school and left home to seek her fortune. Eleven years later, she was still seeking.

The ebbing tide had left the sand littered with the former homes of myriad sea creatures. In the bright moonlight, she spotted several round white seashells, like silver dollars scattered on the sand, and bent down to pick one up. Its surface was etched with a five-petaled flower. Farther down the beach she found a strange, puffy green shell adorned with lines and spots. To a city girl, the shells seemed as pretty and mysterious as stars. She slipped several into her pocket before starting back toward the mansion. *This is the life I want. Maybe if I play my cards right with Peter Winslow...*

Voices coming from the promenade interrupted her thoughts, but they were too far away for her to hear what they said. A midnight tryst perhaps? She approached quietly, trying not to interrupt. Suddenly the voices stopped. As Lizzie passed the statue of the half-dressed Aphrodite, she saw a shadowy form running across the lawn, but she couldn't make it out or even tell if it was male or female.

She continued on, nodding to statues of Poseidon and Apollo, until she neared the bronze fountain of the nymph riding the dolphin. On the ground beside it lay a dark mound. Perhaps someone had drunk too much and fallen asleep on the damp grass. Curious, she stepped closer.

The man lay on his back, his legs crumpled at an awkward angle, his arms flung out at his sides. A huge, dark stain covered the front of his white shirt. It took Lizzie a few moments to realize what she was looking at. When she did, a high, strangled cry burst from her mouth.

Shaking, she raced to the gentlemen's quarters and pounded on the door. "Sid, come quick!"

Her half-asleep friend opened the door, pulling a maroon robe over his yellow pajamas. "Lizzie, what the hell? This better be good."

"It's Henry. I think he's dead."

"What?" Sidney frowned as if he didn't believe her, as if he couldn't comprehend her words. "Are you drunk? What sort of nonsense is this?"

She grabbed his hand and pulled him after her. "This way, over by the fountain. Hurry!"

He followed her at a trot to where the body lay, bleeding into the soft grass. He knelt and gingerly lifted Henry's wrist, checking for a pulse.

"Is he...?" Lizzie asked.

Sidney nodded. "Afraid so."

"We have to get help," she cried. "I'm going to wake the housekeeper and tell her to call the police."

"Okay, I'll get dressed and meet you at the big house in a few minutes."

Lizzie sprinted toward the mansion and slipped through the servants' entrance. She didn't know where Mrs. Greely, the housekeeper, slept so she wandered down the gallery that ran along the back of the house, calling out until a startled, stiff-backed woman emerged from a room off a back hallway, tying a robe over her nightgown.

"Keep your voice down, do you want to wake the whole house?" the woman said angrily. "Whatever is wrong with you?"

"Mrs. Greely, please telephone the police. Someone has murdered our saxophonist."

"Murdered? Who?"

"Henry Ives, my colleague. He's dead. I just found his body out there." She pointed in the direction of the bronze fountain. "If you don't believe me, go out and look for yourself."

"That won't be necessary."

"Please notify the police. *Now*. The murderer may still be nearby."

"Stay right here," the housekeeper ordered.

Apparently convinced by the horrified expression on Lizzie's face, the bony woman shuffled away to make the phone call, leaving Lizzie standing alone in the shadowy hallway near the kitchen, uncertain what to do next. She took a few deep breaths, trying to calm herself, but her heart kept beating wildly against her ribs.

A few minutes later, Mrs. Greely returned. A stocky man with a fringe of graying hair around his otherwise bald head accompanied her. He snapped on several electric lights.

"I am the head butler, Charles Reardon," he told Lizzie. "I have telephoned the authorities, and I'm now going to inform Mr. Winslow of this unfortunate situation. Remain here, miss. Mr. Winslow and the police will undoubtedly want to speak with you."

Holding himself in an erect manner that to Lizzie looked very formal and self-important, he mounted the curving marble staircase that led to the mansion's second floor. Mrs. Greely remained at her side, as if she feared Lizzie might run off somewhere. Neither servant had offered her a word of condolence, a chair, or other comfort.

"Mrs. Greely, I wonder if I might have a cup of tea to help settle my nerves. This is a frightful shock."

The housekeeper's stern expression softened a bit. "Certainly. I'll make some."

Lizzie followed her down a narrow hallway whose starkness made it seem even farther removed from the elegance of the mansion's social rooms than it actually was. In the enormous kitchen, she sat on a three-legged stool beside a worktable, while Mrs. Greely heated a kettle. She leaned her elbows on the table's zinc surface and rested her chin in her hands. *Who would want to kill Henry?* she asked herself. *Nobody other than the Winslows and the help even knew he was here. This must all be a terrible mistake.*

Mrs. Greely placed two china cups on the table. "Milk or sugar?"

"Sugar, please."

The matron poured their tea and took a seat across the table from Lizzie. With a shaking hand, Lizzie lifted her cup. The two women drank in uncomfortable silence, waiting in an empty kitchen that usually bustled with activity.

Lizzie had nearly finished her second cup of tea when the butler and a tall, striking, middle-aged man entered the room. He wore a handsomely tailored gray suit, crisp white shirt, and silk tie, as if dressed for a day in town. Although his eyes seemed tired, he was freshly shaven and his silver hair was neatly combed.

"I am Zachary Winslow," he said to Lizzie, "and you are?"

She stood and extended her hand. "Elizabeth Crane. I'm a member of The Troubadours, from New York City. Your wife hired us to entertain your guests this week."

"Oh, yes. And the deceased?"

"My colleague, our saxophone player Henry Ives."

Winslow's left eye twitched and his mouth hardened. He cleared his throat. "You're certain he's dead?"

"I found him lying on the ground near the bronze fountain, his shirt soaked with blood. My business partner checked for a pulse and found none."

"What makes you think he was murdered? He could have injured himself."

That idea hadn't occurred to Lizzie. She struggled to imagine how such a thing might have happened.

"Perhaps I should have a look before the police arrive. Would you be kind enough to come with me, Miss Crane?"

The last thing she wanted to do was gaze down again at Henry's gruesome, lifeless body, but Winslow's question sounded more like an order than a request. Leaning on the table for support, she pushed herself up. She felt so shaken and confused that she wondered if she could have jumped to conclusions. Maybe Henry wasn't dead after all; maybe she should check the body one last time to make sure. Maybe his life could still be saved.

"Charles, when the police arrive show them outside," Winslow said.

"Yes, sir." The butler opened a drawer and withdrew a flashlight, which he handed to Winslow.

Lizzie had to hurry to keep up with her host's long strides as they crossed the mansion's back terrace and down the steps to the lawn. Before they reached the fountain, she saw Sidney rushing toward them.

"Mr. Winslow," she said, "may I present my colleague, Sidney Somerset. Sid, this is our host, Mr. Zachary Winslow."

The two men shook hands. "I wish we could've met under better circumstances," Winslow said.

"So do I, sir."

Lizzie gestured toward the fountain. "Over there."

Winslow directed his flashlight beam on the bronze nymph, then let it drop to the body lying at the fountain's base. He held the light fixed there for a moment before moving on. Lizzie and Sidney followed him. He shown the light on Henry's once-handsome face, now contorted in a grimace, his skin blanched a waxy yellowish-white.

Lizzie clapped her hands over her mouth, afraid she might vomit. Beside her, Sidney shuddered. Winslow scanned the area with the flashlight, perhaps searching for a killer lurking nearby or some sign of a struggle. Finally, he aimed it into the circular pool at the bottom of the bronze sculpture, where something silvery glinted from beneath the water.

Lizzie stepped closer and gasped. "A knife. The murder weapon?"

"I suspect you may be right," Winslow said, keeping the flashlight's beam trained on the knife.

"*Now* do you believe he was murdered? I mean, people don't usually go around stabbing themselves to death with knives."

Winslow glanced at her, a wry smile on his face. "Unless they're in one of Shakespeare's plays."

Before she could reply, they heard a car pull into the parking area; two men got out. One of them held his own flashlight to illuminate the way. Lizzie watched as a beefy policeman and a shorter, thinner fellow in uniform made their way through the night toward the trio standing by the fountain. Nervously, she linked her arm through Sidney's.

The officers stopped and the bigger one spotlighted Henry's body with his torch. Lizzie searched the cop's face for a reaction but saw none. *I suppose, being a policeman, he's seen such things before.*

Having acquainted himself with the corpse, the policeman stepped up to Winslow and introduced himself. "I'm Sergeant Mulvaney. This is Officer Connolly."

"Thank you for coming so quickly. I'm Zachary Winslow." He shook hands with both men. "This is Elizabeth Crane, who discovered the body, and her associate Sidney Somerset."

"Yes, Mr. Winslow, we know who you are. And what is your relationship to Miss Crane and Mr. Somerset?"

"They're performers from New York City. My wife hired them to entertain our guests here this week."

Lizzie glanced at Henry's lifeless form on the grass. "The deceased is, uh, *was* our saxophonist, Henry Ives."

"I see. Well then, I'll want to speak with you both right away."

"Aren't you going to search the premises for the murderer?" Sidney asked.

Mulvaney's tone was cool and pointed. "First, we can't assume there *is* a murderer—cause of death has yet to be determined. Second, if a murderer does, in fact, exist, my guess is he absconded long ago. And third, we haven't an inkling who to look for, unless you two have some notion of who might have killed your associate. Which is why I need to have a word with each of you—separately."

"Of course," Sidney agreed.

"Mr. Somerset, I'll begin with you."

Lizzie fixed her gaze on the shiny brass buttons on the big cop's blue uniform. Now that the adrenaline rush had passed, she suddenly felt very, very tired. *If only I could go to sleep and wake up to find that this was all a bad dream.*

"After I've interviewed these two, I'll be wanting to speak with the members of your household, Mr. Winslow."

Winslow raised his eyebrows. He glanced at his watch. "It's nearly two in the morning."

"As soon as possible."

"Very well, I'll have Charles and Mrs. Greely round up the staff."

"Family members and guests as well."

Winslow's expression hardened and he straightened his shoulders. He stared down his long, narrow nose at the policeman and Lizzie had the impression he was accustomed to intimidating people. With a trace of annoyance in his voice, he said, "You don't suspect my family, do you, Sergeant?"

"A man has died, apparently of unnatural causes, on your property.

Someone may have seen or heard something that could help us in our investigation. Until I know more, Mr. Winslow, I suspect everyone." Mulvaney adjusted his cap and stared back. "For the time being, please advise everyone not to leave the Wingate estate without first consulting with me. Failure to comply with a police investigation could result in serious consequences."

"Surely that doesn't apply to me."

"I'm afraid it does, Mr. Winslow. My apologies, but until we have a better understanding of what took place here, I want all of you to remain available for questioning."

"Now see here, Sergeant. I have a business to run and that often requires me to travel."

"And I, too, have a job to do, sir. I hope to resolve this matter quickly and with the least amount of inconvenience to you. Now please, alert your household and tell them I'll be wanting to ask them some questions."

Overruled and dismissed, Winslow turned away sharply and strode angrily toward the mansion. His heels slammed silently into the lush grass with each step.

Sergeant Mulvaney motioned Sidney toward the gentlemen's quarters, leaving Lizzie and Officer Connelly standing awkwardly beside the bronze fountain. They tried not to look at one another or the bloody body of Henry Ives.

She sat down on the edge of the pool at the fountain's base. Once again, she glanced into the water at the knife. *Just a few hours ago Henry and I shared a drink together. Now he's dead. Murdered. Stabbed.* She shivered, as frightful images rose in her imagination. Scores of times she'd seen actors knifed onstage, but never the real thing.

She wondered how Melody would take the news. Ever since Henry joined their group, Melody had fantasized about having a love affair with him. Lizzie flashed back to their conversation only a few days before coming to Wingate. The two young women sat at a corner table in their favorite Village speakeasy, toasting their good fortune at having gotten this engagement. The trip to Massachusetts would be the nineteen-year-old blonde's first time away from home and she bubbled with excitement.

"What do you make of Henry?" Melody asked.

"In what regard?"

"He's so good-looking and talented. And he knows rich people like the Winslows."

Lizzie rolled her smoke-colored eyes. "Poor little bunny. I hope you're not stuck on Henry, because in case you've forgotten we have an unbendable rule about getting romantically involved with your coworkers."

"I know, I know. I just—"

"Just nothing," Lizzie cut her off. "Look, Melody. You're a sweet, pretty girl from a nice family. You have gobs of talent. You could have the whole world at your feet. Besides, we know almost nothing about Henry Ives, other than that he might be the next Eduard Lefebre."

"Who?"

"Only the best saxophonist ever to play in America." Lizzie stirred her drink with a swizzle stick, feeling responsible for Melody as if they were sisters instead of coworkers. "Anyway, Henry has only been with us a short time. Don't give him so much credit. Really, it was good luck that we landed this event—not just Henry's influence. The previously scheduled entertainers got invited to perform in London and cancelled at the last minute. Mrs. Winslow had already planned her summer season and she was left up a creek without a paddle."

And now Henry Ives was gone. His death had not only crushed Melody's hopes for a happy-ever-after but Lizzie's dreams of fame and fortune as well. Who, why, and other unanswerable questions arose in her mind, but she was too tired to pursue them.

Officer Connelly turned his back to the sea breeze and lit a cigarette. The flare from the match illuminated a small white object about the size of a radish, lying on the grass near Lizzie's feet. She bent down and picked up the pretty heart-shaped shell, ran her fingertips over its ridged surface, and slipped it into her pocket along with the others she'd gathered earlier on the Winslows' private beach. Then she folded her arms on her knees and rested her forehead on them.

Just as she began to doze, Sergeant Mulvaney called her name.

# Chapter Four

*"Only he who is without anything is without enemies."*

— *Rafael Sabatini, Captain Blood Returns*

"Come with me," Mulvaney ordered.

Lizzie raised her head and looked up at the Winslows' mansion, where dozens of golden lights had begun to appear in the windows. The staff must have received the master's order by now. She imagined the serving girls in their cramped chambers on the third floor, nervously preparing themselves for questioning by the police. *How frightened they must be. Most likely there's more than one illegal immigrant among them.* The thin, wall-eyed Officer Connelly still stood at his post beside the fountain, smoking a cigarette. Its bright orange tip glowed in the indigo night. With a long sigh, Lizzie stood and followed the stocky police sergeant into the guesthouse.

Usually, she relied on her arresting beauty to give her the upper hand in difficult situations. This time, however, she sensed she'd have to call upon other resources. She lifted her chin and squared her shoulders so that she seemed to look down on him even though he was a few inches taller. With a haughtiness befitting a queen, Lizzie marched ahead of Mulvaney into the parlor of the gentlemen's quarters, where she'd laughed and drunk bootlegged gin with Henry Ives only a few hours ago. Everything looked the same as she remembered it—the stone fireplace, the leather sofas, and chairs, the billiard table. And yet everything had changed.

She recalled Henry's response when she'd first asked him about sailing. "I was practically born on a boat. I'm from Gloucester, the oldest fishing village in America. If you look across the bay you can see its coastline from here."

"Where's Sidney?" she asked the big Irish policeman.

"I'll ask the questions," Mulvaney said. "Have a seat."

Ignoring him, she went into the kitchen and rummaged around in the cabinets until she found a coffeepot and a can of Cuban roast. While the coffee brewed, she stalked down a long hallway, calling out for Sidney. When no one answered she canvased another part of the building. Finally, his voice responded from behind a closed door.

She rapped on the door. "Sid, what's going on?"

"I'm taking a bath."

"*Now?* The cop's out here. What did you tell him?"

Lizzie felt a strong hand clamp onto her shoulder. A no-nonsense voice said, "Come with me, Miss Crane." She struggled to extricate herself, but Mulvaney's vice-like grip held her firmly.

Grudgingly, she accompanied him back to the kitchen where the coffee percolated aromatically. She took two china cups from a cabinet and filled one for herself, then offered the other one to Mulvaney.

"Thanks," he accepted, not waiting for cream or sugar.

As she seated herself in one of the spacious parlor's club chairs, she contemplated momentarily the incongruity of the delicate china cup in Mulvaney's big, gnarled hand. *A hand that may have bashed many a jaw, or worse.* He sat facing her, drinking with an unexpected degree of grace. He didn't lift his pinkie, but he didn't slurp or spill any coffee either.

The caffeine cleared her head and Lizzie sighed emphatically. She was accustomed to charming men in order to get what she wanted—or to avoid what she didn't want—and now seemed like the right time to put her skills to work. She leaned back in the chair and propped her feet up on the cocktail table, giving the sergeant a nice view of her bare, shapely ankles beneath the rolled-up legs of her trousers. Mulvaney glanced at them, but his expression seemed more amused than lascivious.

Eying him over the rim of her cup, she asked, "Okay, Sergeant. How can I help you find the person who murdered my friend?"

"You can begin by telling me everything you know about Henry Ives."

"We met at the Cotton Club in Harlem, about six months ago."

"Why did you form an alliance with him?"

"My friend Sidney liked him. They played music together sometimes. Henry blew a swell sax, and he was easy on the eyes. We thought he'd be an asset to the group."

"Did you have, uh, a romantic relationship with Ives?"

She shook her head and smiled up at him from beneath dark lashes. "I never mix business with pleasure, Sergeant. Each demands my utmost attention, and if I tried to blend them they'd both suffer."

"What do you know about his past?"

"Not much. We'd only worked together briefly." Lizzie drained her cup and stood up. "I need another cup of java before I answer any more questions. What about you, Sergeant?"

He held out his cup and she carried it into the kitchen. When she returned, Mulvaney was standing at the bar, studying a half-empty bottle of gin.

"I could book you and your friends for this," he said.

"Is that a threat?"

"Statement of fact."

"The *fact*, Sergeant, is that the 18th Amendment does not prohibit drinking spirits—only manufacturing, selling, and transporting them. You have to admit, none of those activities is taking place. This bottle is just sitting here, minding its own business."

He raised an eyebrow and accepted the coffee cup she offered. "I'm not interested in a bit of booze anyway—unless it's somehow tied to your friend's death. I'm in homicide, not vice."

Lizzie shifted the conversation away from the liquor. "What about the knife the murderer used to kill Henry? Won't it show the killer's fingerprints?"

"Slim chance. Any fingerprints probably washed off while it lay in the fountain. And if the killer's prints aren't on record, we'd have no way of identifying him anyway. We'll test the knife, you can be certain of that. I've already asked Officer Connelly to bag it for the folks in forensics."

Mulvaney stepped away from the bar and slowly made his way around the parlor, his eyes roaming from bookcase to fireplace to billiard table. Her eyes followed his maneuvers, wondering what he was looking for and what he saw that she didn't. For a big man, he moved with surprising grace and Lizzie imagined him waltzing to the music of Jack Denny and his orchestra.

"According to Mr. Somerset, the deceased was responsible for this engagement between your group and the Winslows," Mulvaney said.

Lizzie sunk down in the leather club chair again, her bravado starting to ebb. What had started out as a terrific opportunity to make some serious money and enhance their reputation had turned into a tragedy. Catherine Winslow, no doubt, would send The Troubadours packing. Their chances of ever working this circuit again had gone bust. *Just when we were on the threshold of success*, she lamented. *Will we even get reimbursed for our traveling expenses?*

"That's right," she answered.

"Mr. Ives was associated with the Winslows?"

She felt certain he already knew the answer to that question, but replied, "So he said."

"In what capacity?"

Lizzie felt the depressing weight of the whole experience fall on her shoulders like a wet cloak. She drank the last of her coffee and set the cup down on the cocktail table.

"I don't know, Sergeant. Perhaps you should ask Mrs. Winslow about that."

"Did Mr. Ives have any enemies? Anyone who might have wanted him dead?"

"Not that I know of. But I didn't know him well."

Mulvaney studied her from beneath his wooly caterpillar eyebrows, then waved his big hand. "That will be all for now, Miss Crane. But be assured, we're not finished here. Don't think about going back to New York or anywhere else until I give you permission."

When Lizzie emerged from the gentlemen's residence Officer Connelly was still standing guard beside the bronze fountain. She tried to ignore him and Henry's body as she headed across the rolling green lawn toward the mansion. As she approached the back terrace, she saw a petite woman wearing a moss-green dress, followed by two Boston Terriers.

"Miss Crane," the woman called. "May I have a word with you?"

Catherine Winslow descended the stairs from the terrace, the dogs following obediently at her heels, and stood on the bottom step next to a large stone urn blooming with purple and red petunias. She waited for Lizzie to come to her. As Lizzie drew nearer, she noticed her hostess scowling at her appearance: her trousers, bare ankles, and tousled hair. Mrs. Winslow, by comparison, appeared elegantly coifed and attired as if for a society luncheon, despite the early hour and the fact that a man's murdered body had just been discovered on her property.

"Certainly, Mrs. Winslow," Lizzie said, squaring her shoulders.

"My condolences. Your friend's death…such a terrible thing."

"Thank you. Yes, it is. We're quite stunned."

With Mrs. Winslow standing on the step and Lizzie ankle-deep in the dew-drenched grass, the two women were nearly at eye level. Lizzie wanted to ask about the Winslows' relationship with Henry Ives, how the family knew the dead saxophonist, and did their hostess have any idea who might have wanted to harm Henry. But Catherine Winslow said quickly, "I'm confident the police will soon apprehend the guilty person."

"I sure hope so."

The older woman shifted her attention to the petunias for a moment and pinched off a dead blossom. "In the meantime, I do hope you and your colleagues will remain here at Wingate and continue with the plans we've arranged."

*Well, that's a stroke of luck,* Lizzie thought. *Maybe we can salvage something from this nightmare after all.* "Yes, of course. I hope we can minimize the tension caused by this unfortunate disruption—"

"Good, that's settled. Oh, and Miss Crane, I'd appreciate it if you would keep this matter as quiet as possible. My guests will begin arriving today and I don't want this gruesome event to upset them or distract from my daughter's betrothal party."

"Hard to keep news of a murder quiet," Lizzie said. *It'll be in the papers and it's already on the lips of every servant.* "But I promise they won't hear about it from me."

"Thank you. Good day, Miss Crane."

Mrs. Winslow turned away and climbed the steps to the terrace with her terriers in tow. Lizzie waited until the woman and the dogs had disappeared into the mansion before following.

* * *

Melody perched on the edge of her narrow bed, locks of her blond hair twisted up in strips of cloth to curl it. Her white cotton nightgown hung loosely about her slender form and her blue eyes stared at Lizzie in horror.

"Henry's dead!" she wailed.

"I know."

"Someone stabbed him," Melody cried, tears running down her cheeks. She looked as pale as a corpse herself. "All the serving girls are talking about it. One of them stopped me on the way to the bathroom just now and told me. It can't be true, can it?"

"Sorry, Mel. It's true."

Melody shook her head and fiddled nervously with the amethyst pendant she wore at her throat. "How can you be sure?"

"I found his body."

"No!"

She rushed to the window of their third-floor bedchamber and pushed aside the pretty lace curtains an earlier occupant had tatted. Below, the lawn still lay swathed in shadows. Melody looked down at the two men in uniforms who stood beside the bronze fountain of the naked nymph riding a dolphin, conversing with several other men holding flashlights. Between them, a tarp covered a lumpy form.

"The police are down there," she said.

Lizzie joined Melody at the window and placed an arm around her younger friend's thin shoulders. "Yes, and they're going to want to ask you questions about Henry."

"What kind of questions?"

"How you knew him, did he have any enemies, was he involved in anything that might have caused problems, that sort of thing."

"But I barely knew him. I mean, I wanted to know him better, but he was…"

"An enigma."

"What?"

"A mystery. We worked with him, but we didn't really know him." Lizzie couldn't even recall ever having had a serious conversation with him about anything other than music.

"Henry and I will never be sweethearts now." The younger woman dabbed at her tears and blew her nose into an embroidered handkerchief. "Who would want to murder him?"

"I suppose everyone at Wingate is asking that very question," Lizzie answered. "Except the person who did it, of course."

Melody leaned her head against Lizzie's shoulder, her plaintive sobs gradually easing into soft, animal-like whimpers. "I've never talked to a policeman before. What should I tell him?"

"The truth." Lizzie patted her friend's arm, wishing she could offer some useful advice. "You don't know anything, right?"

"No. Not really. Like you said, I barely knew Henry."

"Okay, get dressed. I'll come downstairs with you. Don't be scared. But don't say anything more than you absolutely have to. Keep your answers brief and to the point. Crying is good too—it makes men uncomfortable and the cops may go easy on you if they see you're distraught."

Melody nodded and began gathering her clothes and toilet articles. Clutching them to her chest, she said, "Thanks. I'll be back in a jiffy." She opened the bedroom door, but then turned back to her friend. "This is the worst thing that's ever happened to me. I'm glad you're here to help me through it."

Lizzie forced what she hoped was a supportive smile. "May it truly be the worst thing that ever happens to you."

\* \* \*

While Sergeant Mulvaney questioned Melody, Lizzie sat cross-legged on the outdoor stage near the gentlemen's quarters, having been banned from the interrogation despite her protests. As she watched the morning sky turn gray, then aqua, she wondered for the hundredth time who might have killed Henry, and why.

She rubbed her temples, trying to ease the tension in her head so she could think clearly. Her colleague might be dead, but she still had a show to put on. A show without their stellar saxophonist. A show that could make or break their career. Did the three of them have it in them to carry off this event, in the wake of Henry's unexpected death?

She heard a door slam and looked up to see Melody scurry away from the gentlemen's lodge. Clutching her skirt in her fists, the young woman rushed toward the Winslows' mansion. While she ran, she turned her head nervously from side to side, as if she expected a villain to leap from the bushes and accost her at any moment.

"Melody!" Lizzie shouted after her. "What the—?"

Behind her Sergeant Mulvaney's voice boomed. "Miss Crane."

She watched Melody's slim figure grow smaller and smaller as her young friend neared the mansion's back terrace. Angrily, she stood and faced the police sergeant, hands on her hips. "What did you say to Melody?"

"I merely impressed on her the seriousness of the situation. I reminded her that she could be the next victim."

"You don't really believe that, do you, Sergeant?"

Mulvaney raised a bushy eyebrow. "To be sure, Miss Crane, I do."

# Chapter Five

*"So we beat on, boats against the current, borne back ceaselessly into the past."*

— *F. Scott Fitzgerald, The Great Gatsby*

Even before she entered her third-floor bedchamber Lizzie smelled breakfast. A tray of food and a coffeepot sat on the bureau. She touched the china pot. *Good, still hot.* A cinnamon crumb cake, she noticed, had already been cut into.

Melody stood at the window, munching cake and dropping crumbs on the floor as she watched the goings-on below.

"I see you're not too grief-stricken to eat," Lizzie teased, glad that her friend hadn't collapsed in despair.

Melody turned around. "They've taken Henry's body away."

Lizzie poured herself a cup of coffee and joined her younger colleague at the window. A lad with the dark curls of the Black Irish was pouring buckets of water on the blood-stained grass, trying to wash away the mess, or at least dilute it enough that no one would guess a man had died there.

"Oh, look." Melody pointed to the driveway that led up to the manor house. "Someone's coming."

A shiny, silver Bentley pulled into the granite-paved parking area and stopped. The driver's door opened and a tall, slender man with hair that shone like a dark flame stepped out. Lizzie waited to see if someone else would emerge from the car, but the man appeared to be alone.

"Do you think he's one of the Winslows' guests?" Melody asked, obviously intrigued.

"One would assume. You know what they say about redheads, don't you?"

"What?"

"Hot!" Lizzie fanned herself with one hand and laughed when Melody blushed.

"Do you think he passed the hearse on the way?"

"Must have. There's only one road in and out of this place." Lizzie sipped her coffee and watched as Charles the butler greeted the copper-haired man and escorted him into the mansion. "Mrs. Winslow met me on the back terrace as I returned from my little chat with Sergeant Mulvaney. She asked me to hush up Henry's murder. Doesn't want to scare off her guests, it seems."

"But everyone's talking about it."

"I know, and of course it's impossible. But here's the good news. She wants us to stay on and finish the program."

"Even without Henry?" Melody asked.

"Obviously we'll have to make some adjustments. I doubt we can find a replacement saxophonist at this late date. You've got your flute and violin, right?"

"Yes."

"And your tap shoes?"

"Yes."

"Good girl." Lizzie's brain shuffled through the troupe's repertoire, searching for acts they could put on without the fourth member of the group.

Fortunately, the skit *Porcelain and Pink*, with its infamous bathtub scene, only required three actors—they wouldn't have to scrap that one. *Damn it, Henry, why did you have to go and get yourself killed now?* she lamented. She felt like a high-wire artist tumbling through space without a net to catch her. Yet she had to keep up appearances, buoy the group, and prevent them from collapsing.

Melody wiped crumbs from her Cupid's bow lips and asked, "What did that policeman talk to you about?"

"The same things he talked about with you, I suspect. What did I know about Henry's past, did he have any enemies, was I aware that he'd gotten us this engagement with the Winslows. I told Sergeant Mulvaney what I know, which isn't much."

"Just before you came up I overheard two chambermaids talking in the hall," Melody said. "One of them remembered Henry, from two summers back. Said she'd seen him strolling down the promenade to the sea with the older Winslow girl, Florence—and on more than one occasion. What do you make of that?"

Last night, while Lizzie sat drinking martinis with Sid and Henry, the saxophonist had spoken wistfully about his chance meeting with Florence Winslow. "I liked her immediately. And she liked me," he'd said. If the chambermaid could be believed, that initial meeting had apparently blossomed into something more.

Another motorcar, a robin's egg blue coupe, rolled up the long driveway. From their elevated vantage point, the two young women watched as it circled the parking area and then stopped. This time, a man in a linen suit and a plump woman wearing a green suit and matching cloche hat got out. The butler met them, as he had the red-haired man who'd preceded them. Two servants hurried toward the motorcar, gathered up the couple's bags, and carried them into the mansion.

"The 'quality' are beginning to arrive," Lizzie said.

Melody's expression brightened. "Maybe I'll meet a millionaire while I'm here—even marry one."

"You might at that." Lizzie patted her friend's cheek, glad to see the pretty young blonde rebound so quickly. *We may get through this yet.* "I'm going to take a bath, then have a chat with Sidney."

* * *

Lizzie fastened a regiment of tiny buttons that ran down the front of her simple, beige linen frock from clavicle to mid-calf. She rolled up her stockings and slid her feet into low-heeled leather pumps. She powdered her nose and swiped a splash of color on her lips. A night without sleep had left her eyes bloodshot with dark circles below them, but after a nice hot bath, she felt ready to face the day. She hooked a circlet of pearls—a gift from a long-ago admirer—around her neck and studied her reflection in the tarnished mirror above the bureau of her sparsely furnished bedchamber. *I could pass for the wife of a respectable businessman,* she thought and laughed at the unlikely possibility of ever becoming a housewife and raising a passel of children. Then she made her way downstairs, dodging servants who scurried about, busily tending to the new arrivals.

She tried not to look at the bronze fountain and the stain on the ground beside it as she crossed the lawn to the gentlemen's quarters. Before she could knock on the door, however, Sidney opened it in a state of high pique.

"I'm being shunted off to the *stables*," he grumbled. "What do they think I am, for god's sake, a *groom*?"

She pushed past him into the parlor, where last night's memories hung like specters. "Why? Because of Henry?"

"Charles, the butler, informed me that this building is intended to house the Winslows' unmarried male guests, who've already started moving in." He waved his hand to indicate a collection of suitcases and trunks stacked along the wall near the fireplace. "It appears I fall into the category of 'the help' not 'guest.' They've taken away my luggage—and all our props. I barely had a chance to dress before they gave me my walking papers."

Unlike Lizzie, he'd always lived a life of privilege and considered the change in accommodations an insult. He'd never been good at rolling with the punches, she knew, and too many upsets so soon had shaken his bearings. He felt a need to control things, but neither of them could have controlled the events of the past twenty-four hours. *Whatever will I do if Sidney buckles now?*

"Don't be a pill. Melody and I are rooming with the chambermaids, you know. It's not so bad—we're hardly ever in our room anyway except to sleep. Say, maybe you'll get to bunk with the cute Black Irish lad I saw just a little while ago," Lizzie teased him. "Anyway, being among the help has its advantages. The servants always know everything that goes on—maybe they can help us figure out who bumped off Henry."

"That fat copper thinks one of *us* did it."

"That's baloney. Why would we want Henry dead? We're left in a pickle without him."

"And how. We're going to have to scratch half the bits we'd planned to do." Sidney ran a manicured hand through his thinning hair. "I can't believe this is happening."

"What about Henry's luggage? Did you look through it? Maybe it holds some clues to his death." *Why didn't I think of this before?* she scolded herself.

"No go." Sidney shook his head. "Cops confiscated it, lock, stock, and barrel."

Lizzie snapped her fingers. "Hold on, I've got an idea. Didn't Henry say he came from someplace not far from here? Gloucester, I think it was?"

"Yeah, so?"

"Let's take a trip to Henry's old stomping grounds and see what we can dig up. Better we leave now before Mulvaney gets wind that we're gone and puts us in manacles. Besides, it's a lovely day for a drive."

Sidney's scowl dissolved; apparently, her suggestion pleased him. "Now you're on the trolley. Collect Melody and I'll meet you at the breezer in half an hour."

\* \* \*

They drove east through the town of Ipswich, Massachusetts, its streets lined with clapboard cottages dating back to the 1600s, then for several miles through farms and pastureland where livestock grazed on lush green grass, and on into Essex. Melody's eyes grew wide with amazement as they passed a shipyard where an almost-finished schooner perched in a cradle, awaiting its day at sea. Its masts soared high above the nearby buildings. Even without its sails, the wooden ship was a beauty. Other boats of varying types crowded the Essex River.

Lizzie recalled Peter Winslow's sailboat *Rhiannon* and thought it seemed like a toy compared to these vessels. "The Essex shipyards have been famous for 200 years," she said. "During their heyday in the middle of the last century, they built a ship a week here. Of course, that's declined now, because these days more boats are being made of metal."

Sidney chuckled. "You sound like a history teacher. How do you know all that stuff?"

"Dear Sidney, I keep telling you, I *read*. Just because I never finished high school doesn't mean I'm ignorant."

A narrow road led them over a stretch of marshland where snowy egrets and blue herons perched on legs like stilts, hunting food in the shallows. A sparkling ribbon of water wound through the tall marsh grasses and fishermen in dories dipped their lines in it. In the backseat, Melody bounced about like a little girl, exclaiming with delight at each new sight. Everything seemed to enchant her: clam diggers probing the wet sand for mollusks, roses cascading over white picket fences, flocks of wild turkeys scurrying alongside the road trying to decide whether or not to cross.

With the Buick's top down, the northeast wind kept the heat of the late morning sun from being uncomfortable. Lizzie tightened the chin ribbon of her hat so it wouldn't blow away. Despite her lack of sleep, she felt energized by the nice weather and the prospect of learning more about Henry's past. *This seems more like a pleasure outing than a murder investigation,* she thought. *Shouldn't I feel more grief-stricken over my colleague's death?*

Sidney, getting down to business, interrupted her thoughts. "Now that Henry's gone, we'll have to revise our program again. Damn, I'm going to miss his horn."

The mention of Henry reeled Melody back from her traveler's romp to their present dilemma. Tears sprang into the young flutist's eyes and she dabbed at them with her handkerchief.

"Who'd want to kill Henry?" Melody asked.

"That's what we're going to Gloucester to find out," Lizzie answered.

"Is what we're doing dangerous?"

"What do you mean?"

"Sergeant Mulvaney said whoever murdered Henry might want to kill the rest of us too."

"Poor little bunny, he was just trying to scare you," Lizzie said. "He wanted to trick you into opening up and revealing something about Henry."

"But I don't know anything."

"You're not in any danger," Sidney insisted. "You've never done anything even vaguely shady in your entire life. You probably don't even know how to play Blackjack."

Apparently, he meant to comfort Melody, but to Lizzie, his reassurance sounded hollow. None of them had the slightest idea why Henry had been brutally slain, or what the killer's motive might have been. Recalling her colleague's body awash in blood sent a chill up Lizzie's spine. Maybe Mulvaney was right. Maybe someone *did* want to eliminate The Troubadours, although she hadn't the foggiest notion who or why.

Tall trees arched over the road as they continued motoring across the western part of Gloucester. It seemed as though they were driving through a dark, green tunnel. Whenever they came upon another automobile Sidney sounded the breezer's horn. When they passed a horse-drawn conveyance, however, he slowed down to avoid startling the animals and they all waved. After her brief spate of tears, Melody resumed her role of sightseer.

Sidney and Lizzie bantered back and forth, selecting and rejecting acts for the coming week.

"We'll keep it upbeat," Lizzie said. "We want to distract the audience. My guess is that by tomorrow most of them will have heard about Henry's murder, no matter how hard our hosts try to hush it up."

# Chapter Six

*"They that go down to the sea in ships..."*

— *Gloucester Fisherman's Memorial (Psalm 103:23)*

As they entered Gloucester's city limits, Lizzie could easily see why seamen had settled this crook of land three centuries ago, and why it remained a center of the fishing industry to this day. The mile-wide harbor was sheltered by Eastern Point peninsula and its breakwater for more than two miles before it opened out into the north Atlantic. Dozens of vessels—mostly working boats, but some pleasure craft as well—sailed, motored, and bobbed on the sparkling green water. Lizzie tried to imagine it filled with barks, brigs, and schooners, perhaps even a frigate or two, as the artists Fitz Hugh Lane and Winslow Homer had painted it years ago.

They rolled to a stop at a drawbridge, poised upright to allow a parade of fishing boats to pass from the Annisquam River into the harbor. Sidney switched off the engine.

"Looks like we're in for a wait," he said.

Lizzie noticed a shop with a green-and-white-striped awning on the opposite side of the street. "I'm going to see if they have any Coca-Cola. Anybody else want one?"

"Yes," her companions answered in unison.

"We should've brought a picnic lunch," said Melody.

Sidney lit a cigarette. "I'm sure we can find a place to eat in town."

Grabbing her purse, Lizzie stepped out of the car. Two other vehicles had stopped behind them, and she felt the drivers' eyes appraising her as she crossed the street.

The shop's interior was dark and cramped, with a worn wooden floor and ceiling-high shelves laden with all manner of supplies. A sign at the back said "Live Bait," the source of the store's pungent odor. An elderly man sat on a high stool behind the counter, reading a newspaper. He looked up at her and nodded.

"What might you be wanting today, miss?"

She pointed to a large red ice chest. "Three Coca-Colas, please."

As the shopkeeper slid off his stool and limped over to the cooler, Lizzie plucked a paperback traveler's guide from a rack and flipped through it. The old man lifted the cooler's heavy lid, pulled out three bottles, and set them on the counter.

"Fifteen cents," he said. "You taking that book too?"

"Yes."

"Two bits total. Want those bottles opened?"

"Yes, please." She reached for her coin purse and withdrew a quarter. "I'm looking for a fisherman named Henry Ives. Do you happen to know where I might find him?" She gave the shopkeeper a pretty smile. News of Henry's death wouldn't have gotten around yet—the police might not have even notified his next of kin.

"Nope. Ain't seen him in a good long while."

She flashed back to the night of Henry's murder, to the darkly handsome and annoyingly aloof saxophonist who'd sat with her drinking gin in the parlor of Wingate's gentlemen's quarters. The colleague about whom she knew so little. "But you do know him and his family?"

The old man shrugged. "I suppose I do. What's your interest in him?"

"I heard he's a swell musician. I wondered if he might be playing someplace around here."

"That's all you heard?"

She cocked her head to one side, feigning innocence. "Is there something else?"

The shopkeeper picked up the quarter she'd placed on the counter, rang up the sale, and dropped the coin into the cash register drawer. "Good day to you, miss."

"I don't understand…"

But the man had perched himself on the stool again and held up the newspaper, blocking his face. Lizzie slipped the traveler's guide in her purse and gathered up the Coca-Cola bottles. As she pushed the screen door open with her foot, she saw the drawbridge slowly descending into place.

"Just in the nick of time," Sidney said as she handed him a bottle and then passed one to Melody.

Settling herself into the passenger seat of the Buick, Lizzie said, "I just had a peculiar conversation with the shopkeeper of that store." She related the exchange to her friends.

"What does it mean?" Melody asked.

"Sounds kind of fishy to me," Sidney replied. "No pun intended."

"Ob-vi-ous-ly. We know Henry wasn't murdered because he blew a sour note," Lizzie pointed out. "Now I'm even more curious to find out what skeletons he had tucked away."

They drove along the recently completed Stacy Boulevard, where pedestrians and motorists were enjoying the sunshine and sea air. A bronze statue of a larger-than-life fisherman grasping a ship's wheel stood on a pedestal, looking out over the harbor. As the three performers wound their way into town, along narrow streets bordered by brick buildings, sea captains' mansions, and clapboard cottages, the stench of fish grew stronger.

Sidney pulled over and parked the car. "Let's walk down to the docks," he suggested. "Maybe we can find someone who knows—knew—Henry."

"I think Melody and I should go alone," Lizzie said, opening her door and stepping out onto the running board. "The fishermen might be more willing to talk to two pretty ladies than to a fella like you, Sidney. They might even beat you up."

"Bushwa," he said, but Lizzie could see his expression change as he considered the possibility. "Well, maybe you do have a point—you've always been able to wrap men around your little finger, Bearcat."

"Why don't you find a nice coffeehouse or a restaurant where we can eat lunch?"

Sidney climbed out of the breezer and held the back door open for Melody. "Okay, but be careful. I'll meet you back here in, say, half an hour?"

"I'm a fast worker," Lizzie said, "but it might take longer to dig up some dirt. We'll be back as soon as we can."

* * *

Vessels of all sizes clogged the inner harbor, from open seine boats and paint-chipped dories to graceful, seagoing schooners with masts like great trees. Longshoremen unloaded caches of fish from moored boats and shuttled supplies onboard ships that would soon head out to sea again. Seagulls squawked and circled overhead. Nearby, what looked like fields of fish lay drying in the sun. The smell was so strong Melody held an embroidered handkerchief to her nose.

As the two women stepped onto a rough wooden pier, a young man about Melody's age approached them. Long days in the sun had burned his skin as brown as a potato's.

"You ladies lost?"

Lizzie lifted her hat brim and gazed up at him with her big, smoky eyes. "What makes you think that?"

The man chuckled. "We don't often see your kind down here on the docks."

"Oh? And what 'kind' is that?"

"Well...*ladies*. You're not fish wives and you're not..."

She heard the implied word he'd left unspoken: prostitutes. She flashed him a fetching smile. "We're tourists, from New York. We wanted to see the renowned Gloucester fleet."

"Most of it's out on the water. You're looking at the rest," he said, sweeping his arm in a wide arc to indicate the mélange of boats bobbing on the incoming tide. "Finest in the whole U.S. of A."

Lizzie let her eyes roam up and down his body, making sure he noticed her appraising him. Although he was only an inch or two taller than her, he was well-muscled from years of hard work, and when he smiled his eyes crinkled at the corners in a pleasing way.

"Which of these boats is yours?" she asked.

The young man shook his head modestly. "I'm no owner, just a simple fisherman. I crew on the *Lorelei*—over there." He pointed to a vessel tied up about a hundred feet away.

"Lorelei…wasn't she a German mermaid who caused ships to sink? Doesn't sound very auspicious. Aren't you afraid of being jinxed?"

He shrugged. "I wouldn't know about that."

Lizzie snapped her fingers, as if she'd just remembered something. "Say, you wouldn't happen to know a musician named Henry Ives, would you? I heard him play music in New York, but I recall someone saying he's originally from Gloucester."

The man's smile faded. "Heard the name."

Lizzie turned to Melody. "I think he might even have been a fisherman once upon a time, or maybe his family fishes. Do you recall?"

Taking her cue, Melody said, "Yes, I seem to remember that."

"Lots of fishermen in Gloucester," he said.

An older, taller, and more weatherworn man shuffled toward them. His left leg, rigid as an iron stake and somewhat shorter than the right one, threw a hitch into his gait. He pulled off his soiled cap and wiped his forehead with his shirtsleeve.

"Good day ladies," he said, then nodded curtly to the younger man. "You'd best be getting back to your work, lad."

"A good day to you, too, sir," Lizzie said. "I was just telling the gentleman here that my friend and I are visiting from New York. We've heard ever so much about Gloucester's famous ships and we wanted to see them for ourselves."

"Uh-huh."

The young fisherman hurried away without so much as a backward glance.

"A man we met in New York told us about them," she continued. "His family hails from here and he praised your town to the high heavens. Maybe you know him—a fisherman named Henry Ives?"

The man settled his cap back on his head, frowned, and crossed his thick arms over his chest. "You look like nice young ladies, so I'm gonna give you a piece of advice. Stay away from Henry Ives. He's no good, his family's no good, and nothing good'll ever come of that lot. Now get yourselves off this dock and go back to where you came from before you end up in a pile of trouble."

"What do you mean?" Lizzie asked. She and Melody exchanged confused looks.

The man turned his head and spat tobacco juice into the water. "Go on, now." Realizing they weren't likely to glean any information here, the two women headed back toward the street where Sidney had parked the motorcar.

"What do you suppose he was talking about?" Melody asked as they picked their way along a dirt alley between two boarding houses. Laundry hanging on clotheslines between the buildings flapped in the wind.

"I don't know, but I don't think he's just chewing tobacco."

"Maybe we shouldn't get involved. If it's dangerous..."

"Don't you want to know who killed Henry?"

"Well, yes, I guess so. But shouldn't we let the police solve it?"

"Poor little bunny, you're right. I shouldn't drag you into this. It sure sounds like our pal was up to no good, and I intend to find out what pies he had his fingers in."

They rounded a corner and spotted Sidney sitting in the green Buick convertible, reading a newspaper.

"Hello, Sidney," Lizzie called out and waved.

"Any luck?" he asked as they approached.

"A complete waste of shoe leather." Lizzie related their dead-end exchange with the fishermen. "Henry doesn't seem to have many friends around here. Did you have better success finding a place to eat?"

"Affirmative." He folded the newspaper, tucked it under his arm, and got out of the car. "This way."

They walked two blocks down a street paved with local granite, past women chatting over white picket fences, past a vendor selling fresh vegetables from a horse-drawn cart. Flowers of every color bloomed in window boxes. Perched high on a hill overlooking the town and the sea they saw a mission-style church with twin domed towers.

"This is a pretty town," Melody said.

"That's why so many artists come here," Lizzie said. "What do you say we drive around after lunch? I bet we can find some of the places Edward Hopper painted."

Sidney stopped and held a door open for the two women. "Here we are."

Paneled with oak-aged to a golden-brown, the restaurant's interior smelled of fried fish and cigarette smoke. Several locals seated at the long wooden counter looked up from their meals to size up the out-of-towners. No one smiled, but no one seemed hostile either. A stout woman behind the counter waved them to a corner table.

Hand-written menus tucked into a wire rack sat on the table beside salt-and-pepper shakers, a bottle of catsup, and a jar of tartar sauce. Lizzie opened a menu and perused the lunch offerings. Seafood and more seafood.

"Hope you like fish," she said to Melody.

When a young waitress came to take their orders, Sidney pointed at Lizzie and said, "This lady will have the cod cakes."

"I don't even know what cod cakes are," she protested, but she was too hungry to argue.

"All the more reason to try them," he told her. "And the other lady will have a big bowl of clam chowder."

"At least I know what that is," Melody said.

"It's not like what we get in New York," Sidney explained. "Here they make it with cream instead of a tomato base. It's darb—you'll love it. And I'll have fish and chips. And three Coca-Colas, please."

After the waitress left, he lit a cigarette and spread his newspaper out on the table. "Look at this," he said, pointing to an article.

Lizzie and Melody leaned together and read the piece Sidney had indicated. It described the arrest of a Gloucester captain and crew after the Coast Guard boarded their ship and found the hold filled with illegal alcohol.

"How unfortunate," Lizzie sighed. "All that juice dumped in the harbor."

"Or confiscated and kept by the cops." Sidney lowered his voice and tapped the newspaper. "But that's not why I wanted you to see this. When I read it, and then you told me how those fishermen reacted when you asked them about Henry, well, I started wondering if our boy might have been mixed up in the whole business. I remember, back in the City, he could always get his hands on plenty of hooch."

A chill ran up Lizzie's spine and her mind started racing. In colonial times, distilleries thrived in Gloucester. The Triangle Trade brought molasses from the Caribbean to New England for rum-making. The region then shipped manufactured goods to West Africa and exchanged them for slaves, who were transported across the Atlantic to labor on the sugar plantations in the West Indies.

"You think Henry was smuggling booze and that's why somebody killed him?" she asked.

But before he could answer, the waitress brought their food and they stopped talking to eat.

# Chapter Seven

*"Manners are a sensitive awareness of the feelings of others. If you have that awareness, you have good manners, no matter what fork you use."*

— *Emily Post, Etiquette*

W hen they arrived back at Wingate, the parking area was crowded with motorcars. Lizzie spotted a Cadillac Touring Phaeton, a Packard Speedster, an Alfa Romeo convertible, a cream-colored Bugatti, and a cherry-red Stutz among them. Although most of the license plates showed that they hailed from the northeastern states, she noticed one from California and another from Texas.

*Imagine, driving all the way across the country*, she thought. *How exciting that would be!*

She still remembered the very first automobile she'd seen, at the age of eleven: a Model T Ford. It was love at first sight. When she later discovered its nickname "Tin Lizzie" she told everyone she met that Mr. Henry Ford had named it after her. Since then, she'd been fascinated with motorcars. Although she'd driven Sidney's prized Buick roadster and several cars that belonged to various suitors, she'd never owned one of her own. *One day I will*, she promised herself.

She slipped off her duster coat, laid it on the front seat, and climbed out of the breezer. Melody followed suit.

"Well, I'm off to the stables to rub shoulders with the other servants," Sidney grumbled.

Lizzie rapped on the car's door. "Stop grousing, Sid. It's only for a week. Besides, some of those shoulders might be pretty nice. Keep your ears open—maybe you'll hear something about Henry."

But before he could drive away, a skinny young housemaid with a galaxy of freckles splashed across her cheeks hurried toward them. Lizzie recognized her as the same girl who only yesterday had lugged their suitcases up three flights of stairs. She curtsied, lowering her eyes in deference.

"Begging your pardon, ma'am, but Mrs. Greely requests that you come with me, if you please."

"What if we don't please?" Lizzie said. The girl's worried expression suggested she might be reprimanded if she failed to fulfill her duty. "Oh, all right. Lead on, then."

"Would the gentleman be good enough to come too?"

Sidney's face expressed annoyance—or was it apprehension—but he parked the Buick between a Jaguar and a glossy black sedan manufactured by the brand new Chrysler Corporation. Then the three Troubadours followed the serving girl down a back hallway Lizzie hadn't noticed before and into a small, sparsely furnished sitting room near the kitchen.

*A parlor for the help?* she surmised as she switched on an electric light. *At least it has a radio.*

The succulent scent of roasting meat wafted around them, teasing her taste buds. Suddenly, it seemed a long time since lunch.

"Would you please wait while I tell Mrs. Greely you're here?" the serving girl asked.

Sidney nodded and lit a cigarette. Lizzie fiddled with the radio dial, trying to find some music to listen to while they waited. After a few minutes of struggling with static, she gave up and seated herself on a brown mohair davenport. Even through her linen dress, the coarse material felt scratchy on the backs of her thighs.

"What do you suppose is going on?" he asked.

49

"Beats me. Maybe there's news about Henry."

Melody sat beside Lizzie, her eyes filling with tears. "Poor Henry…"

*She can sure turn the waterworks on and off,* Lizzie thought. *It's a good quality in an actress, though.*

Several minutes later, the stork-like housekeeper entered the modest sitting room. She stared down her long, pointed nose at each of The Troubadours in turn, her thin lips drawn in a tight line of disapproval. Her prim, navy-blue dress with its stiff white collar and her tidy hat gave her a military appearance.

"You are not to leave the premises without consulting with me first," she said sternly.

"Are we under house arrest?" Lizzie asked, a hint of sarcasm in her voice. She stood and speared the woman with a steely glare. "Mrs. Greely, we are *not* servants and we do not answer to you."

Mrs. Greely took a step back. Almost apologetically, she said, "No one knew where you'd gone."

"You still haven't told us what this is about," Sidney interrupted.

"Mrs. Winslow wants to speak with you immediately. Follow me."

As the trio tagged along behind the matron, like schoolchildren on their way to the principal's office, Lizzie wondered how old Mrs. Greely was. *Probably not as old as she looks.* Her brown hair, pinned back in a tight bun, showed streaks of gray. Her tall, thin form more closely resembled an ironing board than a female figure. Still, she moved with energetic determination and her formidable presence gave her a no-nonsense air that dared anyone to contest her orders. *What an old killjoy,* Lizzie thought.

She led them into an enormous formal dining room where two young women wearing white aprons and starched caps moved down either side of a long mahogany table, laying out silverware, linen napkins, and a series of crystal goblets. Tall vases held gladioli in shades of yellow and coral. Catherine Winslow stood at a Chippendale lowboy, arranging flowers in another vase. Lizzie noticed she still wore the same moss-green frock she'd had on earlier that morning. As the group entered, Catherine turned and smiled at them, though without warmth.

50

"Ah, our wandering Troubadours have returned," she said. "Thank you, Mrs. Greely. That will do."

The housekeeper nodded, then departed, the heels of her sturdy shoes clicking down the hall.

"I was concerned that you might not be back in time to entertain my guests tonight," Mrs. Winslow said, softening her tone.

"We're not scheduled to perform until tomorrow night," Sidney reminded her. "We contracted for six performances, not seven."

"And I contracted for four entertainers, not three."

"It's hardly our fault that our colleague was killed," Lizzie said. "If he hadn't come here, he might still be alive."

Mrs. Winslow narrowed her eyes and glared at Lizzie. "We don't know whose fault it is, do we?"

Sidney patted Lizzie's arm, a signal not to say anything more. "What sort of performance did you have in mind for tonight, Mrs. Winslow?"

"I've heard marvelous reports about your skill at the piano, Mr. Somerset. I hope you'll favor us with musical accompaniment during supper." Catherine Winslow gestured toward a Steinway baby grand nestled in a shell-shaped niche at one end of the dining room. "I'm quite fond of Chopin, but perhaps Debussy or Brahms? Of course, Vivaldi and Pachelbel are always pleasant. Something calming and not too *au courant*. My guests have traveled a long way and I want them to feel relaxed."

"Background music?"

"Why, yes, you could put it that way. We'll save the livelier fare for tomorrow evening, shall we?" She turned and focused her cool gaze on Melody. "And you, dear. I understand you're an accomplished flutist."

"Some people say so, ma'am."

"Perhaps you'd be good enough to play a few songs for my guests?"

"Yes, ma'am."

"Miss Crane, what instrument do you play?"

"The oldest instrument of all. I sing," Lizzie answered. "Although on occasion I've been known to strum the ukulele."

Mrs. Winslow frowned ever so slightly, a trace of disappointment in her voice. "Oh. Is that all? I'd thought tonight we'd have only instrumental . . . *background* music." She glanced at a handsome antique grandfather clock, apparently calculating the time remaining before supper. "In that case, I suppose we won't need you this evening after all, Miss Crane."

Lizzie didn't know whether to feel relieved or insulted at having been dismissed. *I could go to bed early and try to make up for not getting any sleep last night.* The idea had definite appeal.

"Mr. Somerset," Mrs. Winslow continued, "would you be kind enough to prepare a list of the pieces you and Miss Fitzgerald will perform tonight and give it to me within the hour, so I may have time to make any adjustments, if necessary?"

Lizzie knew Catherine Winslow's sudden change of plans had addled Sidney. *He doesn't like surprises, and he's had more than enough lately.* But she admired his ability to maintain his actor's poise.

He nodded. "Certainly, Mrs. Winslow."

"And tomorrow morning, we'll go over your entire repertoire for the next few evenings. You too, Miss Crane." Her mouth smiled, but her eyes remained icy. "Just to make certain we're all in agreement."

*The iron fist in the velvet glove,* Lizzie mused. *Well, she's the client, and money talks.*

\* \* \*

"Which do you think I should wear?" Melody asked, holding up one dress, then another. "I feel so ill-prepared."

Lizzie watched her pretty young colleague sift through her wardrobe. Their garments lay in piles on twin beds in an empty maids' room where Mrs. Greely had grudgingly allowed them to stash their clothing. Their own tiny bedchamber had only a row of hooks on the wall—no chifforobe or closet. Adequate, perhaps, for serving girls, but certainly not enough for two New York performers. Finally, Melody held up a calf-length frock embroidered with colorful Chinese birds and flowers on a black background. Gold mesh cap-sleeves echoed the golden designs that embellished the two-tiered skirt.

"Yes, that's the ticket. You'll knock 'em dead in that dress." As soon as she spoke, Lizzie regretted her choice of words, but Melody didn't seem to notice.

Hugging the gown to her delicate frame, Melody examined herself in the cloudy mirror. "Whatever will you do tonight, Lizzie?" she asked.

"I'll be here with you, of course."

The flutist seemed confused. "But Mrs. Winslow said she only wanted background music…"

"Don't worry, poor little bunny, I won't sing," Lizzie assured her. "But I want to be privy to the dinner conversation and anything else that may transpire this evening. I'll sit quietly and study our audience, you know, to get a sense of what they're about. It will be fun to watch the quality dine—do you suppose they read Emily Post or do they inherit their table manners like blue eyes? Jeepers, I hope they're not all fuddy-duddies like Mrs. Winslow. Who knows, I might even gain some insight into our pal Henry."

Melody twirled before the mirror, surveying her image one more time before hanging up the elegant gown. "Surely, you don't suspect the Winslows of being involved in Henry's death, do you?"

"I haven't the foggiest idea who knows what, or who may or may not have played a role in Henry's murder. That's what I plan to find out. Tonight, while you and Sidney perform, I'll survey the guests. I'll listen to their conversations, watch their interactions. Perhaps one of them will reveal something."

Melody flopped down on one of the twin beds and rested her chin in her hands. Without the theatrical gown, she looked like a schoolgirl, and Lizzie wondered if it might be better to dress the petite blonde in something more winsome to accentuate the impression of innocence. Deflect suspicion of guilt away from The Troubadours. Of course, she reminded herself, the Winslows' guests might not know anything about Henry or his untimely demise. The papers probably hadn't picked up the story yet, and Catherine Winslow would do everything in her power to suppress the unpleasant details until after the week's festivities had ended.

"What are you going to wear?" Melody asked.

From the batch, Lizzie plucked an indigo silk frock embellished with hundreds of tiny, sparkling beads and held it before her, gazing at her reflection in the bureau's mirror. Its simple lines and deep color wouldn't compete with Melody's more flamboyant dress, yet its cut would reveal a rakish length of shapely calf and ankle, and its plunging neckline would show her unfashionably full bosom to advantage. No doubt Peter Winslow would be at dinner tonight, and she wanted to impress him.

"What do you think of this?"

"It's lovely," Melody answered.

"Yes, I think so too."

They carried their gowns down the hall to their own bedchamber. At the door stood the freckled maid they'd encountered previously, holding a tray draped with a white linen towel.

"Your supper," she said, lowering her deep-set eyes deferentially.

Lizzie opened the door and signaled for the girl to enter. "Thank you. Please put it there on the bureau."

As the maid set the tray down, Lizzie dug in her purse for a coin to tip her. "By the way, I'm Lizzie Crane and this is Melody Fitzgerald. May we know your name?"

The girl seemed surprised that Lizzie would care to see her as a person, not just a servant. "Tess O'Hare, ma'am.

"How did you come to be employed at Wingate?"

"Me older sister, Marie, is Miss Florence Winslow's personal maid," Tess replied proudly. "She brought me into service a year ago."

"And how old are you, Tess?"

"Fourteen, ma'am."

Lizzie pressed the coin in Tess's calloused hand and closed the girl's fingers around it. "Thank you for bringing our supper, Tess. I expect we'll see more of you in the coming days."

"Yes, ma'am. And thank you."

As the girl backed out of their room, Melody said, "You're going to spoil the maids if you keep tipping them, you know."

"I certainly hope so," Lizzie replied.

She pulled the linen cloth from the tray, revealing a panoply of culinary delights. Thick slices of roast duck lay on plates next to carrots and spears of asparagus drizzled with a creamy sauce. Fresh-baked rolls nestled in a basket, accompanied by a generous lump of butter and a dish of golden honey. A white china bowl held a medley of chilled apple chunks, raisins, and walnuts.

"What's this?" Melody asked, poking the apple bits with a fork.

Lizzie examined the mix closer. "I think it might be a Waldorf salad." Noticing Melody's confused expression, she explained, "The Waldorf-Astoria hotel in New York served it to President Coolidge when he dined there last year. It's all the rage now."

Melody spooned some of the fruit salad onto a plate along with the other offerings and sat on her bed, holding her meal on her lap. "I never imagined I'd be eating like the President."

Lizzie filled her own plate and sat facing Melody. From under her mattress, she withdrew a silver flask of scotch and poured two fingers' worth into a water glass. "Want some?"

"No, thanks."

"No opening night jitters to calm? It's genuine brown plaid."

"Truly, I feel fine."

Lizzie shook her head. "You amaze me, Mel. Cool as a cucumber. I've been at this infinitely longer than you and I still get butterflies before I perform." She hoisted her glass to toast her friend. "Break a leg."

# Chapter Eight

*"You didn't take your clothes to parties; they took you."*

— *Elizabeth von Arnim, The Enchanted April*

From the alcove, Lizzie had a clear view of the Winslows' elegant dining room and the thirty-six guests assembled there. She'd never before seen so many gorgeous gowns and such magnificent jewelry together in one place at one time. By comparison, her own stylish and rather elaborate wardrobe seemed tawdry. *Oh, to have their money and access to these ladies' dressmakers!*

Zachary Winslow presided at the head of the long Chippendale table, his silver hair sparkling in the light dispensed by a crystal chandelier. If he weren't so stern, he'd be a very handsome older man. His brow furrowed as his skeptical gaze moved from one guest to another, apparently examining rather than enjoying his companions. At the table's foot, Catherine Winslow held court. Dressed in a shimmering turquoise gown, she reminded Lizzie of a mermaid floating on a sun-kissed wave—alluring and dangerous. A jeweled tiara perched in her golden hair and a necklace of aquamarines and pearls circled her slender neck.

Peter Winslow sat on his mother's right. Lizzie's heart skipped a beat as she gazed at his handsome, tanned face and trim form. Tonight he wore a perfectly tailored tuxedo. *Custom-made in London,* she assumed. Her mind drifted back to their meeting yesterday on the beach at the edge of the estate as he pulled his dingy ashore, his wet white trousers rolled up to expose his muscular calves. She sighed inwardly, and as she did, Peter Winslow turned away from his beautiful dinner companion and smiled at Lizzie.

Seated at her father's right, Florence Winslow looked plump and sullen. Despite her lovely gown of peach-colored silk, which should have accentuated her fair skin and light brown hair, she seemed drained of color. The swarthy man beside her, with coarse dark hair, heavy eyebrows, and a prominent nose, attempted unsuccessfully to engage the young woman in conversation. To Lizzie, his movements seemed oddly formal and a bit awkward, and his severe attire made her think of people from the previous century. *That must be Flo's fiancé, Count Nikolai Ivanovich.*

Across the table from Peter, the copper-haired man Lizzie had observed this morning from the window of her bedchamber chatted amiably with young Winslow. At closer range, she noted that the man was even more attractive than he'd appeared from three stories up. Next to him sat a pale woman so delicate and perfectly formed that she could have been a porcelain doll.

Among the other guests, Lizzie spotted a heavy-set middle-aged woman with an overbite that scraped her lower lip every time she forked a piece of food into her mouth and a horse-faced girl of perhaps eighteen, decked out in so many jewels that she could have been an advertisement for Tiffany. The older woman was discussing the "coming out" of her daughter, whom Lizzie presumed to be the bejeweled girl.

"It's such a delight to dine with you and your esteemed guests, Zachary," she said in a loud voice to their host and anyone else whose attention she might manage to catch. "As you know, we've been so involved this summer in Newport with Evangeline's season that we've had little time for enjoying pleasantries with our dear cousins."

"You honor us with your presence," Zachary Winslow said coolly.

The woman turned to Florence Winslow, whom Lizzie guessed was about the same age as the horse-faced Evangeline. "Flo, do you regret not having had a season of your own? Missing out on the excitement, the balls. It's what young girls dream of."

"Flo and Count Ivanovich have more than enough excitement ahead of them," Catherine Winslow countered. "After their wedding, they'll travel throughout Europe and then go on to live in the count's castle in Hungary."

Lizzie lost the train of conversation as servants swept in to clear away empty soup dishes and set out plates of lightly baked halibut. Candlelight flickered on the faces of the scions of industry whose names appeared in the pages of the *Wall Street Journal* and the privileged young people who would follow them to positions of power. Although she didn't recognize most of them, a few of the men looked familiar and she made a mental note to learn their names and more about their businesses while she was here at Wingate.

From the dining room's shell-shaped alcove, Sidney shifted into a romantic piece by Frédérick Chopin, written for a solo piano. Melody, breaking with tradition, stepped forward and accompanied him on her flute. As she drew heartfelt notes from the silvery instrument, Lizzie noticed the swarthy gentleman seated next to Florence Winslow lay his hand over hers. After a moment, Florence pulled away. A tear slid down her cheek and she dabbed at it with a lace handkerchief.

Servants cleared away the halibut dishes and set out plates of roast duckling, along with dill-buttered potatoes, asparagus in Hollandaise sauce, and what appeared to be the same Waldorf salad Lizzie and Melody had enjoyed earlier in their upstairs room. Water glasses were filled, coffee cups topped off. Girls in gray dresses and starched white aprons refreshed the guests' goblets with wine. No one seemed in the least concerned about Prohibition or how the Winslows had acquired the evening's libation.

Animated conversation flowed up and down the dinner table. At a distance, however, Lizzie had a hard time deciphering most of it. With Sid's piano and Melody's flute playing nearby, she only picked up bits and pieces of what was said.

Halfway into the duck course, Sidney began playing George and Ira Gershwin's song "The Man I Love." Under other circumstances Lizzie would have accompanied him, singing the moody and heartfelt piece. But Catherine Winslow's stipulations had relegated her to an observer's position tonight and she sat back silently, admiring Sidney's skill on the ivories. Caught up in the melody, she momentarily tuned out her surroundings and the *illuminati* dining before her, and let herself be swept up in the music.

Suddenly, the sound of glass shattering and a woman's startled cry rose above the piano's refrain. Florence Winslow jumped up from her chair and stared, aghast, at the red stain splashed across the front of her peach-colored gown. Her overturned wine goblet leaked Bordeaux on the linen tablecloth. For a moment, Lizzie flashed back to the ghastly image of Henry's blood-soaked torso. Florence grasped her bodice with both hands, her face drained of color, and hurried away from the table as a kitchen girl rushed in to clean up the mess.

The count stood and started to follow his fiancée, then hesitated, uncertain, and turned to Zachary Winslow for guidance. Apparently not wanting to draw further attention to his daughter's faux pas and subsequent leave-taking, their host shook his head ever so slightly. The dark man sat down again.

Throughout the interruption, Sidney played on as if nothing had happened. *The consummate professional*, Lizzie thought with admiration. While servants cleared away the remnants of the mishap, he shifted to a neutral piece by Brahms. Before long, the group at the dining table returned to their food and conversation, without giving another thought to Florence Winslow's abrupt departure. The night was young, and much remained to be enjoyed.

\* \* \*

In consideration of her out-of-town guests, whom she explained would be tired from traveling and would prefer an early evening, Catherine Winslow asked Sidney and Melody to continue playing for only an hour or so after the dessert dishes had been removed. Tomorrow night, when everyone felt adequately rested from their journeys, Wingate would host a full program complete with drama and dancing.

After consuming Venetian ice cream and assorted cakes, some of the gentlemen departed for the billiard room. Others wandered out to the veranda, where they could smoke their Cuban cigars without offending the ladies. *No doubt glasses of port will circulate among the billiard players,* Lizzie surmised, *and flasks of whiskey among the cigar smokers.*

"I'm going to snoop around a bit," Lizzie told her colleagues as she stepped down from the alcove stage to follow the guests. "Carry on."

"I don't think anyone can even hear us anymore," Melody lamented, glancing around the empty dining room and down the vast gallery that stretched beyond it.

Lizzie patted her on the shoulder. "Poor little bunny, you're probably right, so just play for yourselves. You've done a splendid job tonight. The muses must be pleased."

# Chapter Nine

*"There are all kinds of love in this world, but never the same love twice."*

— *F. Scott Fitzgerald, The Great Gatsby*

A number of the ladies had removed to an octagonal-shaped game room, situated near the billiard parlor. As servants scurried about carrying trays of tea, coffee, and after-dinner sweets, the women seated themselves at card tables to play bridge, mahjong, and backgammon.

The aromas of a dozen or more different perfumes swirled around Lizzie, each trying to drown out the other, as she entered the chamber. As unobtrusively as possible, she eased her way to the room's windowed wall, trying not to attract attention to herself. Protocol in such matters baffled her—would these women invite her to join them or frown on her presence? Her position in the Winslow household remained tenuous and unclear, though she guessed these upper-class ladies—and certainly Catherine Winslow—looked down their Patrician noses at her. Some of the younger ones, though, might consider her and the life of a New York performer glamorous.

She strolled around the perimeter of the game room and stopped at a window seat overlooking Wingate's grassy promenade. From here, she had a clear view of the bronze fountain where Henry Ives had bled to death. She sat down, sipped her glass of ginger ale—surreptitiously laced with gin she'd

61

purloined from the gentlemen's quarters—and watched the group of ladies shuffle their cards and tiles. Most of them ignored her, though she noticed Catherine Winslow occasionally eyeing her with veiled curiosity.

The heavy-set woman with the overbite dealt cards to the three others at her table, including the debutante Evangeline and the chestnut-haired beauty who'd sat beside Peter Winslow during dinner. Lizzie couldn't help admiring the lovely young woman's emerald-green gown, studded from neckline to hips with rhinestones arranged in a shimmering pattern that resembled a Manhattan skyline. Idly, she wondered if the lady was a fellow New Yorker.

As the women picked up their hands, the horse-faced Evangeline said, "I so envy Flo, traveling through Europe with a genuine Russian count."

"He's rather beastly looking, though, don't you think?" the chestnut-haired beauty asked.

"Oh, I don't know, he just seems, well, *foreign*. And he's older, of course," Evangeline replied. "Still, it's so romantic—like a fairy tale. Imagine living in an honest-to-goodness castle."

"He hasn't any money," her heavy-set mother stated as if revealing a dirty secret. "He lost his property and most of his fortune during the Revolution and had to flee to Hungary. Even his title means little now that the Communists are in power in Russia. Oh, he still holds some land near Budapest, inherited from his mother's family, and a rundown old castle that no one could bear to live in." She shivered as if the idea were too bleak to consider.

"How do you know that?" asked the fourth woman in the group, a nearsighted matron who used a magnifying glass to see her cards.

"One has one's sources," Evangeline's mother answered smugly, as if enjoying her moment. She turned to Peter Winslow's chestnut-haired dinner companion at her left. "Bid, dear."

"One spade."

"But if they're in love," Evangeline said, "what does money matter?"

The woman stared at her daughter in disbelief, as if Evangeline were a silly child. "Money is the *only* thing that matters."

Pretending to view the expansive gardens and lawn below, Lizzie moved slowly along the outer wall of the game room. For the most part, she directed her gaze out the windows as she eavesdropped on conversations, sifting through the dross of their discussions for tidbits of information.

"Will Florence rejoin us this evening?" asked a striking woman with ebony hair and olive skin. Her coloring and slight accent suggested a Mediterranean heritage, perhaps Italian or Spanish. "I felt so sorry for her, spilling her drink at dinner like that. How embarrassing."

Catherine Winslow, seated at the Mediterranean woman's table, carefully arranged mahjong tiles. "Flo's a bit distracted these days—nervous and excited about the wedding, as you might imagine. Not quite herself. She needs her rest."

"Yes, of course," agreed the olive-skinned woman.

A petite blonde with charming dimples sighed. "Her beautiful gown, ruined. At first, I thought it was blood, that maybe she'd been cut by the broken glass."

"Heavens, child, don't even *think* such things," the olive-skinned woman said.

Lizzie lingered a while longer in the game room, catching snippets of conversation here and there, but nothing that seemed relevant to Henry's murder. No one even mentioned it. Apparently, Catherine Winslow had managed to squelch word of the crime for the time being.

After a bit, Lizzie moved outside to the terrace, where several couples and a number of single men smoked and conversed in the soft, salt-scented air. Fireflies flashed here and there. Gaslights illuminated the undulating promenade for guests who chose to stroll among the marble statues.

She spotted Peter Winslow standing alone, face upturned to the sky, apparently studying the stars. "Ahoy, Captain Winslow."

He lowered his eyes and turned to Lizzie, scanning her from head to toe and then back up again. "Well, hello there. I waited all evening to hear the lovely Miss Crane sing. Alas, I was disappointed."

"Your mother forbade it. I believe she thought I might be distracting."

He laughed, his eyes crinkling pleasantly at the corners. "Oh yes, indeed."

"What did you see just now in the heavens above?" she asked.

"Fair weather tomorrow."

"A sailor must be able to read the skies, I guess."

He nodded. "His life could depend on it."

"And will you take advantage of this proffered fair day to sail *Rhiannon?*"

"You remembered her name."

"I have a good memory, especially for people and things that intrigue me."

He lit a cigarette and offered her one, but she shook her head. "Thanks, but we singers have to protect our voices, you know."

"Of course," he said. "Could I entice you to go sailing with me tomorrow morning, Miss Crane?"

"Please, call me Lizzie." She fingered a rhinestone clip in her bobbed hair and turned her face toward Ipswich Bay, although it was too dark to see the ocean. "It's a very attractive invitation, but I'm afraid your mother has other plans for me. She's scheduled us for a full evening of entertainment tomorrow night and insists on previewing every detail in advance to make sure it all meets with her expectations."

"Sounds like Mother," he said. "Too bad. I'd hoped to show you a few of my favorite places that can only be reached by boat."

Lizzie looked up at him coyly. "You mean you won't be sailing with the lovely lady who sat beside you at dinner tonight?"

Peter waved his hand dismissively. "A contrivance of my mother's. As you've no doubt noticed, Mother likes to control things."

"Sorry, I didn't mean to pry," she apologized.

"My parents—Mother especially—would like to see me engaged to someone they approve of, rather than leaving me to my own devices. The 'lovely lady' you referred to is the daughter of a fabulously wealthy shipping magnate—a good catch as they say. But I have no intention of marrying to suit my family."

"Unlike your sister, Flo?"

He eyed her skeptically for a moment, then nodded. "Exactly."

"How did Florence manage to meet a Russian count?"

"I think my parents ordered him through the Sears catalog."

Lizzie laughed. "A mail-order husband?"

"I was joking. They met through friends of the family. It all happened pretty fast."

"Is that why she didn't have a 'coming out' season? I mean, the purpose of coming out is to snag a suitable husband, right? So, if your sister had already made her match, the whole auction-block business would have been pointless."

Peter chuckled at her bluntness and nodded again. "You could put it that way. Although, of course, those formalities are starting to go by the wayside."

"Along with arranged marriages, I hope."

"I suspect it might be difficult to force you to marry someone against your will, Miss Crane—Lizzie. You seem to be quite an independent person."

"What reasonably sane female would give over control of her person, finances, and liberties to a man if she had a choice in the matter?"

Peter took a drag on his cigarette and exhaled smoke into the night air. "Perhaps if she loved him?"

"What a romantic you are, Peter Winslow. I must say I find that rather endearing."

Suddenly, Peter slapped his palm against his forehead and groaned. "I must apologize for my atrocious manners. I've been horribly inconsiderate, given the loss you've suffered. Can you ever forgive me? My sincere condolences regarding the death of your friend—and under my family's roof, so to speak. I am deeply sorry. If there's anything I can do…"

Seizing her opportunity to probe into the secret life of Henry Ives, Lizzie said, "Thank you. It's just awful, to be sure. My friends and I don't quite know what to make of it all. We're trying to put the best face on things, of course, so as not to upset your family's guests and interfere with your sister's party, but I admit it is difficult. Say, I believe you knew my colleague, isn't that so?"

Peter flipped the ash off his cigarette and gazed out across the lawn. After a few awkward moments, he answered, "We met a time or two."

"I understand your sister, Flo, knew him too. Henry told me he'd met you both while sailing, and that he'd visited here at Wingate two years ago."

"I feel dreadful that he died in such a violent way and worse still that he died while a guest of my family. I only hope the police can solve the case quickly and give you and your friends resolution in this sad matter."

Lizzie couldn't decide if Peter's regrets were genuine, or if he was simply worried about the shadow a murder might cast over him and his family. However, she did notice he'd dodged her mention that both he *and* his sister knew Henry and that their association may have extended beyond a brief meeting. She leaned closer to Peter and laid her hand lightly on his arm, recalling Henry's words: "I liked her immediately. And she liked me."

"Did Henry and Flo have a personal relationship?" she dared to ask.

Again, he took his time before responding. When he did, he surprised Lizzie with his candor. "I believe they were in love."

\* \* \*

Lizzie accompanied Sidney to his car as the evening drew to an early close. His accommodations in the stables were half a mile away from the Winslow mansion, and he had no intention of walking that far in the dark wearing a tuxedo and dress shoes.

She slipped her arm companionably through his. "You gave a fabulous performance tonight, Sid. Even when Flo smashed her wineglass and bolted away, you didn't miss a note."

"Yes, I thought I did a darb job," he agreed. "Especially on such short notice. Melody played well, too, don't you think?"

"Ab-so-lute-ly. She's a natural."

He plucked a wilting carnation from his lapel and tossed it on the ground. "So, Sherlock Holmes, did you find out anything about our boy Henry?"

"In fact, I did."

"Don't keep me in suspense. Spill."

"I talked with Peter Winslow, who admits that he and his sister Florence knew Henry. Furthermore, he believes Flo and Henry were in love."

"Ah-ha, so Henry's insinuations were accurate. I wonder if Mama and Papa Winslow knew."

"Hard to say."

Sidney loosened his tie. "What do you make of it all?"

"Frankly, the whole thing's a jumble to me. It's intriguing to be sure, but does it cast light on Henry's murder? If anything, I'd say this just muddies the waters."

"Sleep on it, Bearcat. Tomorrow may bring insights we haven't anticipated yet."

Sidney ruffled her hair casually, as if she were his kid sister. He'd treated her that way since the first time they met seven years ago, at a restaurant in the Village where he played piano and she waited tables.

"Speaking of tomorrow," he continued, "We have to meet Catherine Winslow at ten in the morning to go over our repertoire. I think you and I should connect at nine to finalize details and make sure we're copacetic, okay?"

"Your place or mine?" Lizzie teased.

"How about on the beach at the end of the promenade? I haven't had time to even see the beach yet, let alone take the waters."

"You're on." She hugged him quickly, then stepped back as he climbed into the Buick. "Sweet dreams."

# Chapter Ten

*"Life is a lot like jazz...it's best when you improvise."*

— *George Gershwin*

A s Peter Winslow had predicted, the day dawned sunny and clear, with only a wisp of haze hugging the horizon. Lizzie stood at the window of her tiny bedchamber watching a team of groundskeepers mowing, pruning, and otherwise tidying the already meticulously groomed promenade. Two young gentlemen guests dressed in crisp white outfits played a game of tennis. Several other early birds strolled about the grounds or lounged on the back terrace, taking in the sea air.

She spotted Catherine and Florence Winslow in the rose garden, standing amid the multicolored blossoms, supervising two men digging a hole in the rich, chocolaty soil. When the diggers had finished, Mrs. Winslow knelt beside the hole to inspect their work. After a few moments, she stood again, apparently satisfied, and motioned to the men. One gardener grasped a new rosebush that lay at his feet, plunked it in the hole, and held it upright while the other man shoveled and packed dirt around its roots. The Winslow women waited as one of the men watered the new addition to the rose garden, then they turned and walked back toward the mansion arm-in-arm.

\* \* \*

When Lizzie arrived at the Winslows' private beach she saw several sailboats cutting through the blue-green water. Their triangular white sails reminded her of the wings of seabirds unfurled and gliding on the wind. She searched for *Rhiannon* among them, but the sloop wasn't in the cove. Apparently, Peter Winslow had taken her out on the morning tide. Lizzie couldn't help wondering if the chestnut-haired debutante had sailed with him.

Sidney sat on the beach, smoking a cigarette and gazing out to sea. He'd rolled up the legs of his trousers and dug his bare feet ankle-deep in the white sand.

"Top of the morning to you, Sir Somerset," she called, and he waved her over.

"Glorious day," he said. "Sure beats the heat, noise, and stench of the City, wouldn't you say-ski?"

"Any day-ski."

As she dropped down beside him, he shifted away from the serenity of the setting and launched into business. "So, tonight I think I should open with a piano medley, fifteen minutes or so," he suggested. "After the audience has had a chance to get settled in, I'll introduce us. Then I'll start playing 'Everybody Loves My Baby'—that's the cue for you and Melody to come on stage and dance."

Lizzie nodded and added, "How 'bout we wear those short pink outfits with the sequins?"

"That should get the men's attention and raise a few eyebrows among the women."

"Then let's not share that little detail with Catherine Winslow—she might get in a lather because our gams are nicer than hers. What do you think, about seven minutes of tap?"

"More or less. We'll gauge it by the audience's response. If they're enjoying it, I'll play another song or two. Just keep going 'til you hear me start to wind it up, then you can wave, throw kisses, and prance offstage."

They bounced around several possibilities, Lizzie proposing songs and Sidney approving or vetoing them. A few yards away, waves rippled onshore making a soft shushing sound. She removed her shoes and stockings and dug her toes into the cool sand. Leaning back on her elbows, she let the morning sun kiss her cheeks. *If only I could stay here like this forever . . .*

"It's such a lovely day. I suppose we'll be performing on the outdoor stage tonight, wouldn't you say?"

He stubbed out his cigarette in the sand and lit another. "That's my guess, unless our hostess has other plans."

"We'll have to stake out a room in the gentlemen's quarters for dressing and props, now that you've been ousted."

"Don't rub it in," Sidney grumbled.

Lizzie scooped up a handful of sand and let it trickle through her fingers. She still felt apprehensive about opening this important engagement tonight without their saxophonist. Sid's expert piano and Melody's winsome flute needed the solid foundation Henry's horn had provided. Without that anchor, they skimmed the surface like an untethered boat. Moreover, she worried about what the Winslows' guests knew of Henry's murder, what their reaction might be, and how it would affect The Troubadours' image.

"What about Henry's family? Do you think the police have told them yet?" she asked.

"Most likely, unless they had as much trouble as we did, getting the locals to give up the goods."

"If the Ives family isn't on the level—and I pos-i-tive-ly got that impression—the cops surely know who they are and where to find them. Getting them to give it up might be another story, though."

Sidney stood and brushed sand off the seat of his trousers. "Let's walk down the beach a ways."

They waded in the icy water for a while without talking. Squawking gulls swooped by and sandpipers skittered about, searching for a meal. Overhead, a few fleecy white clouds floated past. Now and then, Lizzie bent to pick up a seashell or a bit of beach glass, tucking it into her pocket to join the rest of her gathered treasures.

"I feel like we should *do something*," she said. "A friend of ours has been murdered, and I feel so helpless. If we can't solve the crime and bring the killer to justice, at least we should somehow mark Henry's passing, don't you think?"

"A funeral you mean?"

"Well, we can't have a real funeral without the body, and the cops have seized that. But maybe a memorial service anyway."

"Let's wait 'til we get back to New York, so his friends there can come," Sidney suggested.

From what she'd witnessed thus far, it didn't seem that Henry Ives had many friends around here who might want to attend. Sidney had a point.

"Besides," he continued, "we don't know what's doing with his family. They'll probably arrange something themselves. And we've got our hands full at the moment. Okay by you-ski?"

"It'll have to do-ski."

Sidney put his arm around her shoulders and gave her a brotherly hug. "I'm not trying to make light of what happened. I've known Henry longer than you, although I can't say we were ever close. It's just, well, everything's so balled up. I feel overwhelmed and unable to deal with it right now. I have to focus on this job. It's all I can do to just keep putting one foot in front of the other."

Lizzie slipped her arm around his waist and hugged him in return. The incoming tide swirled around their ankles as they walked. A light breeze tousled her dark hair. By now the frigid water had numbed her feet and for the first time since Henry's death, she felt almost peaceful, sloshing through the foaming waves that broke on shore.

"So, back to business," she said, pushing her concerns about Henry aside for the time being. "We should probably sing a few more songs, then take a short break and come back with a dramatic sketch. Something comical, considering the circumstances. Even if the guests don't know about the murder, it will be easier on us."

"What? Not your lascivious bathtub scene?" Sidney teased.

"Not on opening night—I don't want to give Catherine Winslow anything else to fuss about. How about O. Henry's *While the Auto Waits*?" she injected. "It's short and light, and despite its apparent criticism of the upper classes, it turns the tables at the end. I'm betting the Winslows' guests will be amused, not offended. Besides, we already know our lines by heart and we don't need many props or costumes, although it might add a touch of authenticity if you drove the Buick down to the stage and parked it beside the front-row benches."

"Hmm, there's an idea. Who'll play the chauffeur, now that we're a man short?"

Lizzie snapped her fingers. "How about Thomas, the cook's son? I get the impression he's gaga about theater—he'd love the chance to perform. I know he's just a child, but he's tall for his age…with a little makeup and a uniform, I believe he could pull it off. He'd only have a few short lines."

"Swell! I'll talk to him as soon as we finish meeting with Mrs. Winslow. By the way, what time is it?"

"Probably almost ten. We'd better head back."

Sidney sighed. "Damn, Lizzie, we're really at a loss without Henry. We're good at what we do, but musically, well, we're a bit thin without his horn. We're okay for—"

"Background music," she interrupted. "But not for dancing."

"Right."

"What do you suggest?"

"I know a saxophonist in Boston, an older fella who doesn't perform much anymore, but he's supremely talented. We played together years ago when he still lived in New York. His name's Joey Golick. Plays trumpet too. What would you think of asking him to join us? Just for this engagement, nothing long-term?"

"If you're sold on him, it sounds like a good idea to me. I agree, we need to add some octane." As they reached the fringe of wild salt grass that bordered the beach, Lizzie brushed sand off her feet and slipped on her shoes. "I suppose we'll have to get Madame Winslow's okay before we bring someone else on board."

"I suspect you're right. Do you think we'll need to let Sergeant Mulvaney know too?"

"Let's plead ignorance on that one. He didn't forbid anyone coming to Wingate, just told us not to leave."

As they walked toward the Winslow mansion, Lizzie hooked her arm through Sidney's and laid her head against his shoulder. "Sid, why can't I meet a heterosexual man I like and get along with as well as you?"

\* \* \*

At ten on the dot, Mrs. Greely led the three Troubadours into the mansion's aviary, where Catherine Winslow sat on a white wicker settee awaiting them. To Lizzie, it seemed an odd place for a business conference and yet she enjoyed the tropical ambiance. Mourning doves cooed, brilliantly colored parrots screeched, and miscellaneous songbirds flitted about, trilling their melodious tunes.

In this glassed-in anteroom, which had been designed to capture the morning light, a jungle of plants vied for space and attention. Sitting beneath an oversized philodendron, whose fan-shaped leaves reminded her of the ears of the elephants she'd seen in the Bronx Zoo, Lizzie felt like a shrunken Alice in Wonderland. Melody seemed enchanted with the birds and followed their movements intently, not a bit interested in the humans' conversation. *Perhaps she's studying birdsongs to play on her flute,* Lizzie mused.

Catherine Winslow wore a lovely pale yellow daytime frock that complimented her golden hair and alabaster complexion. As the three Troubadours seated themselves, a servant brought a tray of aromatic coffee and set it on a small table in front of the manor's mistress. No pastries or other dainties, Lizzie noted. *I hope that means she's planning on a short meeting.*

The serving girl poured steaming coffee into cups while Sidney began laying out the program, they'd cobbled together on the beach only an hour ago. As she had so many times before, Lizzie admired his ability to get exactly what he wanted, while somehow making the client believe she'd orchestrated the whole thing herself. His good looks and slightly effeminate behavior worked to his advantage—women never felt threatened or overpowered by him, and men didn't consider him a rival. Mrs. Winslow even responded favorably to his suggestion of bringing in another horn player to replace Henry Ives and offered to let him use Wingate's telephone to ring up Joey

Golick.

After Sidney finished outlining the evening's entertainment, Mrs. Winslow lifted her coffee cup—with her pinky finger raised, Lizzie observed—and gazed at him coquettishly. *Good heavens, is she actually flirting with him?* Lizzie wondered, amused.

Having agreed to the repertoire Sidney had proposed, their hostess said, "After the dramatic piece, I would be most grateful if you would play dance music for a bit—perhaps an hour or two—so my guests can unwind and enjoy themselves."

"Certainly, Mrs. Winslow. I had expected, due to the beautiful weather, that we'd be performing on the outdoor stage tonight, but there's no dance floor there," he pointed out. "Would your guests enjoy dancing on the dew-dappled grass beneath the shining stars? Perhaps we can string up outdoor lights and create a veritable fantasyland. I dare say it might be most romantic."

"Why, yes, Mr. Somerset, that sounds quite pleasant," Catherine Winslow answered. She held out her hand and a small bird with a yellow body and black wings perched on her finger.

"Of course, we'll require a dressing room and a staging area for our props. Could you please allocate a room in the gentlemen's quarters for that purpose? One close to the stage. And we'll need the assistance of a few of your staff to arrange the sets." Sidney lit a cigarette and paused a moment before suggesting, "By the way, given that one of our cast has been, uh, suddenly and unexpectedly prevented from participating in this evening's entertainment, I wonder if you'd give permission for Thomas Appleby to fill in tonight in a very minor dramatic role?"

"Thomas Appleby…"

"Your head cook's son."

"Oh, yes. Hazel's boy. But he's just a child, isn't he?"

"He's fourteen and tall for his age. With a false mustache and some makeup, no one will recognize him," Sidney insisted. "Besides, he'll only have to speak a few words. Truly, we have no other options to draw upon at this late date, unless you have some suggestions?"

"If you can assure me he's capable…"

"I believe he is. Quite."

"Well, then, I must trust your judgment, Mr. Somerset, mustn't I?"

Sidney rolled out his most obsequious tone and endearing expression. "Mrs. Winslow, my only wish—and I speak for my colleagues as well as myself—is to provide enjoyable entertainment and a pleasant diversion for you, your family, and your most esteemed guests."

Lizzie stifled a smirk and let Sidney do what he did so well.

"One more thing," Catherine Winslow said. "Would you please dedicate your entertainments to my daughter, Florence, and her fiancé, Count Ivanovich?" She leaned her pretty blond head toward Sidney, as if to engage him in a private moment, and lowered her voice. "Flo's been so, well, distant these past few days. My hope is to draw her out and lighten her spirits. She didn't have a formal coming out season last year, so this week's enjoyments are my modest way of trying to make it up to my daughter."

"Of course, Mrs. Winslow," Sidney promised, clapping his hands. "What a lovely idea."

# Chapter Eleven

*"Any woman or man who would write the truth of their lives would write a great work. But no one has dared to write the truth of their lives."*

— Isadora Duncan, *My Life*

While Sidney went with Mrs. Winslow to telephone the replacement saxophonist, Lizzie and Melody meandered into the kitchen in search of Thomas Appleby's mother, the head cook. Servants scurried about the commodious kitchen, sliding trays into ovens and setting pots on burners to simmer. Youngsters washed and peeled vegetables. Kitchen maids chopped all manner of foods on wooden cutting boards and stirred undefined mixtures in huge pottery bowls. The aromas wafting through the steamy space made Lizzie's mouth water, but the oppressive heat made her swoon.

They found the plump, red-cheeked cook rolling out dough for piecrusts, flour up to her elbows.

"Mrs. Appleby, I'm Lizzie Crane and this is my colleague Melody Fitzgerald, from New York City. As you know, we're performing for Mrs. Winslow's guests this week."

The cook laid down her rolling pin and wiped her palms on her apron. Sweat dappled her forehead. "Pleased to meet you both. Have you enjoyed the victuals I've sent to you these past few days?"

"We have indeed. Thank you ever so much for all the delicious meals you've provided for us. Your talents put New York's famous chefs to shame." Lizzie patted her stomach. "I believe I've already gained five pounds since we got here."

"You're welcome, miss, I'm sure," the cook replied, grinning at Lizzie's compliments. She puffed herself up and turned her head from side to side like a bird, apparently trying to see if anyone else had heard. "Is there something you're needing now? A biscuit, perhaps, or a piece of fruit? Lunch is still a bit away."

"Thank you, no. We've come about a different matter: to ask permission to engage your son, Thomas, in a short play this evening. I have the impression he's interested in the theater."

"Lord, that's all he cares about," Mrs. Appleby said. "Longs to go to the moving picture shows, but of course we haven't the money or the means to travel to places where they have theaters and such."

"With your permission, we'd like to invite Thomas to play a small role in a dramatic piece we're staging tonight for Mr. and Mrs. Winslow's guests. I believe your son would be perfect for the part, and we'll gladly compensate him financially for his efforts."

Mrs. Appleby wiped her forehead with the back of her arm, leaving a white streak behind. "Goodness, miss, do I hear you saying you want my Thomas to be an actor?"

A girl of about Thomas's age withdrew a huge tray of pastries from the oven and plunked them down on the worktable for Mrs. Appleby's approval. The plump cook snatched one, blew on it, and then popped it into her mouth. After a moment of chewing she nodded, then turned to Melody. "Try one, miss. You look as though you could use a bit of fattening up."

Melody waited a few moments for the pastry to cool before she devoured one.

"It would only be for this evening," Lizzie explained to the cook. "He'd be on stage for just a few minutes, but we'll need to rehearse with him for a bit this afternoon. Could you excuse him from his regular duties for, say, an hour? Mrs. Winslow has already given her okay."

Mrs. Appleby drew herself up from her work, puffed out her ample bosom, and lifted her head with pride. "My Thomas, an actor!"

"Please send him around to the outdoor stage near the gentlemen's quarters at about two o'clock. And we'll need him to show up again right after dinner has been served to dress for the performance."

The cook steepled her flour-dusted palms together beneath her chin, and her eyes grew moist. "Thank you, miss. You've made a young boy's dream come true. However can I thank you?"

"Just keep sending us delightful food."

\* \* \*

As the two performers crossed the lawn toward the outdoor theater, Ginny Winslow raced to meet them. The twelve-year-old girl wore a blue-and-white checked gingham frock and a wide-brimmed straw hat that shielded her fair skin from the August sun's harsh rays.

"Thomas says he's going to act on stage with you tonight," Ginny said, a note of question and envy in her voice.

"That's right," Lizzie confirmed. "A small role, but an important one."

"Will you be there to watch?" Melody asked.

"One way or another," the girl promised. "When do I get to be an actress?"

"Well, I don't know, Ginny," Lizzie said. "First of all, your parents would have to agree."

"If they did, would you have me?"

After a moment, Lizzie answered, "We could consider it."

As they neared the bronze fountain that had now taken on such nefarious associations, Lizzie noticed a uniformed man standing alone under an ash tree, smoking a cigarette. Instantly she recognized him as Sergeant Mulvaney.

She hooked her arm through Melody's and whispered, "It's that cop, Mulvaney. If you'd rather scoot away, I'll handle him. No need for both of us to suffer through talking to him."

"He doesn't scare me," Melody replied, with false bravado.

"All right then."

She turned to Ginny and pointed at the policeman. After all the upset of the night before last, surely the girl must be aware that a man had died, but Lizzie couldn't imagine what that meant to a child. Did Ginny know Henry, or know of her sister's friendship with him? Could she even comprehend the idea of death?

"We have to go talk to that man now, and he's ever so tiresome. If you want to skedaddle I wouldn't mind."

"I want to stay with you," the girl insisted.

"Very well, but don't say I didn't warn you."

As they came within speaking range, Lizzie called out to Mulvaney with mock gaiety. "Good morning, Sergeant. Have you learned anything more about our colleague? We've been on pins and needles, waiting to hear from you."

The stocky policeman stepped toward them and tipped his cap to the women. Lizzie noticed he was almost entirely bald, with only strands of hair combed over to unsuccessfully hide his otherwise naked skull.

"Good morning," he replied. "Miss Crane, Miss Fitzgerald, I've been waiting to have a word with you. Good morning to you too, Miss Winslow."

"Certainly, Sergeant," Lizzie said. "We're at your disposal."

"Is Mr. Somerset on the premises?"

"You might find him at the stables. Does this mean you have information for us, Sergeant?"

Mulvaney settled his cap back on his head and adjusted it with care. "Let's drive there together and see if we can locate Mr. Somerset. You won't mind riding in a police car, will you?"

"Not unless you plan to haul us off to jail." Lizzie threw him a teasing smile. "We all have the same objective, don't we? To apprehend Henry's killer?"

"We do, indeed." He motioned the women toward the squad car.

"I want to come too," Ginny insisted.

"Very well, hop in," Mulvaney said.

Melody and Ginny climbed into the back of the auto, but Lizzie, not wanting to give the impression that they were being apprehended, slid into the front seat beside the policeman. Sidney, she realized, might still be in the Winslow mansion, trying to get in touch with the Boston musician whom, he hoped, would replace Henry Ives. She tightened the drawstring on her straw hat and leaned out the window, enjoying the breeze on her face. As the sedan rolled down the long, winding driveway toward the front gate, she directed him toward the stables, although she felt certain that Mulvaney already knew the way.

When the cruiser pulled up to the building made of native stone with a cedar shake roof, Lizzie spotted two young men mucking out the empty stalls. The Winslows' guests had chosen to ride some of the horses this morning; the others had been turned out into the pastures to graze. Upon seeing Mulvaney's uniform, the stable boys laid down their shovels and snapped to attention, then unabashedly ogled Lizzie and Melody as the two women exited the cruiser.

A few moments later, Sidney drove up in his Buick convertible. Lizzie wished she'd had an opportunity to alert him to the sergeant's presence, but Sid rolled out his actor's acumen and took it in stride.

"Sergeant Mulvaney," he said cheerfully, holding out his hand. "I hope you've come bearing good news. Have you found our friend's killer?"

Mulvaney grasped Sidney's graceful hand with his own beefy one. "I wish that were the case," he said, "but I have a different reason for being here this morning."

"And what might that be?"

"As we suspected, the knife we retrieved from the fountain near where we found Mr. Ives's body revealed no readable fingerprints." Mulvaney cleared his throat. "I understand that on the afternoon prior to his demise, you and your colleagues rehearsed a dramatic act with a dagger on the estate's outdoor stage."

"Yes, that's true."

"Where is that knife now?"

Sidney threw back his head and laughed. "Surely you don't think *that* knife was the murder weapon?"

"Until I examine it I can't say, Mr. Somerset."

"It's a trick knife, a stage prop," Sidney explained. "It's made of rubber. You couldn't slice Brie with that knife, much less kill someone."

"Ah. Well, then, I wonder if you'd mind showing me how it works?"

"Not at all."

As Sidney went to search for the trick dagger, Lizzie stepped toward Sergeant Mulvaney and intentionally stood close enough to the detective to make him feel self-conscious.

"How did you know about the stage knife?" she asked.

Mulvaney stared out over the landscape momentarily, then shifted his gaze to the stables, as if attempting to avoid eye contact with Lizzie. Finally, he admitted, "Mrs. Winslow told me she and her daughters sat in on a rehearsal your troupe gave where the dagger was used."

"I saw it all. She knelt beside a man and stabbed herself with it," Ginny offered, pointing at Melody. The girl frowned for a moment, as if recollecting the scenario and trying to make sense of what she'd seen. "Of course, he was already dead and she's still alive. At least, I think he was dead…"

"Ginny, dear," Lizzie assured the girl, "that was merely a play, all make-believe. The man was only pretending to be dead and Melody, here, didn't really stab herself—as you can plainly see."

Ginny frowned. "Yes, I see that. But the man. Is he dead or was that a trick too?"

"I'm afraid he is dead. But *not* because of the make-believe scene you saw—he was very much alive at that time. We were enacting one of Shakespeare's classic plays, Sergeant Mulvaney. *Romeo and Juliet*. Perhaps you know of it?"

"Yes, I've heard of it," he replied.

"The man playing Romeo in that scene was my friend, Henry Ives," she said and laid her hand on Ginny's shoulder. "After you observed him in that play, Ginny, someone here at Wingate murdered him. Sergeant Mulvaney is trying to find the killer. If you know anything that might help us discover who killed Henry, we'd all be very grateful."

The girl looked at the young men cleaning the stables, then down at her shoes, uncertain how to respond. "But I don't know anything."

"Well, if you stumble upon something about Henry—even if it doesn't seem important—will you tell me?"

Ginny nodded. While they waited for Sid to return, they watched the young stable hands perform their jobs. Ginny climbed up on the corral's split-rail fence and straddled it in an unladylike manner, as if she were riding a wooden horse. Mulvaney smoked a cigarette in silence. After some minutes had passed, Sidney rejoined the group. He handed the rubber knife to the policeman, who fiddled with it, turning it over and over in his hands before passing it back.

"How does this 'trick' knife work?"

Sidney grasped the prop in his right hand and held up his left. He pressed the rubber knife's point against his palm. As he applied pressure, the blade retracted into the hilt. "As you can see, Sergeant, this 'weapon' couldn't hurt anyone."

"Have you asked Mrs. Appleby, the Winslows' cook, about the whereabouts of all her kitchen knives on the night of Henry's murder?" Lizzie interrupted. "Can she produce alibis for all of them?"

Mulvaney dropped his cigarette butt and ground it out with his shoe. "I'll ask the questions, Miss Crane, and you'll answer them."

She wondered if he might order a search of their luggage and props, but he didn't. Perhaps he didn't feel up to it himself and he hadn't brought his junior assistant, Officer Connelly, along with him. *What have they done with Henry's bags?* she wondered, hoping they didn't contain anything that might reflect badly on the troupe.

Mulvaney drove The Troubadours and young Ginny Winslow back to the mansion and dropped them off. After he departed—with another reminder not to leave the premises—Lizzie asked Sidney if he'd reached the substitute saxophonist.

"Lucked out," Sidney said. "Old Joey was still in bed when I called, and none too happy to be awakened, but he's game for the job. He'll be here late this afternoon."

"Well, there's some good news. But will we have time to practice with him before we perform tonight?"

"Joey's been around so long he knows every song ever written." He ruffled her hair. "Don't worry your pretty little head, Bearcat. He'll be fine."

Behind her back, Lizzie crossed her fingers and petitioned the muses to help them get through the night. "Melody and I talked to Mrs. Appleby and she's pos-i-tive-ly thrilled about Thomas acting in the play tonight. She's going to send him down to the stage to practice right after lunch."

"Then everything's copacetic."

"Except that Henry's been murdered, the cops suspect us of killing him, and we can't go back to New York."

Ginny Winslow frowned at Sidney. "You didn't kill that man, did you?"

"Of course not," Lizzie told the girl. "How could you even think such a thing? The man who died was our friend. Friends don't kill friends. But we want to find out who did it. Remember, you promised to let me know if you learn anything that might help us get to the bottom of this tragedy."

Ginny nodded. "If I help can I be in a play?"

"Don't try to bribe me, young lady." Lizzie pulled one of Ginny's braids playfully. "Now off with you, I have work to do."

# Chapter Twelve

*"I've always wanted to participate in, or at least witness first hand, the rituals of the elite."*

— O'Henry, *While the Auto Waits*

W ith a bit of effort, the Black Irish lad and two other young men maneuvered the piano from the gentlemen's quarters to the outdoor stage. While Sidney made certain the move hadn't thrown the instrument out of tune, Lizzie supervised two servants hanging colored lanterns from the trees nearby. Another man rearranged a sleeping chamber for The Troubadours to use as a dressing room, stashing props and costumes in every nook and cranny.

The sun had passed its zenith when Thomas Appleby showed up carrying a picnic basket. He stood in the grass, shifting his weight from one foot to the other, waiting for someone to tell him what to do until Sidney waved him up onstage.

After the troupe consumed a lunch of sliced ham, potato salad, chilled green beans almandine, and blueberry pie—sent by Thomas's grateful mother—they rehearsed O'Henry's ten-minute skit. Sidney and Melody took the lead roles, Lizzie and Thomas the minor ones. The first time Thomas delivered his three brief lines, he stumbled over the second one and blushed with embarrassment. On his next attempt, he tried to compensate for his blunder by overacting.

"Just relax," Lizzie told him gently. "You're doing fine. Third time's a charm, right?"

He grinned sheepishly, and they went through the whole play again. This time the boy gave a flawless performance.

"See? I knew you could do it." Lizzie gave him a quick hug, which made him blush again. "Now let's see how your costume fits."

Although Thomas was nearly as tall as Henry Ives had been, he weighed about thirty pounds less. Lizzie stitched a few quick alterations while Thomas held the false mustache to his upper lip and studied his reflection in a mirror.

"We'll wait 'til this evening to glue that on. It can feel a bit itchy," she explained. "Now put on your costume and we'll run through the skit a few more times until you're comfortable."

After several more practice runs, Lizzie felt certain the boy had his role down pat.

"Hurry down here immediately after dinner is served to the Winslows' guests," she told him. "And see if you can manage to pinch us a bottle, you know, to calm opening night jitters—mine, not yours."

"Yes ma'am. And thank you, ma'am, for giving me this chance."

"Thank you, Thomas, for helping us out." She patted his cheek. "You're a peach."

As the boy's long-legged strides carried him back toward the mansion, Lizzie sighed and hooked her arm through Sidney's. "Alas, another young dreamer falls victim to the theater's siren song."

\* \* \*

At half-past three, a very plump, very plain serving girl with braids wrapped around her head led Joey Golick to the outdoor stage where Lizzie and Melody were practicing their tap-dancing routine. Sidney stopped playing mid-song and rushed to greet the musician. Joey set down his instrument cases and the two men shook hands and slapped shoulders.

Lizzie eyed the short, thickset Golick, whose kinky salt-and-pepper hair reminded her of a Brillo pad and whose nose hooked like a parrot's beak. His suit, though of good quality, dated back to the war years, suggesting the previous decade had been kinder to him than the present one. She motioned for Melody to follow her down from the stage to meet him.

"May I introduce my colleagues, Lizzie Crane, and Melody Fitzgerald," Sidney said.

The older man's presence seemed to have a comforting effect on Sidney. Lizzie imagined she saw her friend's whole body sigh with relief now that Joey had arrived, knowing he had a compatriot in his corner.

"Glad to have you aboard," Lizzie said. "Thank you for agreeing to join us on such short notice. Sidney says you're the cat's meow."

Melody smiled sweetly. "Pleased to meet you, Mr. Golick."

"Joey, Joey," the man insisted, tugging at his garish tie. "Nice digs you got here, Sid. Nice girls too. You're moving up in the world, eh?"

"I can't claim any of what you see as mine. I'm but a poor troubadour, singing for my supper. Still, it's not a bad situation—food's good and the dough's ducky."

Joey held out his hands, palms up. "What more can a man ask for?"

"Better accommodations," Sidney lamented. "You have a choice of bunking with me and a dozen other fellas above the stables, sleeping on a couch in the prop room, or driving back to your apartment in Boston every night after performances."

"I guess it depends on how old Joey feels at the end of the night. Right now, my friend, let's see to the music."

\* \* \*

By the time Thomas brought their supper—plus a bottle of Kentucky bourbon he'd filched from the Winslows' stock—The Troubadours had finished prepping Joey Golick on the evening's program. Despite her initial reservations, Lizzie had to admit that the old musician knew his stuff. True, he lacked Henry's charm and good looks, but his repertoire included more songs than she'd heard in her entire lifetime. His unflappable nature—the legacy of nearly a half-century of experience—provided a sense of stability for the group during this time of uncertainty.

When Joey excused himself to use the men's room, Lizzie hissed to Sidney, "He's a Jew."

"What if he is-ski? He's a fine musician, and we need him."

"Okay by me, but do the Winslows know?"

"If it rattles Her Highness's cage, I'll handle it."

"Then I guess it's none of my biz-ski."

Changing the subject, Sidney asked, "By the way, Bearcat, did you bring along your red dress with the fringe?"

"Of course."

"Good. I want you to wear it tonight and drape yourself over the piano when you sing about passion and unrequited love. Pull out all the stops."

She smiled sweetly at him. "You mean charm the men with the money?"

"In so many words."

"Dear Sidney, I get the impression that you want me to prostitute myself."

"Most people think all lady entertainers are prostitutes anyway," he reminded her. "Besides, Lizzie, you're twenty-six years old—how much longer can you play this game?"

As his words hit home, she pressed her full lips into a tight line. How much longer indeed? Then she tossed her dark hair, as if shaking off her concerns, and asked, "What about Peter Winslow? Do you think I should set my sights on the young heir?"

Sidney shook his head. "He'll never marry you."

"Who said anything about marriage?"

\* \* \*

Lizzie applied rouge to her cheeks and then dusted her face with powder. Skillfully she lined her smoky-gray eyes with a dark pencil and brushed her lids with turquoise shadow. As she gazed at the effect in the dressing room mirror, she spotted the reflection of Ginny Winslow's face pressed against the windowpane behind her. Quickly, Lizzie pulled her silk dressing gown closed and tied the sash at her waist, then threw open the window.

"Are you spying on me, child?"

"I'm only watching, trying to learn," the girl answered. She slid a leg over the windowsill and climbed inside without waiting for an invitation. "Can I put on some of your face powder?"

"Oh, all right, but be quick about it. I have to finish getting ready."

Ginny took a seat in front of the mirror and began examining the array of cosmetics laid out on a makeshift dressing table. Lizzie snapped open a tortoiseshell compact and offered it to the girl.

"Just a dusting of powder. You're too young for anything more."

Ginny leaned close to the mirror and patted her cheeks with a powder puff. "I told you I'd be here for the performance."

"How did you sneak out of the house without anyone noticing you? Since Henry's death, Wingate is crawling with vigilant servants and guards. I should think they'd have locked you in your bedroom for the night."

"Easy. Our bedrooms have balconies, so we can sit outside in nice weather. All I had to do was climb down the trellises and rain spouts to the ground. Peter showed Flo how to do it ages ago and Flo showed me. It's practically a family tradition."

Lizzie laughed and handed Ginny a tube of pink lipstick. "Here, try this. But be sure your mother doesn't see you painted like a floozy or she'll have my head on a platter."

The twelve-year-old meticulously glazed her thin lips, trying to make the lower one appear plumper to create a fashionable Cupid's bow effect. After she'd finished, she turned to Lizzie for approval. The actress nodded, and Ginny reached out tentatively to touch Lizzie's bobbed hair.

"I wish Mother would let me cut my hair like yours." She yanked her own waist-length, caramel-colored braid, over her shoulder, frowning as if it offended her.

"That might be rather scandalous. Besides, you have such lovely hair."

"I don't want to be lovely, I want to be exotic."

"Well, you have plenty of time to decide these things." Lizzie gave Ginny a quick hug. "Whatever you choose to be, I'm sure you'll be a woman who strikes awe in the hearts of men."

Ginny frowned and mumbled, "Hmph."

"Don't frown, it causes wrinkles. By the way, where do you plan to hide so you can watch us tonight?

"I'm going to climb a big oak tree near the stage and sit on an overhanging branch. I'll have a front-row seat."

"Promise me you won't do anything to distract Thomas or make him nervous. We need him to give a good performance—and he needs to feel proud of his accomplishment."

"I promise."

Lizzie handed Ginny the tube of pink lipstick. "Here, take this. You might find another occasion to wear it."

# Chapter Thirteen

*"Nobody could have put her in the shade, blown out her light that evening; she was too evidently shining."*

— *Elizabeth von Arnim, The Enchanted April*

Dressed in sequined, skin-tight outfits that covered less of their shapely bodies than bathing costumes would have, Lizzie and Melody peered through the window of their improvised dressing room, watching the Winslows' guests saunter into the outdoor theater area and take their seats. Despite the salubrious weather, several women had fur stoles draped around their shoulders. One lady vigorously waved an ostrich-feathered fan, as if shooing away mosquitoes. Another wore a gown that seemed to be fashioned entirely of feathers.

Zachary, Catherine, and Florence Winslow, accompanied by Count Ivanovich, sat in the first row directly in front of the stage. Behind them, Peter Winslow and his beautiful companion took up residence.

While Sidney played a mélange of musical pleasantries, Lizzie studied the gathering crowd. The handsome copper-haired man she'd spotted on the first day of his arrival at Wingate sat directly behind Peter Winslow. At his side was a beautiful brunette wearing an exquisite white gown and matching cape trimmed with silver fox fur. Several other guests she recognized from the previous evening positioned themselves so they'd have a good view of the stage. Lizzie noticed a few people passing silver flasks surreptitiously between them. Searching for Ginny, she looked up at a grand old oak tree near the gentlemen's quarters but saw nothing but summer-heavy foliage.

As the stone benches facing the stage filled up, Sidney shifted to livelier tunes. Lizzie sighed with envy as she eyed the women's outfits, cut in the latest and most elegant fashion, each more gorgeous than the next. She consoled herself, thinking *at least my red frock will stand out in that lovely field of celadon, green, and ivory, like a fire burning across a meadow.*

Earlier, Sidney had advised her to eschew the tight undergarments that would have constrained her full bosom and given her the fashionable, flat-chested figure of a girl. He encouraged her to flaunt her womanly lushness instead.

"I don't give a damn what Paris and New York designers decree," he'd insisted. "Men don't want pencil-thin women, they crave those sensuous feminine curves. You've got a great figure, Bearcat—show it off, and you'll have all those aristocrats falling at your feet."

"Why should I take seriously the opinion of a three-letter fella?" she'd joked.

"Because I'm a keen observer of men, no matter what their sexual preference. And because I want to help you snag the man of your dreams."

Assessing herself in the mirror, she'd realized he was right. Still, she'd felt a bit self-conscious and overexposed as she'd studied her reflection and all that bare skin.

As Sidney played the first notes of "Everybody Loves My Baby," Lizzie nudged Melody and patted her cheeks. "That's our cue. Ready?"

"Whenever you are," Melody answered.

For good luck, Lizzie touched her left tap shoe with her right hand, then her right shoe with her left hand. She did a full-body shimmy, turned full circle, and clapped her hands twice. "Okay, showtime!"

As they pranced on stage, Lizzie thought she saw Peter Winslow wink at her. Seated in the row behind him, the copper-haired man smiled. Sergeant Mulvaney, in citizen garb so as not to make the Winslows' guests uncomfortable, stood in the shadows behind the rest of the audience. She pushed thoughts of all three men from her mind, determined not to let them distract her, and concentrated on her dance steps.

After a few lively and slightly provocative numbers, Sidney, in his spiffy tuxedo, left his piano and joined the two dancing women. Positioning himself between them, he tapped, twirled, dipped, and intermittently lifted the ladies into the air with such pizazz that the audience cheered again and again at their acrobatics. Joey Golick accompanied them on his sax as smoothly as if he'd been working with the troupe for years.

Following a short break, during which The Troubadours changed clothes, the guests smoked cigarettes and tipped flasks under the starry sky. Stage-hands, purloined from the Winslows' cache of servants, arranged the set for the performance of O'Henry's play *While the Auto Waits*. In the dressing room, Lizzie cringed at the noise they made as she readied Thomas Appleby for his debut performance.

As the stage lights came on and the scene opened with Melody sitting on a park bench, Lizzie held her breath. But when Sidney, in his role as a society scion, joined the unshakable Melody onstage, Lizzie relaxed and enjoyed their performance. Even Thomas carried off his brief role with aplomb.

After the play ended—with a twist that made the audience question their own interpretations of reality—Joey Golick took up his sax again and wove tantalizing melodies through the lush, green evening. A few couples rose to dance on the grassy lawn. Others snuck off into the welcoming shadows to profess their love—or at least their desire.

Sidney—once again garbed in his tuxedo, a fresh carnation pinned on his lapel—seated himself at the piano. Lizzie strolled onstage wearing her knee-length, low-cut, red-fringed, body-hugging dress. A shuffling of feet, a soft murmuring, and clearing of throats, rose from the audience. Sid smiled and winked at her. Leaning provocatively into the baby grand's sweeping curve as if it were a lover's body, she launched into the Gershwins' ballad "The Man I Love" with such heartfelt passion that every man in the audience longed to be *her* man, at least for the night.

After several more songs—intentionally chosen to spark lust among the members of the audience—Sidney stepped forward to thank the Winslows' guests for joining them this evening. "The Troubadours of New York

City would like to extend our utmost gratitude to Mr. and Mrs. Zachary Winslow for giving us the opportunity to entertain you wonderful people tonight—and especially their daughter, Miss Florence Winslow, and her fiancé, Count Ivanovich. Tomorrow, we'll offer you another evening of music, dance, and theatrics to delight your fancies, entice your imagination and awaken the romance within your souls," he promised.

He turned to his three associates, who'd taken up their curtain-call positions. As he introduced them yet again, each bowed, smiled, and waved goodnight. "We wish you a most pleasant good evening and look forward to engaging you further throughout your stay at Wingate."

Waves of applause rolled toward the stage, interspersed with more than a few whistles. Lizzie glanced at Catherine Winslow. The lady's countenance didn't reflect happiness, but at least it didn't convey dissatisfaction, which Lizzie took as a good sign. As she bowed for the third time, a girl about Ginny's age hurried onstage to present Lizzie and Melody each with a bouquet of pink roses. Assuming the gift had come from their host, perhaps from the estate's own rose garden, Lizzie turned her smoky gaze on Zachary Winslow. She curtseyed and flashed him her best smile. Following her lead, Melody did the same. Winslow nodded back.

Gradually the audience dispersed. Two stagehands wrapped a tarpaulin around the piano, carefully tying it up like a Christmas package to protect it from the damp sea air. Even so, Sidney fussed about the instrument as if it were a delicate and pampered child.

Servants dismantled the props. Still dressed in her red-fringed gown, Lizzie directed the breaking down procedure, feeling buzzed by the success of the evening's performance. *We did it,* she complimented herself, wishing she could shout it out for the whole world to hear. *After the horrors of Henry's death, we still managed to carry it off.* She signaled a young man to carry the props into the makeshift dressing room and told him to return tomorrow afternoon at 4:00 to set up for the next night's performance. As she handed each man a tip, Lizzie noticed Zachary Winslow still standing in front of the stage, watching and waiting.

Lizzie dipped her head toward him again. "Mr. Winslow, thank you so much for the lovely roses, and for the pleasure of entertaining your guests this evening."

"My pleasure entirely," he said. "Would you care to walk along the promenade with me, Miss Crane?"

His invitation sparked apprehension in Lizzie. Whatever could he have in mind? Would a nighttime stroll with Mr. Winslow seem improper or upset his wife? But given that he was her host and employer she consented. "I'd be delighted," she answered, with something less than enthusiasm.

She took Winslow's arm and they walked down the rolling promenade toward the sea. As they passed, Poseidon, Apollo, Aphrodite, and other marble gods and goddesses greeted them from both sides of the grassy stretch. Gaslights flickered, illuminating their path. Here and there, couples enjoyed the last vestiges of the evening.

"A first-rate performance tonight," Winslow said.

"Thank you, sir," Lizzie answered. "I'm glad you found it satisfying."

He cleared his throat, coming to the point. "Miss Crane, I must admit to being quite devastated by Mr. Ives's death, and sorry for the loss you've experienced. Such an awful occurrence."

"Yes, Henry's death has left us all in a quandary. A terrible shock to be sure."

"Although I have no idea what or who caused your associate's death—or why—I feel an obligation as your employer to offer you some sort of recompense for Mr. Ives's demise during the course of his assignment here." Zachary Winslow cleared his throat again. "I'm prepared to give your troupe a sum of $1,000 to settle the details of your colleague's death."

Surprised, Lizzie tumbled the proposal in her mind. A thousand dollars was a lot of money, more than she'd ever earned in a year, perhaps equivalent to the annual salary of a worker at one of Winslows' shoe factories. She wondered if he paid recompense to the families of workers who died at their jobs in his mills. *What does he expect in return?*

She tightened her grip on Winslow's arm ever so slightly, as the scent of saltwater tickled her nostrils. "I appreciate your consideration, Mr. Winslow, but how can one put a dollar value on a man's life?"

"Of course, one can't," Winslow answered.

"A thousand dollars…hmm, I suppose that might cover funeral expenses and a tombstone, but as for aid to his family, well…not to mention what The Troubadours are out of pocket as a result of Henry's untimely death."

"What would you consider fair, Miss Crane?"

"We haven't been in communication with Henry's family. Do they even know he's dead?"

"I believe notifying the next of kin is Sergeant Mulvaney's responsibility. I suspect he's carried out that sad duty by now."

Before they reached the beach, Zachary Winslow turned her around. Having said his piece, he steered her back toward the house. Lights blazed from every window and trailed along the terrace at the rear of the mansion. As they neared the manse, Lizzie heard laughter and radio music floating on the damp night air.

"Think about it, Miss Crane."

"I will, Mr. Winslow."

\* \* \*

After her bath, Lizzie returned to the bedchamber she shared with Melody. Her young companion sat on her single bed propped up against pillows, writing a letter to her parents in New Jersey. Melody's middle-class family thought she'd taken leave of her senses by joining a theater group and performing in nightclubs, but they were proud of her talent. Despite their reservations, they had agreed to indulge their only daughter in what they hoped was a passing fancy. Now that she'd stepped up from the speakeasies of Greenwich Village and into the posh home of one of New England's foremost families, Melody peppered her letters with details that her mother and father could brag about to their friends.

The pretty blonde looked up from her letter and smiled. "I thought it went well tonight, don't you?"

"Oh ab-so-lute-ly," Lizzie answered. "Thomas turned out a darb performance, spur of the moment and inexperienced as he was. And the rest of us did a splendid job too. I must admit I'm quite proud of us all, rallying under the circumstances."

"Joey Golick played swell," Melody said. "Too bad he looks like an old toad."

"Not many people can match our friend, Henry, in the looks category, but who knows? Maybe women Joey's own age might think otherwise. At least he has a nice smile and a congenial manner. Anyway, his looks don't matter right now. He blows a hot horn and that's our priority." Lizzie bent over and toweled her dark hair. "What do you think about this? After our performance tonight, our host, Zachary Winslow, escorted me along the grassy promenade and offered a sum of a thousand clams to cover Henry's funeral expenses and our costs. What's your take on that, Mel?"

"That was nice of him."

Lizzie stared into the tarnished mirror that hung over their bedroom bureau and ran a comb through her damp hair. "I got the feeling he was offering a bribe."

"Why would he do that?" Melody asked.

"Hush money. To keep the story under wraps."

"But all the papers will publish the story of Henry's death. You can't conceal a murder, especially one involving a prominent family like the Winslows."

"I mean the story about Henry and Florence Winslow's romance. I'm certain Zachary Winslow doesn't want it known that his daughter was involved with a rumrunner—a *murdered* rumrunner at that. Think of the scandal! Wouldn't the papers just love to get wind of a juicy bit like that? He's prepared to offer us a bribe to prevent that piece of the mess from coming to light."

"What did you tell him?"

Lizzie rubbed Pond's cold cream on her face. "I said I'd think about it."

As she slid into bed, she thought, *I wish I knew what the bronze nymph knows.*

# Chapter Fourteen

*"Here's to alcohol, the rose-colored glasses of life."*

— *F. Scott Fitzgerald, The Beautiful and Damned*

L izzie rose earlier than usual, but even so, Melody was already up and gone. She stretched, yawned, and then crossed the tiny bedchamber to the window. Pulling aside the lace curtain, she gazed down at the grounds below. A few guests meandered along the promenade. A spirited couple dressed in white energetically smacked a ball back and forth across the tennis court. At the entrance to the rose garden, Florence Winslow stood watching a gardener prune the bushes.

Lizzie gave herself a quick sponge bath, then slipped on an unpretentious pale blue daytime frock. She fluffed a bit of powder on her face, ran a brush through her coffee-colored hair, and went downstairs to the mansion's sunny morning room where bright chatter competed with the clatter of dishes. Although she wasn't sure if this area was intended only for the Winslows' guests, she decided to test the waters.

Instantly she spotted Sidney. Handsomely attired in a creamy linen suit, a peach-colored shirt, and subtly striped tie, he sat alone at a table for two. He sipped coffee while reading the morning paper, and smoked a cigarette tucked into his signature silver holder. The sun, shining through sea-facing windows, glanced off his forehead and accentuated his growing baldness—a detail of vanity he often sought to conceal with hats and hair dyes. *I'll have to remind him to sit in the shadows,* she told herself.

Sliding into the chair across from him, she asked, "How did you sleep-ski?"

He looked up from the *Boston Globe* and replied, "In the ocean's deep-ski. And you?"

"Quite comfortably, thank you. Given that all went swell last night, I didn't have to do battle with the night frights."

Sidney lifted a china carafe a serving girl had left on the table and filled her coffee cup. "What led our illustrious host to escort you down the grassy promenade after our performance last night, Bearcat? Ordinary lust, or something more intriguing? Do spill."

Lizzie sipped her coffee and signaled to a girl, who approached and took her order. "A poached egg and toast with strawberry jam and gobs of butter." Then smiling at Sidney, she revealed Zachary Winslow's offer.

"Hmm. A tidy sum to accidentally fall in our laps." He tapped ash into a glass tray. "But the complications may not be worth it."

"I thought the same thing. Henry's family and all that."

"Not to mention the appearance of guilt, or at least complicity, that would surely arise if we took hush money from Winslow."

"How would anyone know, though?" She hadn't entirely ruled out the offer. A thousand bucks was a lot of dough. "He's not going to broadcast that he paid us to keep quiet about Henry and Flo. Do you think Catherine Winslow knows about the offer?"

Sidney's gaze shifted up and away from Lizzie, and she turned to see Count Ivanovich making his way toward them across the breakfast room's tile floor. He stopped beside their table and stood there awkwardly until Lizzie finally motioned for him to sit.

"Would you care to take coffee with us, Count Ivanovich?" she said, wondering what the sullen man could possibly want with them.

The count surprised her by pulling up a chair from an adjacent table and positioning himself stiffly on it. "Yes, thank you."

Sidney grimaced, then waved to the serving girl, who brought another place setting. Lizzie noticed a dab of shaving cream at the corner of the Russian's lip and a few dark hairs on his chin that his razor had missed.

After slurping half the coffee in his cup, Count Ivanovich said, "Ever since you are arriving here my fiancée is unhappy."

"I'm sorry to hear it, but I don't see what that has to do with us," Sidney answered.

"The one man is dead, and this is making her sad."

"When someone you know dies, it's normal to feel sad." Sidney held out his hands, palms up, in a gesture of helplessness. "We're all sad about Henry's death. He was our friend and we miss him too."

"But if Miss Winslow is sad, she may not wish to marry me."

Apparently, Lizzie's presence made no impression on the count, for he directed his concerns to Sidney alone. As the morning sun washed across his face, she felt sympathy for nineteen-year-old Florence Winslow, engaged to marry this coarse, older man—never mind the count's title and his landholdings in a foreign country. Flo, from all indications, had once entertained hope of a future with the handsome and talented Henry Ives. How could the pampered young lady be satisfied with this strange, morose Russian who might drag her away, in the wake of her beloved's demise, to a land far from her family and friends and all she held dear?

The servant brought more coffee and the count sipped his pensively. He stared down at the table for several moments, fiddling with his napkin, before turning his brooding gaze again on Sidney. He shrugged and sighed deeply; his shoulders slumped. To Lizzie, he seemed a man trying to extract a bargain, but without any coin to offer.

"You are entertainers," said the count, his voice laced with desperation. "You can make her happy."

"We're doing our best," Sidney answered, "but we can't take responsibility for Miss Winslow's happiness. You're her fiancé. Shouldn't you be the one to make her happy?"

The count's heavy eyebrows knit together above his prominent nose and he glared at Sidney. He clenched his right fist and Lizzie expected that at any moment he might start pounding the tabletop. She got the impression he wasn't used to people contradicting his commands.

"I will do anything to bring happiness back to her. *Anything.*" He stood up abruptly, his shoulders pulled back stiffly as if at attention, his lips pressed together in a tight line. He cast a dark, withering stare at each of them, then turned sharply and strode away from the morning room.

"Looks like he got up on the wrong side of the bed this morning," Lizzie said. "What do you suppose he expects from us?"

Sidney stubbed out his cigarette in the glass ashtray and lit another. "Oh, bother. We don't need another prima donna in the midst of everything else."

"It's an occupational downside of dealing with the quality," she reminded him. "They're all a bunch of spoiled children who think the world revolves around them. Nonetheless, we have a show to put on tonight, so let's concern ourselves with that shall we?" She finished her third slice of toast with fresh butter and homemade jam, probably made from the fruit of the Winslows' orchards. "By the way, have you seen Melody this morning?"

"I saw her strolling in the gardens this morning with an attractively attired gentleman, who seemed quite attentive to our young colleague."

"Good for her, so long as she doesn't lose her pretty blond head over a trifling fancy." Lizzie dabbed at her mouth with her napkin, then pulled out her compact mirror and reapplied her lipstick. "What about Joey Golick?"

"He spent the night on the couch in the prop room," Sidney answered. "I suspect he's still dallying in dreamland."

"Perhaps you should rouse him. I want to run through the music and dance numbers a few times this morning. Joey seems the consummate professional, but we still need to familiarize him with our routines. And I want to rehearse tonight's play again to make sure my illustrious bathtub scene is ab-so-lute-ly flawless."

Sidney chuckled. "Bearcat, if you flubbed every line and sat there dumb as dirt, no one would care in the least."

\* \* \*

Dressed in a chevron-striped skirt and V-necked blouse, Lizzie directed the men allotted to her today as they set up the outdoor stage. The Black Irish lad, who'd washed away Henry's blood after the murder, assisted one of the other workers in moving an old-fashioned claw-foot bathtub onto the stage. Another man positioned a potted palm tree near the tub and laid a bath mat beside it.

"Such a fuss over a smidgeon of skin," Sidney teased, but she knew he hung high hopes on her ability to dazzle the audience with this skit.

"I suppose it all depends on whose skin is on display." Lizzie motioned for one of the men to place a folding Japanese screen so it would conceal the tub until time for her performance. "I think I'll ask them to paint the tub pink, to go along with the play's title, even though the script calls for blue. What's your take?"

"It's up to you." His gaze shifted away, up and over her head. "Top of the mornin'."

Lizzie turned to see Joey Golick standing behind her, disheveled and apparently hungover. His dull eyes were puffy, his skin gray, his jowls loose and sagging like a basset hound's.

"You look like something the cat dragged in," she said anxiously. *Jeepers creepers, I hope he shapes up in time to perform.*

"Where can a fella get a cup of joe?" he asked.

"You might still manage to grab some breakfast up at the big house, but you'll have to clean yourself up first." She studied his pathetic form, then said, "Oh, c'mon. I'll make some coffee. Pull yourself together—we've got work to do."

She let herself into the single gentlemen's lodge, where men in all manner of dress—and undress—shuffled about. Lizzie ignored them and made her way to the kitchen, where she lit the stove and put the kettle on. Some of the men raised their eyebrows and smiled rakishly at the bold young woman in their midst. Others pulled their dressing gowns about them modestly and scurried out of sight.

"I'd think at your age you'd know how to hold your liquor," she chastised Joey.

"Yeah, well, I've got diabetes and heart problems."

"Then you probably shouldn't be drinking at all."

He shrugged. "You only go around once."

After the water boiled, Lizzie spooned instant coffee into a ceramic mug, added water, and handed it to him. "Just don't check out on us now. We can't afford to lose another horn player this week."

Joey cupped his hands around the mug and followed her back outside to the stage. In the cool morning air, the steam rose from the coffee and swirled playfully, like a genie released from a magic lamp.

As Sidney laid out the evening's itinerary, Lizzie studied Joey's doughy face, his deep-set eyes, his sagging jaw dappled with gray stubble. She wondered if he was aware of Henry's bootlegging connections. From what she'd ascertained since Henry's death, Zachary Winslow knew about those connections—and may have made use of them. In fact, that link might have been why the Winslows hired The Troubadours for this engagement.

But that knowledge alone wasn't reason enough to prompt Henry's death. Even if the police realized Winslow was buying illegal liquor from Henry and his family, most likely they would've turned a blind eye. A handful of cash placed in the right hands would've erased any problems. There had to be more to it than that.

# Chapter Fifteen

*"Men and girls came and went like moths among the whisperings
and the champagne and the stars."*

— *F. Scott Fitzgerald, The Great Gatsby*

N ight enfolded the scene like a velvet curtain. Despite her state of
undress, Lizzie felt sheltered and protected by the intimacy of the
small outdoor stage with its subtle lighting and deep shadows,
instead of uncomfortably exposed as she'd expected. In her role as Julie
in F. Scott Fitzgerald's play *Porcelain and Pink*, she slouched down in her
newly painted pink bathtub. Her beige bathing costume mimicked bare skin,
allowing her to tease her audience and leave them wondering whether or
not she really sat naked before them.

Catherine Winslow's edginess at the provocative scene amused Lizzie
perversely. She enjoyed seeing their very proper hostess squirm amidst
her guests' unabashed enthusiasm. Sandwiched between Zachary Winslow
and their elder daughter, and wearing a champagne-colored gown that
shimmered like moonlight, the mistress of the manor seemed uncertain how
to react. Mrs. Winslow had approved the play—and her guests expressed
their delight with cheers, whistles, and loud applause—yet she sat primly in
her front-row seat with a petulant scowl on her pretty face. For a moment,
Lizzie wondered what it might be like for young Florence Winslow to have
such a pill for a mother, especially as the girl embarked upon marriage to a

foreigner and needed advice about her future.

After the skit ended, Thomas Appleby—engaged tonight as a stage-hand—dimmed the lights briefly. A veil of darkness provided cover for Lizzie to dash away to the actors' dressing room—and for the other helpers to reposition the Japanese screen to conceal the pink bathtub. There she met Melody changing into an amber-colored dress with an elaborately embroidered bodice and a petal skirt. Quickly Lizzie donned a poison-green beaded dress with a flared hemline that barely covered her knees, ran a brush through her hair, and refreshed her face paint.

She grabbed her friend's hand and pulled her back onstage. "C'mon, I've got an idea," Lizzie said and signaled for Melody to follow her down into the audience.

Gliding from row to row, the two performers urged men and women to rise up from their seats and dance. With only a bit of encouragement, they got ten couples to join them for a Charleston on the grassy promenade. As Sidney and Joey Golick played popular songs, weaving a musical tapestry around their audience, the dancers kicked up their heels in the salubrious evening air.

Lizzie held out her hand to Peter Winslow and smiled. "May I have this dance, Captain?"

With only a brief nod to his female companion, he accepted Lizzie's invitation and rose to take her in his arms. His hand pressed on the small of her back sent heat waves rippling up and down her body. As he swept her away from the other guests, Peter said, "I can't help wondering if you were really nude in that bathtub."

"Does it matter?"

"No, I suppose it doesn't really. But, tonight my imagination will dwell on the possibility."

"Perhaps I'll show up in your dreams," she teased.

He laughed. "I certainly hope so."

As they glided among the marble statues, to the tune of Gershwin's "Lady, Be Good," Peter said, "I thought you should know that tomorrow morning the papers will reveal the story of Henry Ives's death. I tried to squash it—I have a friend at the *Boston Globe*—but to no avail."

The news sparked a pang of anxiety in Lizzie's chest, even though she'd expected this would happen sooner or later. "What will this mean?"

"For one thing, it may implicate my father in the whiskey trafficking business Henry was involved in."

Feigning surprise, she asked, "You mean Henry was brokering booze? And your father purchased alcohol from him?"

She felt Peter's nod against her cheek. "Not only Father—a lot of people around here relied on Henry and his family to procure their libations."

"But surely no one would think ill of a man of your father's stature."

"You'd be surprised to learn how many people would enjoy seeing my father brought low."

"What about his businesses? The hundreds of people he employs? His contributions to the community?"

Peter shrugged. "Envy can spark all sorts of strange behavior."

They danced in silence for a few minutes, until Lizzie asked, "How will the news affect your family's guests and these events that your mother has arranged for your sister?"

"How our guests will react is anyone's guess. I suppose it depends on how the papers report the story. If they don't make a circus of it, the festivities most likely will go on as planned." He smiled at Lizzie, his lips only inches away from hers. "It's possible that you and your colleagues will be detained here, however, until the killer is found. How would you feel about spending some additional time at Wingate?"

Lizzie smiled back at him. "I can't think of anything that would please me more. I just wish the circumstances were different."

"Well, then, before we're all put under lock and key by Sergeant Mulvaney, would you like to go sailing with me tomorrow?"

"Oh, ab-so-lute-ly."

"Good. The tide turns at 10:42 tomorrow morning. Can you meet me on the beach at quarter past ten?"

"Yes, indeed."

He brushed the backs of his fingertips against her cheek. "Tell no one."

\* \* \*

Still high with the effervescence of the evening's success and too wired to sleep, Lizzie, Sidney, and Joey strolled down to the Winslow estate's private beach. Melody had begged off, saying she had some "personal" things to tend to, which Lizzie knew meant she wanted to spend time with her new suitor. Sidney carried the half-empty bottle of bourbon Thomas Appleby had provided, tucked under his arm.

"Just now, Peter Winslow admitted to me that our Henry supplied Papa Winslow and his friends with hooch," she told them.

"I guess we shouldn't be surprised," Sidney said.

Lizzie juggled the bits and pieces in her mind. "Peter intimated that exposing this information, in light of Henry's murder, could damage the Winslows. Maybe connect our host with bootlegging. What I'm wondering is this: Would Zachary Winslow kill to protect his secret?"

"That bribe he offered you casts suspicion on him," Sidney said.

"Him among others. If not Winslow, then maybe one of his pals wanted to hush up our man. Someone who also relied on the Ives family for booze, but didn't want his illustrious name besmirched. Possibly someone among the guests."

"But they didn't arrive until after Henry was murdered," Sidney reminded her.

Joey interjected, "It wouldn't be hard to hire somebody to slip in here at night and take out Henry. Especially if the guard knew that somebody."

"Somebody from Gloucester you mean?" Lizzie asked.

"From wherever," Joey said and quoted Sir Walter Scott. " 'Oh what a tangled web we weave, when first we practice to deceive!' "

As they approached the beach, Lizzie pulled off her shoes and stockings, digging her bare feet into the sand. Sidney did the same, but Joey kept his shoes on as they strolled along under the light of a silvery moon. Waves rolled onto the beach in lacy ruffles, making shushing sounds as they washed over the sand.

Lizzie dipped her toes in the chilly water. "I keep wondering who would have had the most to lose if Henry had stayed alive."

"In that case, I'd guess Zachary Winslow," Sidney said, as he uncapped the bottle he'd brought along and held it out to her.

She took a swig and passed it to Joey. She thought about the people she'd overheard talking shortly before she found Henry's body, and the person she'd seen running away from the scene. If only she'd gotten a better look at that person maybe she'd know who killed him.

"What about the count? On the night the Winslows' guests arrived, I overheard one of the women say that Ivanovich had lost virtually everything during the Russian Revolution. He's basically broke, unless he managed to smuggle out a bunch of Fabergé eggs. Florence is his bread and butter, as well as his ticket to American citizenship. Maybe he feared she'd run off with Henry, leaving him high and dry. And remember, Sid, he said he'd do *anything* to make Flo happy, which I take to mean that he'd do anything to make sure she goes through with the marriage."

"Including bumping off Henry?" Sidney asked.

Lizzie bent down to pick up a sand dollar glowing white in the moonlight. "There's the jealousy factor as well as the money. You can't underestimate what people will do when the green-eyed monster rears its ugly head."

"I don't have any experience with murder," Joey said, "but from what I've seen in life, the most obvious answer is usually the right one." He handed the bottle to Sidney.

"Are you a betting man, Joey?" Lizzie asked.

"Sometimes."

"If you were to put money on our culprit, who would you choose?"

"Catherine Winslow," Joey said, without hesitation.

His response surprised Lizzie. "Hard to imagine her exposing one of her precious gowns to all that blood. So *very* messy."

Sidney interrupted, "Bearcat, don't you think you're being rather cavalier about a serious matter?"

"Not at all. I think our best bet for dodging Sergeant Mulvaney's suspicion—and he's de-fin-ite-ly suspicious of us—is to figure out who killed Henry. I'm trying to save my skin, and yours too, Sid."

"Why Catherine Winslow?" Sidney asked Joey.

"Lizzie asked who had the most to lose. Like most society ladies, Mrs. Winslow has invested her whole life in this family and all it represents—she's nothing without them. She sure couldn't let Henry gum up the works. My guess is, this ugly business is already starting to put a dent in her social standing."

Lizzie kicked at the rippling waves. Even though she held little affection for Mrs. Winslow, she rued the precarious position women had in society—completely dependent on their husbands—and how they were held to higher standards than men. "It's not fair," she declared.

"You're right, it's not," Joey agreed. "Maybe the old girl is bent on evening the score."

# Chapter Sixteen

*"To be supremely happy for a moment—an hour—that is worth living for!"*

*— Louise Bryant, The Game*

Dressed in a navy-blue middy blouse and white pleated skirt, Lizzie went downstairs to meet Sidney in the breakfast room. She'd barely seated herself when a serving girl brought them soft-boiled eggs in dainty porcelain cups, along with plates of rashers, toast, and sliced peaches.

Sidney surveyed her outfit and raised an eyebrow. "Going sailing?"

"With Peter Winslow," she answered, feeling her cheeks flush with excitement.

He nodded his approval, then handed her the morning edition of the *Boston Globe.* "Take a look at this."

In some ways, seeing the story of Henry's murder printed in the newspaper made it seem even more real than seeing his body. As an actress, she knew the tricks performers used to convey illusions and she realized that some part of her still held on to the idea that the whole affair might have been staged. The facts spelled out in black-and-white type proved otherwise. Despite the warm morning, she shivered.

A photo of Henry and one of Zachary Winslow stared up at her. Lizzie read the piece, which discussed the Ives family's whiskey trafficking activities—apparently, more than one member of the clan was already serving time in prison—but stopped short of mentioning the names of their customers. The writer had merely stated the known facts. He didn't even surmise that Henry might have followed in his family's footsteps, describing him only as a musician. *The Winslows must be relieved,* she thought, *and so am I.* If Peter was right, the light-handed reporting shouldn't ruin the festivities.

"The Troubadours got a mention," she said, "though I wish we'd made the Arts and Entertainment page instead. I wonder if the notoriety will help or hurt us?"

"You know what they say, even bad publicity is good publicity."

"Hmm, I suppose it's better to be infamous than unknown." Lizzie passed the newspaper back to him and dug into her breakfast. "What do we do now?"

"Same as always. The show must go on."

\* \* \*

Lizzie stood on the sandy beach, feeling a bit awkward at having arrived ahead of Peter Winslow. Perhaps he wasn't serious last night when he invited her to go sailing this morning—maybe he'd stood her up. But after a few minutes, she spotted his sloop, Rhiannon, tacking across the bay. Peter waved at her from the stern and she waved back. After dropping anchor, he rowed ashore in a dinghy.

"Perfect day for a sail," he said as he dragged the rowboat onto the beach. "I'm glad you agreed to accompany me, Miss Crane."

"Please call me Lizzie. And may I call you Peter?"

"I wish you would. I think we know one another well enough to be on a first-name basis, don't you? If not, we should rectify that straight away."

He held out his hand and guided her into the dinghy. After she'd seated herself, gripping the boat's wooden sides more tightly than necessary, he shoved the little rowboat back into the water and jumped in.

Pointing at his rolled-up white flannel pants, she said, "You've gotten your trousers soaked coming to fetch me."

Peter laughed. "Occupational hazard for a sailor. I hope you aren't afraid of getting wet."

"Well…"

"I should've asked earlier. Can you swim?"

Lizzie shook her head. She'd been to the Jersey shore a few times, but she'd never done more than wade in the surf.

He handed her a life jacket. "Here, put this on. I know it's not exactly the height of fashion, but it could save your life."

"Dear me, Captain. You don't really think my life is in danger, do you?"

"Of course not. It's just a standard safety precaution." He grinned at her, exposing his perfectly straight, white teeth. "I'd never forgive myself if anything amiss happened to such a beautiful lady under my command."

"Aye, aye, sir." She strapped the lumpy orange vest over her stylish outfit. *So much for trying to look my best.*

Once aboard *Rhiannon* Lizzie asked for a tour. Although she understood almost nothing of what Peter said about rigging and draft and other nautical terms, she admired the sloop's gleaming teak deck and bright brass fittings. The numerous dials, gauges, and array of baffling instruments fascinated her. She marveled at the efficiently designed space below deck, where a sailor could sleep, cook, and wash up, all within a few paces.

"She's beautiful," Lizzie exclaimed.

"That she is," he agreed. "And fast too."

"Do you race her?"

"Not yet. I've only owned her a few months. We're still getting to know one another. Like any love affair, it takes time."

As they came topside again, Lizzie asked, "Shouldn't she have a figure-head?"

"She's rather small for that. But if I decide to have one carved for her would you consider modeling?"

"Ab-so-lute-ly. I'd be honored. That way I could glide upon the waves in proxy—and you'd think of me every time you took to the sea."

Peter laughed as he weighed anchor, and they sailed out across the sparkling blue-green water of Ipswich Bay. Lizzie gave herself over to the motion of the yacht and the fresh, salty scent of the ocean. The peace, freedom, and endless space invigorated her. She could easily understand why Peter Winslow enjoyed escaping this way. As *Rhiannon* picked up speed, the wind whipped at Lizzie's hat; she tied it more securely beneath her chin. It wouldn't do to scald her skin, not when she was in the midst of the most important opportunity of her career.

"I read the article about Henry's murder in the *Globe* this morning," she said.

"Yes, thankfully it wasn't too salacious. I feared a lot worse. I guess the reporter couldn't resist giving some background about the Ives family, but at least he didn't claim Henry was a bootlegger too—or that my father had any knowledge of the family's business."

"How are your guests taking the news?"

"Most of them already knew about the murder. They're not going to let it stand in the way of a good party if that's what you mean."

They sailed east toward Gloucester, never getting out of sight of land. Along the way, Peter pointed out things he thought might interest her. The opening at the end of the Winslows' private beach led to Choate Island, where Revolutionary War battles were fought and a "poor farm" once existed. The salt marshes that bordered the shipbuilding town of Essex. Wingarsheek Beach and the twisting rivulets that branched like a network of arteries to the Atlantic, cutting Gloucester and Rockport off from the mainland. He talked about marine life and seabirds, ocean currents and wind patterns, and the people who'd inhabited this area for centuries.

*He's not only handsome and rich, he's knowledgeable too,* she thought. *I don't think I could ever be happy with a man who lacked intelligence and curiosity, no matter how wealthy he was.*

Peter adjusted the rudder and the sails, causing *Rhiannon* to come about, and headed back toward Wingate. "Say, do you feel like a spot of lunch? Mrs. Appleby packed a hamper for us."

"Oh yes, please. The sea air does stimulate one's appetite," Lizzie answered. "Mrs. Appleby has provided my friends and me with oodles of delicious meals during our time here."

"A real treasure, that woman. Would you rather we ate below deck at a proper table or up here?"

"Up here, de-fin-ite-ly."

"Atta girl." He slid an anchor from *Rhiannon's* deck and it dropped into the water. The sails drooped, at ease.

Lifting the basket's lid, he handed Lizzie a linen napkin and a Delft china plate, then passed her a sandwich of smoked salmon and sliced cucumbers on dark rye bread. He opened a container that held deviled eggs sprinkled with caviar, and another filled with a fragrant rice mixture unlike anything she'd ever tasted before. Digging deeper into the wicker basket, he fetched out two generous slices of raspberry pie and a Thermos vacuum flask. "Shall I pour tea? Or would you prefer..." He withdrew a bottle of wine and two glasses.

"Oh, wine, please."

He filled their glasses and then offered a toast. "To a lovely summer day and an even lovelier lady."

Lizzie tossed her head and smiled seductively at him. After taking a sip of wine, she said, "This wine is lovely too."

"Quite," he agreed and frowned slightly. "However, I'm afraid it's the last bottle I'll enjoy of this particular vintage. It seems my supply has dried up."

"Are you referring to Henry?"

"Sadly, I am." He turned his gaze away from her and looked out at the horizon.

Lizzie seized the opportunity to ask a question that had been bobbing about in her mind for some time. "Were The Troubadours invited to perform here because of your father's, um, connection with Henry?"

Peter leaned back against *Rhiannon's* brass rail. The sun filled his hair with golden highlights. "Actually, my sister Florence encouraged my mother to hire you. Haven't a clue how Flo found out Henry was a member of your troupe, but I'm certain my parents didn't know. If they had, they surely would have vetoed the arrangement."

"But I thought Henry was a friend to you and Flo. You even said you believed he and your sister were in love."

"Love is fine, so long as it flows through the right channels. But my sister's affection for Henry lacked propriety. In fact, her association with Henry caused quite an uproar in my family. People in our position—especially young ladies—can't just go about dallying with whomever strikes our fancy."

Lizzie wondered if entertainers fell into the category of unsuitable companions, and decided they probably did. She thought about the chestnut-haired beauty who'd accompanied Peter these past few evenings, a lady of a certain class who would be considered a proper match for the heir to the Winslow fortune. Then she wondered if his family or friends knew Peter was "dallying" with Lizzie this afternoon on *Rhiannon*? He'd asked her to keep it quiet. If they knew, what would they think? Maybe that he was sowing his wild oats—the rules for men were different than those for women.

She held out her wineglass for a refill. "You said your sister and Count Ivanovich met through friends of your family."

"Yes, they met at a party given by some people my parents know. He's related by marriage to a man my father does business with. As you may know, a lot of Russian aristocrats fled their homeland during the Revolution, and some took up residence in America. Although he still owns quite a bit of property in Hungary, I suspect he'd rather live here. I mean, who wouldn't? I don't know all the details of Flo's engagement—I was away in London at the time it happened—but I suspect you're sharp enough to understand that it's an arranged marriage."

"I thought such things had gone out of fashion."

"Let's say they're edging in that direction. Niko—that's what I call him—isn't a bad sort, really. Unsophisticated and gruff by our standards, certainly. But he's devoted to Flo. He'll take care of her. My sister isn't the sort who can take care of herself."

"You forgot to mention that he's ugly as a wild boar and old enough to be her father."

Peter licked his fingertips. "That's rather unkind. Should looks be a criterion for love?"

"Baloney, she's no more in love with him than she is with this life preserver." Lizzie tapped her ugly orange safety vest. "Flo's marrying him because your

114

parents are forcing her to. Surely you can see the poor girl is miserable. How can they condemn her to a lifetime she'll despise with a man she loathes?"

"I didn't invite you out here today to discuss my sister."

His tone struck her like an icy North Atlantic wave. Without meaning to, she realized she'd impugned his parents' judgment, his sister's behavior, and perhaps the manner in which his entire social network functioned. *If I hope to move among these people, I need to learn to think the way they do,* she scolded herself.

Peter collected their dishes and stashed them in the picnic basket, keeping the bottle of wine at the ready. After weighing *Rhiannon's* anchor, he steered the sloop out into the open bay. Lizzie watched cormorants skimming the surface of the water, diving and resurfacing again and again, searching for their next meal. Seagulls squawked overhead. Occasionally, another sailboat passed them and the occupants waved. Sunshine glinted on the waves, like stars that had fallen from the sky into the deep blue sea. As they tacked back toward the Winslows' private beach, she imagined what it might be like to sail these waters on a moonlit night, or even to live onboard with only the sea as your home and the stars to guide you.

After a long period of silence, Peter asked, "So, Lizzie, what made you decide to become an entertainer?"

"I wanted to be someone else, and acting lets you be anyone you want to be."

"Why would you want to be someone else?"

*If only you knew,* she thought. "My beginnings were rather humble, but I aspire to greater heights." *Oh, damn,* she thought after the words were out of her mouth. *Now he must think I'm a gold digger. I really am chewing on my foot today.*

"Well, from what I've heard these past few days, it's likely that your aspirations will blossom."

"Oh? What have you heard? Do tell."

"Only the obvious," he said. "Lizzie, you're beautiful, talented, and I'm sure you know all that. The Troubadours are a class act. My guess is you'll get a number of bookings as a result of your week here."

She bowed dramatically and said, "Thank you, kind sir. I certainly hope you're right."

"Assuming one of you didn't murder Henry Ives."

# Chapter Seventeen

*"It is up to you to find as many pictures to put on your blank pages as possible."*

— *Emily Post*

"Oh, there you are," Melody exclaimed as Lizzie entered their bedchamber in the maids' quarters. "Sid and I were worried."

"Good heavens, why?"

"Well, it's getting late…we didn't know if you were okay." The younger woman stood in front of the mirror, meticulously applying her face paint.

Lizzie stripped off her sailing garb and plopped down on her narrow bed in her slip. "I went out with Peter Winslow on his sailboat *Rhiannon*. Sid knew where I was—I told him about it at breakfast."

"How exciting!"

Lizzie filled her in on the high points of the day's adventure. When she'd finished, Melody said, "Sounds like he's stuck on you."

"I wouldn't go that far, but I'm doing my best to win him over. Of course, I'm not in his league, still…the Duke of York married a non-royal lady two years ago."

"See, there's hope." Melody ran a brush through her golden locks. "Oh, before I forget, Sid wants to discuss tonight's performance with you."

Lizzie lay back against her bed pillow, arms folded beneath her head. "What's to discuss? Tonight's just music and dance, no theatrics."

"He's thinking of adding a new act. Joey suggested performing the comedy routine he did in the Catskills last month. It's really quite funny."

Lizzie hadn't known their new associate was a comedian—how could that fact have escaped her? Attempting to hide her ignorance of the matter, she said, "Maybe tomorrow. Tonight, let's just go with what we know best. Easy does it. I'll let Sid know."

"Okay," Melody agreed. "There's some dinner left if you're hungry. The German chocolate cake is divine."

Lizzie pushed herself up from the bed and crossed the room to examine the leftovers. Lifting a linen towel, she saw slices of rare roast beef, baby carrots, and creamed spinach with pearl onions. Several dinner rolls and a compote of fresh butter crouched under another towel. Nearby sat a pot of tea, long gone cold. Even though she'd had a more-than-adequate lunch onboard *Rhiannon,* she spooned food onto a plate and took it back to her bed, where she ate off her lap. *Good thing I don't eat this way all the time, or I'd end up looking like the Venus of Willendorf.*

In between bites, Lizzie ran through the evening's list of songs and dance numbers. "Simple as one, two, three," she said.

"One, two, three," Melody repeated.

"So when do I get to meet this mysterious suitor of yours?"

Melody's face lit up, and she touched her amethyst necklace as if it were a good luck talisman. "Soon. His name is Douglas, and he heads up an insurance company in Hartford, Connecticut."

"A big cheese, is he?"

"Yes, I guess you could say that. And he's ever so nice. Sid thought he was swell."

"Sid met him?"

"Well, you know how Sid is. He wanted to make sure Douglas's intentions were on the up and up. Especially since he's a good deal older than me."

Lizzie frowned. "How much older?"

"He's thirty-nine."

Lizzie couldn't help wondering why a successful man that old wasn't married, but she couldn't say that to Melody. "Twenty years, that's quite a bit."

Since she'd first heard Melody playing violin at a wedding two years ago and convinced the girl straight out of high school to join her and Sidney in what would become The Troubadours, Lizzie had assumed the role of big sister to her more sheltered friend. She remembered the evening she'd sat with the girl's nice, middle-class, very dubious parents in their Morristown, New Jersey home, negotiating their daughter's future.

"Mr. Fitzgerald, you're an architect," Lizzie'd said "What if all your designs were just tossed in a closet where no one would ever see them? What if no one ever got to live or work in the buildings you designed? What if you had to spend the rest of your life toiling at a job you despised, not because you didn't have the talent to do something more, but because you weren't allowed to fulfill your dream? Your daughter is a splendid musician. We're offering her a chance to do what she was born to do. If you deprive her of that, she'll never be truly happy."

Eventually, the Fitzgeralds' wish to see their only daughter fulfill her dream won out over their fears of her entering the uncertain musical world. Both Sidney and Lizzie had sworn to do their best to keep the talented young girl safe. Even now that Melody was past the age of consent and legally able to make her own decisions, Lizzie still felt responsible for her colleague's well-being.

"So long as you're happy, I wish you the best."

"I can't wait for you to meet him, Lizzie. Maybe after tonight's performance?"

"Sure thing." Lizzie glanced at the clock on the nightstand between their beds. "We've got an hour 'til showtime. I'll send word to Sid and let him know I didn't drown or abscond with Peter Winslow, though I have to admit it crossed my mind."

She jotted a note on a piece of paper, folded it, and then went out into the hallway where she spotted a maid placing clean towels in the bathroom. Handing the girl the note, Lizzie said, "Please find Thomas Appleby, or another fellow, and ask him to take this message to Sidney Somerset at the stables." She pressed two coins in the girl's hand. "Keep one and give the other to the boy."

\* \* \*

As the night's entertainment drew to a close, Lizzie looked out at the audience, resplendent in their evening finery, and reassured herself *not one of these high-class ladies is better than me.* Peter Winslow's explanation of proper relationships for the gentry had deflated her hopes, despite his flirtatious manner and his earlier declaration that he wouldn't marry just to please his parents. She caught his eye briefly, then shifted her gaze to his beautiful and suitable companion. Lifting her head another inch, she told herself that even though she'd grown up in a cold-water flat in the Bronx and never finished high school, this was America, land of opportunity—and opportunity was knocking on her door right now.

Her burgundy silk evening gown—cut up to her knees in front and emblazoned with tiny crystal beads—trailed behind her as she strolled leisurely to center stage. Diamond-studded bracelets sparkled on her arms, and a garnet the size of a pigeon's egg hung in the shockingly bare crevice between her full breasts. Joey Golick's sultry saxophone accompanied her seductive approach as she began singing Gershwin's "Somebody Loves Me."

As she crooned the song, Lizzie sensed every man in the audience longing to be her lover and every woman longing to be loved. Here and there, a couple leaned closer together; a man took a lady's hand or placed his arm around her shoulders. When she glanced back at Peter Winslow and his companion, she noticed the distance between them had increased, however. The young lady even crossed her arms protectively over her chest. *Does she know Peter spent the afternoon sailing with me?*

She sang several more popular tunes, then the rest of The Troubadours joined her center stage to take a bow. The audience applauded so enthusiastically that all three performed another number together, to the accompaniment of Joey's sax.

In a moment of playfulness, Lizzie invited Zachary Winslow to join her onstage for a dance and he accepted—much to Catherine Winslow's apparent dismay. Melody, following her friend's overture, asked Peter Winslow to dance with her. As Peter accepted Melody's invitation, Sidney approached Mrs. Winslow and bowed before her. She took his outstretched hand and he led her onstage, where he gracefully shepherded her through a waltz. By the time the music ended, the entire audience was standing, cheering not only the performers but their hosts as well.

# Chapter Eighteen

*"These people seemed so enwrapped in snobbishness and the glory of being rich that they had no art sense whatever."*

— *Isadora Duncan, My Life*

From her third-floor window, Lizzie watched two dozen men in bathing costumes line up on Wingate's beach. From her elevated vantage point, they appeared no larger than puppies. A chilly wind whipped in off the ocean and raindrops splattered the windowpane, but the inclement weather didn't deter the men. Suddenly, in response to some unheard signal, they dashed en masse across the sand and hurled themselves into the sea. After a few moments of frenzied activity, during which arms and legs churned up frothy spume, the swimmers returned to the beach and swathed themselves in thick beach towels. They slapped one another's backs in a mystifying sort of fraternity ritual, then sprinted toward the gentlemen's quarters.

Lizzie shook her head. *To think these silly boys will one day rule the nation.* She collected her toilet items, trying not to awaken Melody who lay curled up under her counterpane, then padded down the hall to the bathroom. While water filled the tub, she slathered the latest beauty cream on her face and cleaned her teeth. She brushed her dark hair one hundred strokes, then wrapped her head in a towel and stepped into the steaming water. With the rain tapping against the bathroom window, she recited a childhood rhyme:

"Rain, rain, go away. Little Lizzie wants to play."

\* \* \*

Sidney had nearly finished eating breakfast by the time she arrived in the glass-walled morning room. Without sunshine, it lacked the cheerful ambiance she'd grown fond of during her stay at Wingate. Even the guests taking their early repast there seemed more subdued than usual. Lizzie had barely slid into a seat across the table from him when a serving girl appeared at her side, holding a coffee carafe.

"Thank you," she said as the girl filled her cup. "Would you please bring me an egg over easy with corned beef hash and toast?"

"Certainly, ma'am."

"I won't say 'good morning' because it's not," Sidney grumbled as he stared out the window.

"Sorry I'm late, but don't be a flat tire. It's just a little rain. We'll perform in the ballroom tonight. A change might be nice. Mix things up a bit."

He poked his fork into a slice of pineapple. "You've seen the ballroom, right?"

"Yes, of course."

"You could run surrey races in there. In such an enormous room we'll sound like we're playing toy instruments. Only the people closest to the stage will be able to hear Melody's flute, and even your siren's voice won't carry to the far corners of that arena. The ballroom was designed to hold two hundred people. The Winslows' forty will rattle around in there like marbles on a billiard table."

Lizzie shrugged, undaunted. "Then we'll cordon off a portion of the room to make it more intimate. We'll arrange the chairs close to the stage, so people will feel a more personal relationship with us. But they can still go off and dance in the wide-open spaces if they wish."

"Hmm. It might work." Sidney lit a cigarette and contemplated her suggestion. "I asked Joey to do his comedy routine for you this morning. I want to get your opinion."

The serving girl brought Lizzie's breakfast and she dipped her toast into the egg's liquid golden yolk. "Melody thought it was funny. Might be good to have a bit of variety. Okay, let's give it a whirl-ski."

"That's my girl-ski."

While she ate, Sidney finished his cigarette. She knew he was fretting over the change of venue and the problems a new setting presented. One more hitch in his plans had thrown him out of sorts. *If only he didn't feel a need to control things so precisely,* she sighed inwardly. *But if he weren't such a perfectionist, he might not be such a terrific pianist.*

"Stop worrying. Everything will be okay. Trust me," she said, trying to sound reassuring. "You know I love a challenge."

As the serving girl poured fresh coffee for them, the band of foul-weather swimmers bounded into the breakfast room in high spirits. The men hooted and hollered like a sports team that had just won an important game.

"What are they so fired up about?" Sidney asked.

"Some sort of arcane tribal ritual involving bracing cold water and an excess of testosterone," Lizzie answered. "Let's get out of here."

They strolled down the hundred-foot-long gallery that ran along the rear of the mansion and ended at the ballroom. Oriental carpets cushioned their steps. Rain pelted the wall of glass French doors that opened onto the back terrace. Portraits of Zachary and Catherine Winslow's unsmiling ancestors stared down at them. As they entered the ballroom, with its gleaming parquet floor and hand-painted French wallpaper, Lizzie spotted Joey Golick seated on the stage. Sidney waved and Joey waved back. He jumped down and held out his hand.

"Top of the morning to you," Joey said.

"Likewise."

He seemed more energetic than usual, she noticed. Since his first night of overindulgence, the aging musician had cut down on his drinking, which let her breathe a little easier. Not only did they need him to pull off this engagement, Lizzie had grown quite fond of Joey and worried about his failing health.

"Ready to see my shtick?" he asked.

She smiled and nodded. "Whenever you are."

As Sidney placed two chairs in front of the stage, Joey took his position. He rolled his shoulders, cracked his knuckles, and twisted his neck, like a boxer getting ready for a fight. *Funny, he doesn't go through that rigmarole before he plays his horn,* she thought. As he launched into his routine, Lizzie found herself laughing out loud—and even blushing a time or two at some of the bawdier jokes. By the time he finished, tears were running down her cheeks and her sides ached.

"So, what do you think?" Joey asked.

"I think it's hilarious," she answered. "But I wonder if it will fly here in the hinterlands."

"Too Jewish?" Sidney asked.

"And too New York. I doubt these Yankee Brahmin will pick up on the references or understand the Yiddish expressions." Lizzie drummed her fingers on the arm of her chair. "It's rather racy too. Frankly, I thought it was the bee's knees, but I'm afraid we'll have to run it by Mrs. Winslow first. The lady's a bit of a prude, as you know, and we don't want her getting in a lather."

"Then let's send a message to Her Fussiness inviting her to preview Joey's act and see what she says," Sidney suggested.

He pulled a calling card from his jacket pocket, jotted a note on the back, and glanced around for a servant to deliver it to Mrs. Winslow. An older man in a dark daytime suit stood at the entrance to the ballroom—keeping tabs on the performers, no doubt. Sidney started toward him, with Joey in tow.

Lizzie hung back. "I need time to decide how to configure this room for maximum effect. Catch up with you later, okay-ski?"

"Whatever you say-ski."

Heels clicking on the polished wood floor, she paced off an arc in front of the stage where she envisioned chairs being positioned. Intimate, yet not so close that the music would overwhelm the audience. Maybe she could get a few servants to set up chairs and tables with linen tablecloths and candles, to give the impression of a nightclub instead of a ballroom. Then she climbed onto the stage, cleared her throat, and belted out a few bars of one of Sophie Tucker's songs to check the room's acoustics.

"Excellent," she said as the sound reverberated around her. "But what else should I expect in a ritzy place like this?"

She left the stage and crisscrossed the room to get a feel for how the evening's traffic might flow. Sometimes she danced with a fantasy partner, imagining Peter Winslow's arms around her. As she reached the outer limits of the ballroom, where cold drafts leaked through the floor-to-ceiling windows, an idea hit her: plants. *We need lots of plants to absorb echoes and create a park-like atmosphere. And benches placed here and there, where couples can sit and talk privately.*

Pacing off the area, Lizzie noticed movement out of the corner of her eye and looked around. Ginny Winslow was watching her.

"Ginny! How lovely to see you. Where have you been hiding? I've missed you."

The girl forced a smile, then cast her eyes down at the floor.

Lizzie hurried to her side and laid a hand on the girl's shoulder. "What's wrong? Why so sad?"

Ginny shrugged, without looking up.

"I thought we were friends. Friends talk to each other. Spill."

"I guess..."

Trying to think of a way to get the girl to open up, Lizzie snapped her fingers. "Hey, you know that crumbling old chapel on the way to the stables?"

Ginny nodded.

"Well, I was walking that way the other day and saw something that I've been wanting to show you."

"What?"

"A mama cat with a litter of brand-new kittens. Want to go see them?"

The gray cloud that had been hanging around Ginny's shoulders lifted slightly and her face brightened. "Now?"

"Sure. Why not?"

"But it's raining outside."

"Grab your mackintosh and galoshes and we'll brave the elements." When

126

Ginny frowned dubiously, Lizzie taunted her. "You're not afraid you'll melt in a bit of rain, are you?"

The girl shook her head.

"I'll meet you in the pavilion in ten minutes. And Ginny," Lizzie held a finger to her lips, "this is our secret, okay?"

The girl smiled and dashed off. Lizzie climbed the servants' stairs to the third floor and grabbed a rain cape, rubber boots, and an umbrella, then hurried back down to the pavilion to meet Ginny Winslow. As the pair sloshed out into the drizzle, their boots squishing in the spongy grass, Lizzie struggled to keep up a lively banter. But the only subject that seemed to pull young Ginny out of her doldrums was the promise of seeing the kittens.

"How many are there?" the girl asked.

"Hmm, four I think."

"Can we keep them?"

"I should say so. They catch rodents and snakes too. Very useful animals."

"Snakes?" Ginny shrieked.

"Don't worry, I doubt they're poisonous. This isn't the tropics, you know. Just a few everyday garden-variety snakes."

By the time they reached the old chapel with its tiny graveyard that no one, apparently, had tended in ages, the rain had slacked off to a mere trickle. They tiptoed into the chapel and Lizzie led the way to the former nave, where a pile of fallen stones sheltered the cat's lair.

"Sssh. We don't want to scare them."

Curled up in a tangle of purple cloth—old choir robes, she supposed—lay a gray-and-white cat nursing four kittens no larger than field mice.

"Oh!" Ginny cried, then clapped her hand over her mouth.

With wary golden eyes, the mother cat watched them as they watched her and her brood. Lizzie kept an eye on her young charge, trying to ascertain what was bothering the girl. A sisterly affection swelled in her chest, and she thought about her own younger siblings back in New York. She would have crouched here all afternoon, eyeing the feline family, but finally, Ginny tired of her role as observer.

"Can we pat the kittens?"

"I think it's too soon," Lizzie whispered. "We might frighten them—they can't even see yet. But we can come back whenever you want to visit them."

"I'd like that."

"Next time we'll bring them a treat."

As they trudged back across the rain-soaked grass, Ginny suddenly blurted out, "I hate Count Ivanovich!"

Surprised, Lizzie asked, "Really? Why?"

"He's old and repugnant."

Lizzie wondered how a twelve-year-old girl knew the word *repugnant* but didn't dare interrupt the flow of Ginny's angry commentary.

"I wish Flo was marrying Henry instead. She was happy then."

"What happened between Flo and Henry?" Lizzie pressed.

"Mother and Father didn't like Henry, and they sent Flo away to stay with our aunt in South Carolina."

"When was that?"

"Thanksgiving, the year before last."

"Maybe your aunt wanted Flo to spend the holiday with her."

"But she was gone for Christmas too. She didn't come home until spring." Ginny pushed back her mackintosh's hood and looked up at Lizzie. "I liked Henry. Why would someone want to kill him?"

Lizzie tugged the girl's pigtail affectionately. "I don't know, sweetie, but I'm going to find out."

\* \* \*

Catherine Winslow practically shouted, "I will not have that filthy Jew uttering his vile words in my house! If he cannot behave with a modicum of decorum, I'll have him thrown out on the street where he belongs!"

Lizzie backed away and let Sidney take charge. Steepling his hands in front of his chest, he bowed his head in a subservient manner. Somehow, he managed to gently nudge the irate woman away from the stage.

"I hope you can believe that we never intended to offend or in any way upset you or your guests, Mrs. Winslow," Lizzie heard him say as he guided their hostess from the ballroom, like a border collie herding a sheep. "Mr. Golick's act has received rave reviews from the critics in New York City and—"

"Sorry about your shtick, Joey," Lizzie said.

"I guess she understood the Yiddish."

# Chapter Nineteen

*"It would be such a disappointment to certain members of my family if I were to marry a commoner as we like to call them. . . . I might even be cut off from the family fortune."*

*— O'Henry, While the Auto Waits*

The Black Irish lad and three other men fetched potted trees and plants of all sorts from the Winslows' conservatory, atrium, and pavilion. Under Lizzie's direction, they arranged the greenery throughout the northern half of the ballroom to replicate a lush park with winding pathways where guests could stroll leisurely between dances. The young Irishman wrapped the shrubs with extravagantly expensive strings of electric lights to create a romantic ambiance, while the other men carried in wicker chairs and settees. Someone even located a statue of an indiscernible deity and positioned it amidst the flora. They seemed to find the whole endeavor of bringing the outdoors indoors amusing.

Two more men shuttled a long dining table and fourteen chairs onto the stage. Then they unfolded the Japanese screen Lizzie had used in her bathtub scene and positioned it to hide the furniture until The Troubadours were ready to perform Alice Gerstenberg's one-act play *Fourteen*.

"I hope our illustrious hostess won't object," Sidney said as he watched a woman servant laying the table for a formal dinner.

*He's still reeling from Catherine Winslow's reaction to Joey's act,* she realized. "I can't imagine why she would. It contains no dirty words, no exposure of human flesh, and no off-color jokes."

"But it does mock Mrs. Winslow's role as a society hostess."

"Hmm. True. But without Joey's comedy routine we need something to break up the evening's performance so it's not all music. I'm guessing she'll envision herself as far superior to Gerstenberg's silly and superficial character Mrs. Pringle. The rest of the audience, I suspect, are well acquainted with women of this sort—perhaps their own mothers or wives—and that should garner us a few laughs." She combed her fingers through her dark brown hair and let out an overly dramatic sigh. "Besides, I can't think of another act we're all familiar with to fill up tonight's performance—unless you think we should just sing and dance and entertain the masses."

He lit a cigarette and blew a series of smoke rings at the ceiling. "I guess I'll have to trust your judgment on this, Bearcat. By the way, the idea of creating an indoor park to break up the ballroom is brilliant—and it lends a note of enchantment to the setting. Yet there's still plenty of dance floor for those who want to shake a leg."

Nodding her head with mock modesty, Lizzie said, "I know, Sid. I'm a genius."

\* \* \*

The Winslows' guests flowed into the ballroom, each couple more splendidly attired than the last. Sidney and Melody played Baroque instrumental pieces as the audience took in the park-like setting, the cloth-covered tables and chairs in front of the stage, and the lighting configured to bring out the best in the elegant hall as well as the beautiful people who occupied it.

"Jeepers creepers, I think I'm underdressed," Lizzie muttered as she once again envied the gorgeous outfits these upper-class ladies wore. In response to the cooler temperatures, more than half the women sported mink, fox, or ermine wraps. Her own strapless, floor-length gown—the first of several she'd don during the course of the evening—encased her hourglass figure seductively. A heavy, gold, Egyptian-style necklace circled her throat and dozens of gold bracelets sparkled on her right arm from wrist to elbow. She'd purposely left her other arm bare, just to make people wonder about the disparity and what it might mean.

When she heard Sidney's piano introduce the first bars of Ida Cox's song "Wild Women Don't Have the Blues," Lizzie made her way to center stage. With Joey's sax accompanying her, she lost herself in the music, captivating the audience with her sultry voice and queenly presence. She realized the song's feminist message might annoy Catherine Winslow, but she didn't care. *This is why I'm a performer,* she thought. *This thrill of communicating through a medium that transcends the words, briefly taking people out of their ordinary lives and inspiring them to touch what lies deep in their hearts.* The rainy weather, the Winslows' arrogance, even Henry Ives's death faded into the background momentarily as she crooned the tune.

For twenty minutes, Lizzie worked through a repertoire of popular songs. Then she, Melody, and Sidney exited the stage to change outfits for the play. Joey stepped into the spotlight, hugging his sax, while two servants removed the Japanese screen that concealed the set.

As Thomas Appleby dimmed the electric lights and Joey's last few notes faded into the darkness, Sidney entered dressed as a butler. He lit the candles on the dining table laid for fourteen guests. A moment later, Lizzie joined him as the excitable Mrs. Pringle, wearing a curly wig and a garish three-layered pink gown that flounced when she walked. She couldn't make out Mrs. Winslow's reaction to the play, but her guests laughed and clapped and seemed thoroughly delighted.

After The Troubadours finished their performance and took a final bow, Zachary Winslow approached Lizzie and asked her to walk with him. A number of guests, she noticed, had made themselves at home in the "park," where servants delivered refreshments. She took his arm and allowed him to escort her from the ballroom into the gallery.

"I understand you've been asking about my daughter Florence."

Taken aback, Lizzie wondered if Peter had reported their conversation to his father. *How dare he!* Annoyance bubbled up in her, but she had to accept that Peter Winslow's allegiance was first, and probably always would be, to his family despite his pretense of independence.

"Only because she seems so unhappy for a young woman about to be married," she replied.

"And, I suspect, because you're aware of her association with your colleague Henry Ives."

"My *deceased* colleague."

"Yes, well." Winslow cleared his throat before continuing. "My daughter was young and impressionable when she met your associate. When my wife and I sensed that she had become, shall we say, infatuated with him and the glamour of the musical world, we put a stop to it. We sent Florence to stay with my wife's sister in Charleston until the girl got over her adolescent fantasies."

They nodded to guests as they made their way down the long arcade, pretending to be engaged in polite conversation. Thick Persian carpets cushioned their footfalls. Winslow studied Lizzie's face, as if trying to determine how much she'd gleaned from what he'd said, but her expression gave nothing away.

"I expect you know about Henry Ives's questionable background," Winslow continued.

"I didn't before coming here, but I do now."

"Then surely you can understand why an association between my daughter and someone like him was simply out of the question. As her father, I'm responsible for protecting Florence and safeguarding her reputation. When he showed up here last week, for this event to celebrate my daughter's engagement to Count Ivanovich, well, you can imagine how surprising and awkward it was for all of us."

"Of course, I admire your wish to take care of your daughter, Mr. Winslow, and I'm sure you want the best for her," Lizzie said. "I'm also aware that Henry supplied you with alcohol."

If Winslow was surprised by her accusation, he hid it well. "Miss Crane, as I've expressed before, I'm deeply sorry for your loss and regret that Mr. Ives's demise took place here at Wingate. I'm asking you to stop interfering in my daughter's life. This whole situation has been difficult for her. As a young woman yourself, surely you can feel some compassion for Florence and what she's been through."

His words tumbled about in her mind as she tried to interpret what he meant. What was the truth behind Zachary Winslow's plea? Was he really concerned about Florence's well-being? Or worried about the risk connected with his own illicit activity? Did he fear that Lizzie might go to the police with the information? Neither of them had mentioned Winslow's earlier offer of hush money. Whatever his motivation, she redoubled her determination to learn more about what Flo had "been through" and whether it had anything to do with Henry's murder.

* * *

After the women had retired to play bridge and the men to smoke cigars, Lizzie supervised the servants dismantling the set on the ballroom's stage.

"Leave the plants and park benches in place," she told them. "The weather's still uncertain—we may end up performing indoors again tomorrow."

"I think it went well tonight, don't you?" Sidney asked. "Our hostess didn't cast kittens over the play and everyone seemed to enjoy the indoor park."

"Oh, quite," she agreed. "I wouldn't be surprised if a few of them rendezvoused here later tonight for a cuddle."

"I saw you talking with Winslow after the show. Was he complimenting our performance?"

"Among other things. He asked me to stop poking about in his daughter Flo's life."

"Well, he and I are in agreement there."

Trying to deflect an argument, she asked, "By the way, do you know where Melody is?"

"I suspect she's with her new suitor," he answered.

"You've met him. What did you think?"

"Seems like a decent enough fella."

"But he's nearly old enough to be her father. And Mel's such an innocent."

CHAPTER NINETEEN

"Might be a good idea to have a birds-and-bees talk with her."

Lizzie sighed. "I know. I haven't had time—the past couple days have been ab-so-lute-ly frantic."

They followed the servants out of the ballroom. The men carried away the dining table and fourteen chairs, the women gathered up the dishes and glassware.

"Speaking of suitors," Sidney said, "I'm surprised you haven't snagged a sugar daddy yet. What's the problem, Bearcat? You're not losing your touch, are you?"

Lizzie fiddled with one of her earrings.  "In case you haven't noticed—which I find hard to imagine—virtually all these gentlemen, even the unmarried ones, came here with female companions. The rest are either flat tires or gray-haired grandpas. Melody may have snagged the only available member of the species worthy of consideration."

"What about young Winslow? I thought you had designs on him."

"He's escorting a lady too. Someone his parents consider an acceptable match, which of course I'm not."

"But you spent an afternoon sailing with him."

Lizzie shrugged. "Frankly, I think he's just after some nookie. I may not stand a chance at marrying him, but I'm not giving it away for free."

# Chapter Twenty

*"I frequently hear music in the very heart of noise."*

*— George Gershwin*

When Sidney arrived in the morning room for breakfast, he found Lizzie reading the paperback traveler's guide she'd purchased the day they visited Gloucester.

As he sat down she said, "I think we should go on another little sightseeing trip."

"What?" he balked. "Don't we have enough to do here? Besides, Sergeant Mulvaney told us not to leave Wingate without his okay."

"Hooey. What's he going to do, throw us in jail? If he had enough evidence to arrest us he would've done it already. Anyway, you can be sure Mrs. Winslow won't let him disrupt her party by hauling away her performers now."

She glanced out the window and noticed Florence Winslow strolling through the rose garden. Despite the drizzling rain, the young woman held no umbrella and her head was bare. Her brown hair hung limp around her shoulders and she moved as if she were sleepwalking. Periodically, she stopped to sniff a blossom or caress a flower's petals, but plucked none. Lizzie recalled Zachary Winslow's appeal last night, to leave his daughter alone. To Lizzie, it seemed that Flo felt very much alone, despite her family, fiancé, friends, and all the hubbub swirling around her. None of the fun and frivolity that should accompany this week's celebration in her honor appeared to have brightened the young bride-to-be's mood.

A serving girl approached their table, interrupting Lizzie's thoughts, and filled their coffee cups. After she'd taken their breakfast orders, Sidney lit a cigarette and frowned at Lizzie from across the table.

"All right, spill. What sort of outing are you conjuring up in that pretty head of yours?"

She held up the guide and pointed to a picture of an enormous resort overlooking a rocky coastline. "A visit to the Oceanside. It's billed as the biggest hotel east of the Mississippi. According to this booklet, it has a theater that can hold 400 people, as well as a ballroom, impressive dining facilities, formal tea gardens, tennis courts, a bathing pavilion, swimming pool, and plenty of shops. It occupies a whole block, with accommodations for 3,000 people. The Davis Cup tennis tournament was played there in 1912, and it says here that the resort attracts 'national and international leaders of business, politics, culture, and society.' "

Sidney took a sip of coffee before asking, "Where is this grand hotel?"

"A place called Magnolia, a short distance south of the city of Gloucester. It sounds like a pretty ritzy affair. I think we should check it out and see if we might perform there. Really, Sid, we have to pursue this opportunity while we're here in the neighborhood. It could lead to bigger and better things."

"You may be right, Bearcat."

She tossed her head and shot him a playful smile. "Of course, I'm right."

The serving girl brought two plates of eggs Benedict and set one in front of each of them. In the center of the table, she placed a bowl of strawberries from the estate's orchards, along with a pitcher of cream. "Will there be anything else?"

"Thank you, no. This looks delicious," Lizzie said.

They'd barely begun eating when Joey Golick entered the morning room. His shoulders slumped and he shuffled toward their table as if his feet were encased in concrete. His dark eyes seemed dull and purple circles hung beneath them; his skin looked waxy. *Oh no*, Lizzie thought, *he's back on the bottle.*

"Top of the morning. You're up early," Sidney greeted him.

Joey took a seat and nodded at them. He rubbed his temples, inhaled a rasping breath, then coughed into his napkin. "Yeah, well, sometimes I wake up and can't go back to sleep. An old man's curse. Might as well get up and get going." He turned his coffee cup upright and signaled to the serving girl.

"Lizzie and I were just talking about driving out to a resort called the Oceanside today. It's not far from here, and it looks pretty swanky. Maybe we could arrange to do a show there. It's got a theater and a ballroom."

Joey's face brightened. "Hey, I know the Oceanside. Played there a few times myself. Got a cousin who works in the kitchen, Benny Kaplan. You're right, it's a ritzy joint." He rubbed the thumb and the first two fingers of his right hand together. "High-end clientele. People come up from New York for the whole summer and bring their entire household staffs with them—maids, cooks, chauffeurs, the works."

The serving girl reappeared at their table and filled their coffee cups. "What would you like for breakfast, sir?" she asked Joey.

He shook his head and waved her away. "Nothing, just coffee."

"What a stroke of luck that your cousin works at the Oceanside. It's a small world truly. You must come with us, Joey," Lizzie insisted, laying her hand on his arm.

"When are you going?"

"We have to be back in time for tonight's performance, but otherwise we don't really have a timetable," Sidney answered.

The saxophonist nodded a few times as he contemplated the trip. "Be nice to see Benny again. It's been years…okay, give old Joey an hour."

Sidney glanced at his wristwatch. "Great. It's 8:20 now. How about we meet in the parking lot at 9:30?"

After finishing her breakfast, Lizzie climbed to the maids' quarters on the third floor and eased the door to her bedchamber open, trying to avoid its annoying creak that might wake Melody. But her friend was already sitting up in bed, propped against a pile of pillows, writing a letter to her parents. A cup of tea rested beside her on the counterpane.

"Morning," Lizzie said. "How'd you sleep?"

"Like a baby. It must be the sea air. I feel so *good* here."

Lizzie rolled her eyes and chuckled. "Sounds like something more than sea air to me. Are you seeing Douglas this morning?"

"Not until lunch. He has some business to take care of this morning."

"Sid, Joey, and I are planning to take a drive to a resort near Gloucester to see about a possible booking there. You're welcome to come along if you like, but I can't guarantee we'll be back by lunchtime."

"Would you mind very much if I didn't go with you?" Melody asked.

"Of course not. It might turn out to be a total bust, and I wouldn't want to impose on your time with Douglas." Lizzie checked her reflection in the tarnished mirror that hung above the bedroom's bureau, then picked up her pot of rouge and rubbed a little on her cheekbones. She fluffed her face with powder and colored her full lips with lipstick. "I'll let you know if anything significant happens."

Satisfied that her face was in order, Lizzie sat on the edge of her twin bed and looked at her young colleague who glowed with the first flush of love. "Melody, uh, this is a bit awkward, but now that Douglas is courting you, well, I wondered if you know about where babies come from and all that."

She expected Melody to blush, sputter, clam up, or act indignant because Lizzie had brought up the subject. Instead, the pretty blonde giggled.

"Silly, of course, I know. I'm not a child—I'm nineteen years old. I should be married by now. Don't worry, Lizzie. I won't do anything foolish."

Lizzie sighed with relief and tried to make light of the inquiry. "Good, because we can't afford to lose another member of the group right now. And I still haven't met this man who's captured your fancy."

"I don't mean to pry, but I am curious since you brought it up," Melody said. "Why haven't you married and had children? I know you've...had men in your life. Don't you believe in love?"

"Poor little bunny, of course, I believe in love. I just don't believe in ruining it by getting married."

# Chapter Twenty-One

*"If you have to ask what jazz is, you'll never know."*

— *Louis Armstrong*

A light rain splattered the Buick's windshield as they approached the grand hotel. Only steps from the ocean, the red-roofed building rose six stories high with at least a thousand windows looking out to sea. Domed turrets stood at the corners. Not far from the main structure, several "cottages"—each a multilevel structure larger than the Winslows' mansion—provided additional housing for hundreds of guests. Lizzie stared out the breezer's window at the landscaped grounds, tennis courts, and swimming pool, trying to take it all in.

"It's a modern-day castle," she exclaimed as Sidney parked and shut off the motorcar.

She grabbed her umbrella and hurried through the drizzle to the covered porch that wrapped around the front and sides of the hotel. While Sidney and Joey made their way toward the entrance, she scanned the spectacular shoreline. Even the clouds and rain couldn't diminish its beauty. During the week she'd spent here on the Massachusetts coast, she'd marveled at the way the ocean's color constantly shifted, from aqua to emerald green to silvery blue to hematite. She tried to imagine what it might be like to have the leisure and the means to stay here for the entire summer, taking in the salubrious salt air, the sunshine, and the exquisite beauty that awed her at every step.

Her thoughts slipped back to the night Henry died. She remembered him sitting in a leather club chair near the fireplace in the gentlemen's lodge, his feet propped up on an ottoman, drinking gin as he told them he'd met Florence Winslow in a place called Magnolia.

"Let's see if we can find my cousin Benny," Joey said as they entered the lobby.

He paused briefly, his eyes roaming about the spacious room, and Lizzie wondered if he was reminiscing about better days. Leaving her two associates to speak to a man at the front desk, she meandered into a pleasant ballroom with a dance floor. The floral Axminster carpet and the wicker armchairs and tables gave it a cheerful, relaxed atmosphere, unlike the Winslows' formal ballroom. At one end of the room, she noticed a grand piano and envisioned Sidney playing it. Next, she strolled through an enormous dining room that afforded guests a fine view of the pool and tennis courts.

"We're in luck," Sidney's voice interrupted her thoughts. "Joey's cousin is on his way to meet us."

"That's swell," she said.

"Benny's one of the chefs here," Joey said, pride evident in his voice.

"It's a foot in the door," Sidney said. "And the fact that you've already played here, Joey, well, that's a hell of a recommendation."

Lizzie let out a dramatic sigh and said in a teasing manner, "Dear Sid, I realize that bookings and marketing are your forte, and I'm merely a stage director, but if it hadn't been for me, you'd never have even known this place existed. A little credit please?"

"You're right." He put his arm around her shoulders and gave her an enthusiastic hug. "This was a darb idea, Bearcat. Glad you talked me into it."

A few minutes later, a rotund, middle-aged man with dark, piercing eyes and a nose like a hawk's beak met them in the dining room. His puffy white hat reminded her of a giant mushroom. Except for his florid complexion, he and Joey looked so much alike that Lizzie already felt she knew him. When he spotted Joey, his face lit up like a movie marquee. The two cousins fell into one another's arms, hugging and slapping each other's backs, tears glistening in their eyes. They lapsed into Yiddish, alternately laughing and crying.

Lizzie signaled Sidney to follow her. "C'mon, let's give the fellas time to catch up."

At one end of the dining room, double doors opened into a theater where both live acts and moving pictures entertained the hotel's guests. She could easily imagine The Troubadours on the stage, performing in front of hundreds of people. Pictures of men and women in evening attire more glamorous even than that of the Winslows' guests flashed through her mind. She envisioned newspaper headlines praising The Troubadours, posters in the entryway, fans asking for autographs, famous musicians from New York and Chicago befriending them.

"Ethel Barrymore, Maude Adams, and Clara Kimball performed here," she told Sidney. "What do you think?"

"Impressive. Very impressive."

"If we finish the Winslows' party in good stead, I bet we could get a booking here."

"The operative word is *if*. I'm afraid Henry's specter could haunt us for a long time."

Waving her hand as if trying to chase away his ghost, she stepped back from the theater's entrance and crossed to one of the L-shaped dining room's windows. The drizzle had sent the tennis players and swimmers off to find other forms of amusement, perhaps to shop at the hotel's posh stores or to get their hair done at its upscale beauty salon. Here and there, guests read newspapers and drank coffee. A few others had claimed tables near the windows, in anticipation of lunch. A pretty young woman supervised two toddlers roughhousing on the carpet and an elderly couple sat in a corner holding hands.

Sidney took a seat at a round table set for four and lit a cigarette.

"Remember that night at Wingate when Henry told us he'd delivered 'fish and such' to a party in Magnolia?" Lizzie asked. "That's when he said he met Florence Winslow."

"Yeah, so?"

"This would be a swell site for a party. I can't help wondering if this was the place he meant and what sort of 'provisions' he might have delivered."

"Where are you going with this, Bearcat? Don't tell me you dragged me all the way out here on another sleuthing exposition."

"My objective was professional, of course. Wouldn't it be the bee's knees if we could play here?" She began pacing, as she sometimes did when she wanted to process an idea. "But while we were motoring, I kept thinking about how Henry apparently conveyed spirits to lots of people around here. Doesn't it seem logical that he might have supplied this hotel too—and I'm not just thinking seafood? This isn't some cozy mom-and-pop guesthouse. The rich and famous stay here, and I'm sure some of them would like to unwind with a cocktail at the end of the day or enjoy the gift of the grape during dinner."

"You've got a point."

She circled the table where Sidney sat puffing on his cigarette in its silver holder. "Okay, here's another speculation. It's a long shot, but hear me out." She held up her right index finger. "Point number one: We know that long before The Troubadours entered the scene, Henry and Zachary Winslow were acquainted." She raised another finger. "Number two: During the past few years, the shoemaking industry in Massachusetts has been on a downhill slide due to competition from factories in the south with cheaper labor; hence Winslow's profits have been declining markedly." Lifting a third finger, she said, "Which leads me to number three: Did Winslow turn to rum-running in order to prop up his flagging shoe business, and did he partner up with Henry's family in the operation?"

"What if he did?"

"Maybe he knows a lot more about Henry's death than he's letting on. Maybe he isn't as 'sorry' as he pretends to be."

Sidney exhaled a lungful of smoke. "If Henry and Zachary Winslow were in cahoots, it wouldn't make sense for our host to bump off his colleague. Why kill the golden goose?"

"Unless something happened to stir up bad blood between them."

"Such as?"

"Last night Winslow told me that when he realized Flo was sweet on Henry, he sent her to stay with an aunt in South Carolina for several months until she got over her crush. It wouldn't do for a girl of Flo's station to get mixed up with someone like Henry. Peter said the same thing. So when our pal showed up again last week, Papa Winslow had to make sure his daughter and Henry wouldn't renew their romance."

"And you believe he killed Henry to keep that from happening? Really, Lizzie, I think your imagination is running amok. Besides, the Winslows hired us because of Henry—why would they invite him back to Wingate if they thought he and Flo might get together again?"

Lizzie stopped pacing and sat down across from Sidney. "I can think of two possible reasons. One, to show Henry that Flo was getting married. Two, to kill him."

Sidney shook his head. "I don't know, Bearcat, it sounds pretty convoluted…"

"Except neither of those possibilities is true," she continued. "Peter Winslow told me Flo convinced her parents to hire us—she knew Henry was part of our group, but they didn't. Imagine their shock when they realized the fox had returned to the hen house."

Before he could reply, Joey and his cousin pushed open the doors that led from the kitchen and crossed the dining room to join them. Lizzie thought she noticed a slight bounce in Joey's step—he looked happier than he had at any time since she'd met him. Apparently, this rendezvous with his cousin had pumped new life into the aging musician. He introduced Benny Kaplan to Lizzie and Sidney, and the men shook hands.

"Joey told me about your friend's death. *A shvartsen sof*," Benny said. "I read about it in the papers, of course, but I didn't make the connection until Joey says he's playing with you, filling in for your friend. My condolences."

"Thank you," Sidney said. "We were fortunate that Joey could join us just in the nick of time. He's a phenomenal musician, but you know that already."

"So you're performing at Zachary Winslow's shindig, eh?"

"Do you know the Winslows?" Lizzie asked. "I think he and his family

144

may have stayed at this hotel."

Benny shook his head. "Heard of him. Big shot. Seen his name in the papers. I wouldn't know if he stayed here, but you could check if he signed the guest book."

"Good idea. By the way, did you ever meet our deceased colleague, Henry Ives? He was a fisherman from Gloucester. I think he might have supplied seafood for a party here two summers ago."

"We get lots of provisioners through here. Can't keep track of them. Lots of parties too."

Lizzie pulled the newspaper article from her purse and showed Benny the photo of Henry.

"Yeah, seems familiar. I remember seeing him around." Benny's funny hat bobbed up and down as he nodded. "Good-looking fella. I thought he dressed too nice for a fisherman."

An attractive couple strolled through the dining room and Lizzie lowered her voice. "I think he might have been involved in liquor trafficking and that's why he was killed."

"I wouldn't know about that. Don't ask." Benny held up his hands as if they were stop signs, then changed the subject. "Say, can you stay for lunch?"

"We've got time, right?" Joey asked, an eager grin on his face.

Lizzie nodded to the chef. "What a lovely idea, Mr. Kaplan. We'd be delighted. What do you recommend?"

"The lobster's to die for," Benny suggested. "I'm guessing you're not Jewish. But you won't go wrong with the smoked ox tongue or the salmon hollandaise."

"Lobster for me," she said without hesitation.

"Make that two," Sidney said.

"Gotta try your ox tongue, Benny," Joey said. "Remember our *bubbe*'s ox tongue?"

"What's not to remember? You think I didn't get my inspiration from her?" He clapped his palm to his chest and turned his face up to the sky momentarily, as if communicating with his departed grandmother, before shifting his attention back to The Troubadours. "Sit, sit. I'll see to your *mitog*.

It's early yet—you're smart to eat before the hordes descend."

After Benny disappeared into the kitchen, Lizzie said to Joey, "I'm glad you got to reconnect with your cousin. He seems like a nice man."

Joey nodded and his eyes glazed over. "A *mensch*. We grew up together in Brooklyn...the stories I could tell."

He took a seat beside Lizzie as a waiter brought a basket of bread, a tray of various relishes, and a plate of sautéed chicken livers for them to nibble on while they waited for their main course. The waiter filled their coffee cups and water glasses, promising to bring their lunch "in a jiffy."

"I could grow accustomed to this lifestyle," Lizzie said with a smile. She gazed out over the empty tennis court and thought, *even if it rained forever I'd still be content just to sit here in this idyllic environment beside the sea, reading books and listening to music.*

While the men talked business, Lizzie excused herself and went to the lobby to peruse the guest book. She flipped the pages back to June 1923 and began running her finger down the rows of names—hundreds and hundreds of them. On the sixteenth, she found what she was looking for: Zachary Winslow's signature.

"I was right," she told Sidney as the waiter served their lunch. "Winslow did stay here, two summers ago."

"So, what's that prove?" he asked.

"Nothing, really. Could be a coincidence, I suppose. It's just intriguing that both Henry and Winslow were here at the same time, just as Henry said."

"What's intriguing is this lobster. Good thing somebody in the kitchen cracked open the shell, otherwise I wouldn't have known how to get at it." A bright red crustacean with huge pincher claws perched on his plate. Sid forked a bite of the sweet pink flesh into his mouth and savored it for a moment before swallowing. "Heavenly." He took another bite, then said to Lizzie, "Stop playing detective and eat your lunch. If Winslow and Henry were partners in the booze biz, they wouldn't choose a classy place as public as this for their meetings."

"I suppose you're right," she said.

But she wasn't ready to give up—and she had a hunch this was the place where Florence and Henry's affair began. Maybe Henry sold only fish to the Oceanside. Maybe Winslow brought his family here for a party and Henry happened to encounter Florence while delivering seafood, exactly as he'd said. But that didn't discount the possibility of the two men secretly meeting later on the beach at Wingate or a sheltered cove in Gloucester or a dozen other places.

After they'd finished eating, Benny stopped by their table to see if they'd enjoyed their meal. By now more than a hundred people had gathered in the dining room, and Lizzie was glad she and her friends had gotten in ahead of the crowd.

"Superb," she said. "I've never eaten lobster before, but I will again, every chance I get."

"This was spectacular," Sidney said and asked for their bill.

Benny held his hands up to stop him. "What, you think I'd charge my own cousin for a meal? Forget about it."

"Thank you, that's very generous of you. You must promise to come visit us in New York and let us take you out to dinner," Lizzie said. "Deal?"

"Deal," he agreed.

"Mr. Kaplan, this has been a divine experience," Sidney said. "I can't thank you enough. I'm afraid we must be on our way, but if fortune smiles on us, maybe we'll have a chance to perform with Joey in this wonderful hotel's theater and enjoy more of your marvelous cooking."

Lizzie extended her hand. "Thank you again for your hospitality. May we meet again soon."

"*Zay gezunt*," Benny said and hugged his cousin one last time. "Don't be a stranger, eh?"

On the way out Joey handed Sidney a business card. "This is the man you want to see about bookings. Call and set up an appointment with him."

Sidney read it, then tucked it in the pocket of his jacket. "This is great, Joey, really great. I can't thank you enough."

"Hey, one hand washes the other, right? Maybe I'll play here with you someday, you never know. And I got to see Benny again."

All the way back to Ipswich, Lizzie's mind kept trying to decipher the alliance between Henry and the Winslows. So long as Zachary Winslow merely imbibed or even served alcohol at his home, technically he wasn't breaking the law—only if he manufactured, sold, or transported the stuff. She recalled Peter's comment about the speed of his sloop *Rhiannon*—a desirable quality if one intends to quietly ferry illicit goods and avoid the detection of law enforcement officials. Gloucester, she'd read, had a long history of smuggling, dating back to the days when the English still ruled the colonies.

One story told of a schooner laden with illegal cargo that docked in the city's inner harbor late at night. Under cover of darkness, lumpers spent the night unloading the goods, knowing that in the morning a customs official from nearby Salem would come calling. But as dawn broke over Good Harbor Beach, only half the ship's cache had been carted off and secured. When the government man arrived to enact his duty, the wily gatekeeper at the Blyman bridge that allowed access from the mainland—the very bridge whose upright position had delayed Lizzie and her companions on their trip into the city—halted him because of a smallpox scare. Anyone from outside who wished to gain admittance to Gloucester must first undergo fumigation, the gatekeeper insisted.

Much to his chagrin, the official spent the rest of the day being smoked to cleanse him of potential disease. Finally, at dusk—after all the merchandise from the schooner had been safely relocated—he was released to go about his job. He searched the schooner, found nothing amiss, and returned to Salem with only a respiratory complaint from the smoke to show for his efforts.

# Chapter Twenty-Two

*"Music is my mistress, and she plays second fiddle to no one."*

— *Duke Ellington, Music Is My Mistress*

By the time they arrived back at Wingate, the rain had ended and the Winslows' guests had resumed their outdoor activities. They whacked balls back and forth across the tennis court, rolled balls around on the bocce court, rode horseback across the open meadows, and bathed in the chilly surf.

"Even though the weather's improved, I think we should hold tonight's performance indoors," Lizzie told Sidney as they ambled down the long, sea-facing gallery that led to the grand ballroom. "After the rain, the mosquitoes will be horrific."

"Fine by me," he agreed. They paused at the ballroom door and studied the indoor park. "It would be a shame to let all this go by the wayside after only one night."

"What do you think about playing hot jazz tonight? Maybe a dance contest?" she suggested.

Sidney glanced around for a place to dump his cigarette ashes and finally deposited them in a potted plant. "I'm game. We've exhausted our dramatic repertoire anyway. I think we'll have to get the go-ahead from Mrs. Winslow for a dance contest, though. You know how testy she can be."

"Will you handle her, Sid? You're the only one of us she likes—you can wrap her around your little finger."

"Sure," he said. "So, what have you got planned for the rest of the day, Madame Director? We still have several hours until showtime."

"Nothing, actually, other than organizing the songs we'll play tonight. How about you?"

"I thought I'd work on my opera."

Lizzie's surprised voice echoed through the ballroom. "Opera? What do you mean?"

"I've always wanted to compose an opera. When I was a little boy, I fell asleep night after night listening to Mozart's *Magic Flute* and Wagner's *Der Ring des Nibelungen*."

"I never realized...why didn't you tell me this before?"

He shrugged and hooked his thumbs in the pockets of his trousers. Suddenly, the talented, confident, take-charge-guy she'd known all these years went shy in her presence.

"Well, you know, fear of criticism and all that stuff. I mean, I'm a jazz musician, playing other people's material, performing at speakeasies and parties. What makes me think that I can actually write something as grand as an opera?"

Lizzie gave him a quick hug. "What made this high-school dropout from the Bronx think she could become a star in the music world? We have to chase our dreams, Sid. They're all we've got. Don't listen to those voices in your head. Don't listen to those other people who discourage you." She tapped her chest. "Listen to your heart."

Sidney hugged her back and pressed his cheek against her hair. "Thanks for the pep talk, Bearcat. I'll try."

\* \* \*

While Sidney retreated to work on his opera and Melody enjoyed the company of her new beau, Lizzie hiked to the old, rundown chapel to check on the new brood of kittens. This time she'd stopped by the Wingate kitchen beforehand and grabbed a piece of fresh cod for the mama cat. As she left the mansion, she spotted Ginny Winslow sitting on a bench beside the tennis court.

"Hi Ginny," she said, taking a seat beside the adolescent girl. "I'm on my way to visit the kittens. Want to come along?"

A spark flickered in the girl's eyes, and then promptly died. "I have a tennis lesson in a few minutes, then a French lesson, and a piano lesson after that."

"Don't you get a summer vacation?" Lizzie asked.

Ginny shook her head.

"Okay, then, I'll let you know how the kitties are doing when I get back."

Still glistening with moisture, the high grass dampened Lizzie's shoes and socks as she crossed the fields toward the old chapel. The humid air hung close around her, thick and sultry, and the sun struggled to break through a cover of clouds. Birds sang cheerfully after the rain. Along the way, she passed trees heavy with red apples, and raspberry and blackberry bushes dripping with ripe fruit. A flock of sheep grazed in the distance. The peaceful scene made her think of a Corot painting.

The churchyard's rusted iron gate creaked as she lifted the latch to let herself in. She pushed open a rotting wooden door and entered the crumbling sanctuary. The rain had left puddles on the stone floor. Once upon a time, it must have been a pretty little chapel. *I wonder who built it and why no one has bothered to restore it now?*

Near the apse, she found the feline family resting peacefully in their nest of purple choir robes. She counted the kittens to make sure they were all still there: two gray tabbies, an orange tiger, and a calico. Lizzie laid the piece of fish near the mother cat. Cautiously, the cat sniffed at it, then rose from her lair and gobbled it down in an instant.

After gently stroking each kitten in turn, Lizzie went outside to the church cemetery. Weathered tombstones stood in the churchyard, most of them dappled with orange or gray-green lichen. She knelt and read the inscriptions on the headstones. A few of the deceased had lived relatively long lives, but most had died before the age of fifty. *Poor Henry,* she thought, *he never saw his thirtieth birthday.* Several of the women in the graveyard hadn't made it that long either, and their ill-fated infants lay buried beside them. She read one inscription:

**Born November 19, 1841, died November 20, 1841**

Lizzie ran her finger over the etched letters on the timeworn stones, wondering about the lives and deaths of the young mothers buried there. How fearful they must have been, giving birth without any knowledge of what might transpire or any recourse if things went wrong. Even if they and their babies survived the ordeal of birth, they still had a long, difficult road ahead of them.

"You! Here, in a churchyard?" a man's voice bellowed.

Lizzie glanced over her shoulder and saw Count Ivanovich standing behind her. His heavy eyebrows were knitted together, his thick lips drawn in a dark scowl.

"Good afternoon to you, too, Count." She stood up and turned to face him. "What brings you here to this tumbled-down chapel?"

"I come here each day. No chapel is in the Winslows' home and I do not drive in America to a church in the town. This is the best place that I can find."

As he spoke, his hands repeatedly clenched into fists at his sides and then unclenched. For the first time, she noticed the Russian Orthodox cross hanging on a chain around his neck.

"But you," he continued, his voice rising in anger. He pointed a thick finger at her. "How dare *you* come to this holy place? You are an evil woman, a whore who has turned my fiancée against me."

"Hey, wait just a minute, pal. I'm no whore, and if you weren't such a grouchy old bear maybe Flo would like you better."

Color flushed the count's sallow face and his black eyes gleamed. "You are a witch who tempts men with the sin of lust. In my country we stone witches and whores."

"Hasn't anyone clued you in to the fact that it's the twentieth century, not the Middle Ages?"

The count bent down and picked up a rock the size of a baseball. Before Lizzie had a chance to react, he hurled it at her, striking her on the left shoulder.

"What the hell are you doing?" she shouted.

He grabbed another rock. "You are a scourge on the earth. God will not suffer a witch to live!"

Lizzie turned and ran. But before she reached the cemetery gate, a blinding pain burst at the back of her head, and then everything went black.

\* \* \*

An hour before the night's performance, Lizzie lay on her narrow bed holding an ice pack to her head. She'd awakened in the cemetery with a splitting headache and dried blood caked in her hair.

Melody hovered nearby, trying to get her friend to drink a cup of tea.

"I need something stronger than tea," Lizzie grumbled. "See if there's any scotch left in the flask in my suitcase. I think I've got a bottle of aspirin in there too."

"You should see a doctor and notify the police," Melody insisted, her voice laced with concern.

"Not yet. If the cops arrested the count—assuming they believed me—the party would be over. We don't want that to happen, do we? Besides, I think Count Ivanovich may have murdered Henry, but I need more proof."

"Why would he kill Henry?"

"He tried to kill me," Lizzie pointed out. "He may have seen Henry as a rival for Flo's affections and decided to take him out of the picture. As we've learned, the count lost his money and land in Russia when the Communists took over. Florence Winslow is his ticket to financial solvency and United States citizenship. He's desperate, and desperate men do extreme things."

She recalled her late-night walk with Sid and Joey on the beach and their discussion about who had the most to lose if Henry stayed alive. Now, the finger pointed at Count Ivanovich.

"Have you told Sidney that the count attacked you?'

"Not yet. I will when the time's right."

"But what if he kills *you* in the meantime?"

"I'm on to him now. I don't intend to give him another chance to bump me off."

Melody pulled the silver flask from Lizzie's suitcase, then handed it and a bottle of aspirin to her friend.

After washing down two tablets, Lizzie sighed, "Ah, that's better."

"I think you should stay in bed tonight instead of performing," Melody said, pouring a cup of tea for herself.

"No dice. This is our next-to-last night, and I have no intentions of begging off. That would only arouse suspicion and reflect badly on The Troubadours. Besides, I want the count to see me alive and well, despite his evil-medieval tactics."

"Good thing he didn't bring a mace or broad sword with him," Melody teased.

Lizzie gulped some more scotch, then pushed herself up from the bed. The room spun and her vision blurred. She felt nauseous. *Melody's right, I should stay in bed.* As the world slowly rearranged itself around her, however, Lizzie seated herself in front of the bedchamber's mirror and began applying her makeup. She'd washed the blood out of her hair earlier. Now she pulled on a velvet headband decorated with peacock feathers. Behind her, Melody's pretty face expressed concern.

"Really, Mel. I'll be okay. You, Sid, and Joey will shoulder the lion's share of tonight's entertainment. I only have a few songs to do. No theatrics. And if I don't feel up to singing, you'll cover for me, right?"

"Of course."

"Okay, then. Help me into my gown."

# Chapter Twenty-Three

*"She is singing to bring down the chandelier!"*

— *Gaston Leroux, Phantom of the Opera*

S ergeant Mulvaney met the two entertainers at the entrance to the ballroom. Instead of his uniform, the beefy detective wore a badly cut black suit with a starched white shirt and black tie. Even without the uniform, he still stuck out amidst the Winslows' elegantly attired gentlemen guests. Maybe they'd think he was a servant, not a cop.

"Excuse me, ladies," he said. "May I have a word with you?"

"Have we a choice?" Lizzie asked.

"Not one that will benefit you."

He waved them toward a wicker settee in the fanciful indoor park. Electric lights twinkled amid the foliage. In the background, Lizzie could hear Sidney warming up on the piano. The women seated themselves, but Mulvaney remained standing.

"Miss Crane, Miss Fitzgerald, I realize that your contractual engagement with the Winslows ends after tomorrow night's performance. However, we are still conducting the investigation of your colleague's murder—and you were the last people to see Henry Ives alive."

"Except for his killer," Lizzie pointed out.

Mulvaney ignored her remark. "I must insist that you remain here at Wingate until I give you permission to leave."

"You mean we're under house arrest?"

"Call it what you will. But until the police determine that you are innocent or we arrest the person who killed your colleague, you and Mr. Somerset will not be allowed to return to New York. I don't intend to waste the taxpayers' money and my time going through an extradition process. Stay on the premises, where I can keep an eye on you."

*I guess that's both a blessing and a curse,* Lizzie thought. She supposed she could demand that Mulvaney either arrest them or let them go free if he didn't have enough evidence to hold them. Perhaps she should contact an attorney. On the other hand, she couldn't think of anything she'd rather do than spend the rest of the summer at Wingate, walking along the beach, eating Mrs. Appleby's cooking, and getting to know Peter Winslow better. Still, if the detention went on for long, it could hinder their ability to get more jobs and cut into their income.

"How do the Winslows feel about this? I assume you've informed them."

"They don't like it any better than you do, but they have no choice and neither do you."

"How long do you suppose this might take?" Melody asked.

The sergeant shrugged. "I have no idea. You could speed things along by providing information, not only about the murder but anything about the victim's past, who he knew and was involved with, anything at all." Mulvaney tugged at his tie as if it were choking him. "I've tried to keep a low profile while continuing this investigation, to allow you to finish your commitment to the Winslows and to spare them embarrassment. But after tomorrow I plan to turn up the heat."

"You've been swell, Sergeant," Lizzie said, a hint of sarcasm in her tone. "Now if you don't mind, we have a show to do."

He nodded. "I'll be in the audience. Just don't get any ideas about going anywhere else."

Lizzie's vision blurred as she rose and, for a moment, she clung to Melody's arm for support. She paused until the room stopped spinning, trying to ignore the painful pounding in her head, before crossing the ballroom to the stage. She considered telling Mulvaney about today's incident with Count

Ivanovich in the chapel cemetery but held back. She hadn't even told Sidney yet. Besides, if the count thought he'd killed her—or at least driven her away—seeing her onstage, bigger than life, as if nothing had happened might make him believe she possessed supernatural powers.

"I wonder if the good sergeant knows any more than the last time we talked to him," she said to Melody.

"How could you tell? He plays his cards rather close to the vest."

"True. But he's been hanging around Wingate for a week, talking with everybody who lives, works, or visits here, and he still feels a need to confine us. Undoubtedly, he's checked out the Gloucester rumrunners by now, including Henry's family, and come up empty. My guess is either he's still in a quandary or he's getting close to making an arrest and doesn't want to tip his hand. I'm betting on the former."

"Let's hope you're wrong."

"I agree, so long as he's not planning to arrest one of us."

* * *

Tonight, they pulled out all the stops. Sidney spotlighted tunes from Duke Ellington. Joey hauled out his trumpet and played Louis Armstrong's "Hot Five" songs with a flair that would have made Sachmo proud. Once the two musicians got going, they fed on each other's talent and enthusiasm, each trying to outdo the other. The result was pure magic.

Even though each note pounded Lizzie's aching head like a hammer, she loved every minute. With the music swelling inside her, she forgot momentarily about Count Ivanovich, the Winslows, and Henry Ives, and just let herself be transported into the realm where the good times reigned supreme.

After belting out a couple of Marion Harris's favorites, Lizzie signaled Melody to follow her into the makeshift dressing room behind the stage. There they changed out of their formal evening gowns into knee-length flapper dresses adorned with rows of fringe and glittery beadwork. When they returned to the stage, their colleagues had just launched into one of

Ben Bernie's spicier pieces. Even though Lizzie meant to avoid dancing tonight, the music swept her up like a whirlwind and refused to let her go. She and Melody clicked their tap shoes, prancing, twirling, gliding, and sliding with a fervor that brought cheers from their audience. Twice Lizzie's vision blurred and she almost lost her balance, but she recovered without embarrassing herself and carried on.

"And now, ladies and gentlemen," Sidney called out to the crowd, after a pause in the action, "it's time for tonight's dance contest." He announced the rules and then told the contestants to pair up. "My associates and I will serve as judges for three dances. I'm sure it will be a tough call, but our joint decision will be final. So gents, grab your best gals and take your places on the dance floor. History is about to be made."

Couples lined up for the challenge. Lizzie counted twelve pairs of dancers, including Peter Winslow and his lovely debutant. Florence and the count, however, remained seated, as did Zachary and Catherine Winslow.

First, The Troubadours played a swing number, while observing the dancers' grace and smooth, flowing movements. Lizzie watched the red-haired man she'd noticed on the first day of his arrival, skating across the ballroom's parquet floor with such fluid ease that he and his partner seemed to float on air.

For the next number, they chose a Charleston. This time, Peter Winslow and his beautiful companion stood out from the pack. As she watched them, Lizzie longed to change places with the lively deb who, for the moment at least, commanded Peter's complete attention.

The Troubadours opted to play a Lindy Hop for the final number. A skinny, long-legged girl with almost no chest and a pimply youth dominated the floor. Without missing a beat, the young man flipped his partner over his shoulders, swept her between his legs, and spun her around in circles until even the audience watching them felt dizzy.

At the end of the dancing, Sidney stepped to center stage, grinning and dabbing at his receding brow with a handkerchief. "Whoopee!" he said, fanning himself with both hands. "It's going to be hard for my colleagues and me to choose a winning couple out of all this talent, but give us a few minutes to catch our breath and confer. Grab yourselves a Coca-Cola, a smoke, or a smooch while you wait, and we'll be back to announce the winners in fifteen minutes."

As the guests dispersed, The Troubadours retreated into an anteroom off the ballroom that served as a temporary dressing and prop room. Lizzie availed herself of Melody's support and eased herself into the first chair available. Sidney, pumped up from the lively music and excitement, paced about the small space.

"What do you think?" he asked. "Who's our winning couple?"

They deliberated for only a few minutes before deciding on the stunning Lindy Hop couple. Lizzie would have chosen either Peter Winslow or the copper-haired man, but she realized she lacked objectivity. Besides, she was too sore and tired to give it much thought. She pressed her fingertips to her temples, wishing she'd brought her flask of scotch and her aspirin bottle downstairs with her.

"Are you okay, Bearcat?" Sidney asked.

"Not completely."

Concern flashed in his eyes. "What's wrong?"

She waved him off. "I'll tell you all about it after we're finished here tonight."

They repositioned themselves onstage and Sidney seated himself at the piano, where he played a few stanzas from "The Sheik of Araby" to call back the wandering guests. As couples meandered from the indoor park toward the stage, Joey Golick stepped forward and beckoned them with sylvan notes from his sax. When most of the guests had returned to the fold, Sidney strode to center stage.

"Welcome back, music lovers. I don't know when I've seen such a terrific bunch of talented dancers. You all deserve a big round of applause."

He waited while the crowd clapped and cheered enthusiastically. A few men patted one another's backs.

"It's been a difficult decision. You're all the bee's knees, but my colleagues and I have chosen…"

Lizzie had wondered if, in order to please their hosts, they should have

159

chosen Peter Winslow for the honor. But when Sid named the Lindy Hop couple, applause swelled through the ballroom and she saw Peter clapping as vigorously as the rest.

"Come on up here," Sidney called.

The pimply youth and his flat-chested partner approached the stage holding hands, blushing under the attention. *They can't be more than sixteen years old,* Lizzie thought. *Maybe they're Winslow relatives?*

Sidney shook hands with the young man and bowed to the girl. "My friends and I would like to present you with a small token of recognition for the enjoyment you've given us here tonight."

He handed the girl a bouquet of flowers and kissed her on the cheek. Then he held out to the boy a brass plaque engraved with the words: Winners of the First Annual Wingate Summer Dance Contest, August 1925, Ipswich, Massachusetts. The audience cheered as the couple returned to their places and The Troubadours took up their instruments once again.

"When did you have time to have that plaque engraved?" Lizzie asked Sidney.

"When we got back from the Oceanside."

"I thought you were writing your opera?"

He shrugged. "Sometimes the muse doesn't feel like talking, so I drove into town and had the plaque made instead."

"You amaze me, Sid. What a delightful event," she said with a smile. "But you don't really think we're going to come back here every summer to judge a dance contest, do you?"

"Highly unlikely," he answered. "It was fun, though, wasn't it?"

After their evening's performance ended and the Winslows' guests trudged off to bed or went in search of other forms of entertainment, Sidney escorted Lizzie outside to the back terrace. They could see couples strolling down the promenade under the starlit sky, gaslights illuminating their way. Several other guests sat in Adirondack chairs at the far end of the terrace or near the tennis court, laughing and smoking and perhaps passing around a flask.

"What's up, Bearcat?" Sidney asked, lighting a cigarette. "Something's not right. Are you ill? Fried?"

When she told him about the count's assault, he insisted she go to a doctor. "You could have a concussion."

"You know I've got a hard head, Sid. I'll be okay."

"Did you tell Mulvaney?"

"Not yet. Here's the deal. I think the Ruskie killed Henry and I want him to trap himself. He's less likely to step in it if he knows he's being watched."

Sidney shook his head in exasperation. "Jeepers creepers, why won't you stay out of this mess? You could get *really* hurt, or worse."

"We can't stay out of it—we're already in it up to our necks. Unless the good sergeant pinches the count, we could end up sleeping among the servants 'til this time next year, or worse yet, in prison cells. I don't intend to let that happen without putting up a fight."

"I should've known I couldn't talk sense into that hard—and now banged up—head of yours." He sighed loudly, exhaling a cloud of smoke into the night air. "But from now on I want to know everything that happens as soon as it happens—and I do mean *everything*. Will you promise me that at least? If we stick together, maybe, just maybe, I can keep you from getting killed too."

# Chapter Twenty-Four

*"He looked around him wildly, as if the past were lurking here in the shadow of his house, just out of reach of his hand."*

— F. Scott Fitzgerald, The Great Gatsby

Lizzie breathed in the cool night air, heavy with the scent of salt, and tried to make sense of the mess she'd become entangled in during the past week. The lump Count Ivanovich's stone had raised on her head ached, and she fingered it gently. *Maybe Sid's right,* she thought, *maybe I should back off and just let the police do their job.*

Among the couples strolling about the grounds, Lizzie spotted Melody and her suitor, Douglas. Watching the pair, she sent up a prayer to whoever might be listening: *Please let him be good to her.* She'd seen too many women suffer the pains of betrayal, rejection, abuse, deception, and every other sort of heartache in the name of love—Florence Winslow among them. If only she could shield innocent Melody from those wounds.

Gathering up the skirt of her gown, Lizzie descended the stone steps from the terrace to the grassy promenade and wandered down to the rose garden. In the moonlight, the flowers' brilliant colors had dimmed from scarlet, golden-yellow, and bright pink to shades of gray. They made her think of tinted photographs, mere suggestions of their true selves. She lifted the latch of the wrought-iron gate and let herself into the garden. As she bent to smell the blossoms on a particularly fragrant bush, she heard a man's voice behind her.

"My wife and daughter designed this garden together. They're both very fond of roses. Do you know that roses are symbols of love, Miss Crane?"

Lizzie straightened and looked up at Zachary Winslow. "Good evening, Mr. Winslow. Yes, I do know that, and also that each rose has its own unique meaning. During the Victorian period, people composed bouquets of flowers to convey messages. Yellow roses signified friendship and happiness, red ones represented passion. White ones not only meant purity but also secrecy."

In the moonlight, his silver hair glowed like a halo and his stern features seemed softer than usual. His voice, however, was hard and cold. "Miss Crane, I've asked you to stop prying into the lives of my family and me. I've offered restitution to you and your associates for the death of your colleague. Yet you continue to interfere where you shouldn't." He reached out and touched a rose, running his fingertips over its petals with surprising delicacy. "I know you visited the Oceanside Hotel and asked about me. I know you suspect I was allied with Henry Ives and his family."

When she started to object, he silenced her by touching his index finger to her lips. "I have 'eyes' everywhere, Miss Crane. I know where you are and what you're doing at all times. You can't escape my scrutiny. Even when you return to New York—if you are allowed to return—I'll be aware of every move you make."

"My heart goes out to your daughter," Lizzie said, trying to dodge his implied threat. "She seems so sad. As an entertainer, I wish I could somehow make her happier."

Zachary Winslow pulled a Swiss Army knife from his pocket and sliced off a rose stem. Grasping Lizzie's arm firmly so that she couldn't pull away, he pressed the thorns against her bare throat. With exquisite slowness he drew the sharp points inch by inch along her jugular, down toward her collarbone, gently pricking her delicate flesh so that in their wake tiny beads of blood welled up like a necklace of rubies.

"You are my guest and employee," he whispered, leaning in close so that his breath caressed her neck, "but you've overstepped your role. You can be removed. Life is as fragile as these rose petals..."

Lizzie slapped his hand away and the rose fell to the ground. "Take your hands off me, sir, or I'll scream."

"I doubt that." Winslow chuckled and released her. "Think about what I've said as you go to your bed tonight, Miss Crane."

\* \* \*

Still shaking with anger, Lizzie climbed the stairway that led to the maids' quarters. Between the second and third floors, she bumped into a serving girl of about eighteen with broad shoulders and hair bound up around her head.

"Begging your pardon, ma'am," the girl apologized, her face flushing with embarrassment. She backed against the wall of the narrow stairwell to let Lizzie pass.

"No harm done," Lizzie assured her. "Say, I believe we've crossed paths before. You're Florence Winslow's personal maid, Marie. Your sister, Tess, has been tending to us during our stay. Such a sweet girl."

"Yes, ma'am."

Before the maid could regain her composure, Lizzie decided to confront the girl with an idea that had tugged at her mind since Ginny first mentioned Flo's lengthy visit to her aunt in Charleston. "Marie, I have something of great importance to ask you in utmost confidence. Was Miss Florence in a family way when her parents sent her off to stay with her aunt in South Carolina?"

The blush that had risen in Marie's face now drained away, leaving her as pale as a lily. The girl clutched at her apron and stared at her feet.

"Please, Marie. I'm sure you know that Henry Ives—Miss Florence's dear friend and mine—has been murdered. I want ever so much to find out who killed him. Poor Flo seems so sad...we're all worried about her. Her own life may even be in danger. You might be able to save her. Can you help us?"

The girl remained silent.

"You don't have to say anything, just look up at me if it's true."

164

Slowly the girl raised her eyes.

"Thank you." Lizzie slipped off one of her gold bracelets and handed it to Marie. Then she squeezed past the young maid and hurried up the stairs.

As she removed her makeup, Lizzie easily put the pieces together and fingered Henry for the father. No wonder the Winslows got apoplectic when he turned up with The Troubadours. But were they angry enough to bump off Henry?

She tried to imagine Zachary Winslow sticking a knife into the man who'd disgraced his daughter—a man he'd done business with, no less. A man who'd then had the audacity to show his face again at Wingate. Before tonight, she would've considered the head of the manor too proper and aloof for such a violent act. She remembered him presiding at the dinner table in his custom-made London suit, dancing with his wife in the Wingate ballroom. Now the idea of Winslow stabbing Henry seemed more conceivable.

In the bathroom closet, she found a bottle of rubbing alcohol and soaked a cotton ball with it. As she dabbed at the long scratch on her neck, she recalled his threat: "You can be removed." She thought back to the night she'd strolled with him on the estate's grassy promenade when he'd offered $1,000 recompense for her colleague's murder. *Even if he didn't do the deed himself, he could have hired someone to kill Henry.* And yet she'd read that brutal acts of a hands-on nature were usually the work of people who had a strong, emotional connection to their victims. Professional assassins preferred less intimate methods, such as shooting or poison.

Then she considered Mrs. Winslow. The woman's controlled, haughty manner barely concealed her fiery temper. Might Catherine Winslow have stabbed Henry in a fit of rage? Lizzie couldn't rule out the possibility. She recalled Joey's suggestion that Catherine had the most to lose if Henry stayed alive. Then her thoughts shifted back to the count. Did he know about Flo's relationship with Henry and consider him a rival? Maybe the three of them had conspired to kill Henry—and now they meant to eliminate her too.

She frowned at the dark-haired woman staring back at her from the bathroom mirror and said aloud, "What a balled-up mess you've gotten yourself into, Lizzie Crane."

# Chapter Twenty-Five

*"If you want to know what God thinks of money, just look at the people he gave it to."*

— Dorothy Parker, The Natural History of the Rich

The next morning Lizzie wrapped a scarf around her neck to hide the rose's scratch—she wasn't ready to face questions from Sidney just yet. Then she hurried downstairs to join her colleague for breakfast, eager to reveal what she'd learned from Florence Winslow's maid. Upon entering the morning room, she quickly spotted him seated at a corner table that afforded an unobstructed view of the Wingate gardens. Under his blazer, he wore an argyle sweater vest and cream-colored flannel trousers. She found his "sporting look" amusing, considering that Sidney had probably never in his life lifted a tennis racquet or baseball bat.

Turning her gaze to the rose garden below, she saw not only Florence Winslow—whom she'd come to expect, doing her morning ritual check of the blossoms—but also Catherine. Arm-in-arm, the two women strolled along the pathways between the scores of rose bushes, stopping occasionally to sniff the flowers, as if they were calling on old friends.

Lizzie touched the scarf at her throat and mentally cast out yesterday's demons. Although it took all the energy she could muster, she gathered her actress's skills about her. The dizziness caused by the count's assault had subsided, and after a good night's sleep her head ached only a little. She

166

felt almost like her old self again. *Count Ivanovich can't get rid of me that easily—and neither can Zachary Winslow.* As she seated herself across from Sidney, a serving girl appeared at their table with a carafe of coffee and filled their cups. She gazed out the open window and took several slow, deep breaths, then smiled broadly at Sidney as if she were posing for a camera.

"You seem to be in better spirits this morning, Bearcat. Has Prince Charming shown up during the night and offered you his kingdom?"

"Don't I wish. However, I do have some interesting information that may lead us to Henry's murderer."

"Oh?" he said, lighting his cigarette. "Spill."

Lizzie sipped her coffee, then leaned across the table and said in a low voice, "Last night, as I climbed the servants' stairs to my bedroom, I encountered Flo Winslow's personal maid. When I questioned her, she admitted that Flo was in a family way when her parents sent her away. Our man Henry, I take it, was the babe's father."

Sidney puffed on his cigarette in its silver holder, exhaling perfectly formed smoke rings toward the ceiling. "Well, well. The plot thickens."

"I'm certain someone in the Winslow household is our villain in this tangled web, not some rum-running competitor from Gloucester. What do you think?"

The serving girl returned and set a plate of blueberry waffles in front of Lizzie.

"Did I order this?" she asked.

"I ordered for you," he answered. "Bon appetite."

Lizzie poured thick maple syrup on the waffles and took a bite. The tart berries perfectly complemented the sweet syrup.

"Just because Henry knocked up the girl doesn't mean her family took revenge and murdered him," Sidney said.

"True, but think of the embarrassment to the Winslows. That's why her parents sent Flo to stay with her aunt in South Carolina, and why she didn't have a proper coming out. Henry compromised Flo's reputation and her market value, so to speak. He ruined her chance of marrying into one of the really good families."

She paused briefly to eat a few bites of waffle, then continued, "Not only that, her affair with Henry threatened to expose the connection between the Winslows and the booze-trafficking Ives family. What if Henry revealed the relationship between him and Flo? What if she broke her engagement to the count and eloped with Henry when he showed up again here at Wingate? Can you imagine the scandal? Daddy Winslow couldn't risk that."

Sidney stubbed out his cigarette and cut into his waffles. "So, you're fingering Zachary Winslow for the job?"

"He seems the most likely suspect, but I've also got Mrs. Winslow in my sights. And that brute Count Ivanovich, of course." She tapped her head with her fingertips to remind Sid that the Russian had tried to do her in, though for reasons other than Flo's romance with Henry.

"What about Peter Winslow?" Sidney asked.

"Hmm. I hadn't considered him as a suspect. What makes you think he might be to blame?"

"Henry was his friend, right? But our boy betrayed his friend, and in the process, he damaged Florence's reputation. Can you see Peter as an outraged and protective brother avenging his younger sister's honor? Don't let your attraction to young Mr. Winslow put blinkers on you, Bearcat."

Although she couldn't imagine—couldn't *bear* to imagine—Peter Winslow as a murderer, she veiled her thoughts. "I suppose we can't rule out anyone, can we?"

Sidney finished his waffles, then switched the conversation to a professional note. "Shall we cool things down a bit tonight? Lowering the temperature could be a nice balance to last night's heat, and a pleasant finale to the week's events."

"Sounds good to me," she said, glad to turn her attention from murder to music. "What do you think about playing Frank Trumbauer's 'I Never Miss Sunshine' and maybe Ferde Grofé's 'Mississippi Suite'?" Holding her cup with both hands Lizzie sipped her coffee, letting the caffeine do its job, and gazed out at the rose garden. "Jeepers, can you believe we've only been here nine days? It seems like forever."

"If Sergeant Mulvaney has his way, we may be here for a whole lot longer."

"I can think of worse fates."

"Oh, and by the way, Mrs. Winslow wants to have a cake-cutting for the bride and groom after we finish our performance tonight."

Lizzie raised her eyebrows. "Really? I thought couples only did that at their wedding receptions."

"Flo's wedding isn't until January.  One year from the betrothal," he explained. "Considering weather conditions at that time of the year, many of the Winslows' guests won't be able to attend."

Remembering the California and Texas license plates Lizzie had seen on their automobiles, she said, "Then tonight will be a nice fanfare."

"Yes, I think so too," Sid agreed.

"We're set, then, on the evening's tone—cool, smooth, and sensuous? No show-stopping numbers, nothing dramatic…"

"Except that Mrs. Winslow has arranged for a fireworks display over the bay at the end. Thankfully, we're not responsible for the pyrotechnics." He held up his hands and wiggled his fingers. "A piano player needs to safeguard his digits."

Lizzie pushed the last bite of blueberry waffle around on her plate, sailing it like a barge through a river of gooey syrup. "Whatever will we do here, once we've finished tonight's performance? Joey wasn't here when Henry died, so the cops will let him go back to normal life."

"If a musician's life can be considered normal," Sidney said. "I wouldn't be surprised if the Winslows wanted us to continue playing 'background music' during their evening meals. We may have to keep singing for our supper for as long as we're quartered here."

"Maybe they'll invite the neighboring gentry over for a spot of entertainment, while they have us in captivity and on the cheap," she suggested.

"You might even get to hobnob with your famous 'relatives' the Cranes," he teased.

"We're totally at the mercy of the Winslows."

"And Sergeant Mulvaney."

Lizzie finished her coffee and signaled the serving girl to bring more. "Maybe you'll have time to work on your opera."

"And maybe you'll have time to win over Peter Winslow. 'It's an ill wind that blows nobody any good' as the saying goes."

\* \* \*

Only minutes after returning from the breakfast room to her bedchamber, Lizzie heard a knock on the door. She opened it and saw Florence Winslow's personal maid Marie standing there. The girl dropped her eyes as she slipped Lizzie a calling card on which the name Miss Anne Cabot Lawrence had been engraved in a lavish script. Lizzie turned it over and read an address in Newburyport, Massachusetts that someone had written on the back in a pretty hand.

"Who is this lady?" Lizzie asked the maid.

"Miss Winslow's lifelong friend. She requests the pleasure of your visit this afternoon for tea."

"Where is Newburyport? How can I find this Miss Lawrence?"

"Will you be driving an automobile, ma'am?"

"Yes," Lizzie answered, realizing she'd have to come up with a plausible reason for borrowing Sidney's Buick for the afternoon.

"As you pass the gatehouse at the bottom of the hill, turn right and follow the motor-road northeast. You needn't make any other turns at all—you'll run right into High Street. It's only about twelve miles."

"Do you have any idea why Miss Lawrence wishes to see me?"

The girl shook her head vigorously, and Lizzie half-expected her braids to come undone. "Oh, no, ma'am. All she told me was to give this card to you."

Lizzie asked the girl to wait a moment while she fetched a coin from her purse. Pressing it into the maid's hand, she said, "Thank you, Marie. You've been a great help."

\* \* \*

At midday, Lizzie found Sidney on the back terrace, lingering over a smoke while surveying the goings-on among the Winslows' guests. She forced herself to approach him slowly, calmly, as if she were just out for a morning stroll, so as not to rouse his suspicions.

"Oh, hello there," she said. "My, you seem deep in thought. A penny?"

He smiled and replied, "Hello yourself." Then he turned his attention back to the players on the bocce court, who looked to be enjoying a dandy time despite their utter lack of skill at the game.

"What are your plans for the rest of the day? Working on your opera?"

"Haven't decided yet. Truth be told, I'm feeling unnerved by the fact that tonight's our last performance and we haven't a clue what our future holds from here on."

"Maybe we can just relax and enjoy a vacation by the sea. Considering we've had such a trying time thus far, I'd say we deserve it. I expect New York can manage without us for a bit."

Sidney puffed on his cigarette. "You know I need to stay busy. It's not just the dough…I need a purpose. Without a goal, I go to pieces. Once all the guests are gone and we're stuck here alone with the Winslows…"

"Peter Winslow thinks we might receive more engagements as a result of our performance here this week. I'm no psychic, but I dare say he's right. We've made a darb impression. Maybe one of the neighbors will hire us—we've got everything we need right here to keep playing the circuit for months. Perhaps we should pursue that route. Strike while the iron's hot and all that."

"You may be right," he said.

"Why don't you contact the man at the Oceanview that Joey suggested? I'd dearly love to perform there." She studied his slumping shoulders, the way his thumbs tapped on the arm of his Adirondack chair. "Isn't that why we came here? Why we embarked on this path? You've got to admit, we've done a swell job—in spite of Henry's death."

"You're right," he said again.

Confused by his uncharacteristic low spirits, Lizzie asked, "What's eating you, Sid? They can't sequester us here at Wingate for the rest of our lives. First of all, we'll probably get time off for mostly good behavior," she teased. "Second, there are worse fates than hanging out here for the rest of the summer. Naturally, I'll miss Broadway and Tin Pan Alley and the rest of it. But the food's darb and the surroundings are spectacular."

He flicked an ash over the railing into a flowerbed. "I just want to get away from here as soon as possible. Henry's murder, the cops, Mrs. Winslow, and her entire 'above-it-all' lot—I can't wait to put the whole sordid business behind me."

Lizzie laid a hand on his shoulder. *If only I could solve this crime and set us all free.* "Poor dear Sid. I should've realized how ghastly it's been for you. I didn't know Henry the way you did—I didn't know him at all, really. You lost a friend and colleague, yet you still hung in there and handled this event with aplomb—all the week's entertainments, the police investigation, the Winslows, everything. And you never let on that you were hurting." She kissed him on the cheek. "You're a class act, Sidney, the best. I'm lucky to have you for a friend."

He squeezed her hand. "Thanks, Bearcat."

"Um, Sid, I'm a bit reluctant to ask you this, but could I borrow the breezer for a while this afternoon?" She cast her smoky eyes downward, feigning modesty. "Now that it looks like we're going to be detained here for an indefinite amount of time, Melody and I, well, we hadn't counted on this and we need to buy, uh, sanitary products."

Considering how many women were housed under Wingate's roof, surely the staff was well prepared for such occasions and had plenty of feminine items stashed away. All Lizzie would have to do was ask a housemaid for whatever she needed. But men, she knew, were not only ignorant of such matters, they recoiled in embarrassment when confronted with them. The ploy provided a perfect excuse to drive the Buick to nearby Newburyport to meet Anne Cabot Lawrence. If Sergeant Mulvaney chastised her for leaving the property, she'd give him the same story, though he might not buy it as quickly as Sid.

"Sure, sure," he replied absently. "Doesn't look like I'm going anyplace soon." He fished into his pocket for the car's keys and handed them to her.

"Thanks, Sid. While I'm out, is there anything you want me to pick up for you?"

"Yeah, a kind, handsome gentleman who will love me forever."

She tapped her temple in a playful salute. "Aye aye, sir. I'll try to snag one for you and one for me too."

# Chapter Twenty-Six

*"A problem is a chance for you to do your best."*

— *Duke Ellington, Music Is My Mistress*

Lizzie located Sid's dark green convertible among the guests' beautiful motorcars and slid in behind the wooden steering wheel. She started the powerful six-cylinder engine, which Buick had introduced just this year, and smiled as the auto purred to life. After navigating her way through the crowded parking area, she began rolling down the long, steep driveway that wound past a kidney-shaped pond with an arched Japanese bridge, a white-columned building with a domed roof that resembled an ancient Greek temple, and several other whimseys on the way to the main road.

As the car picked up speed, she braked to take a curve. The pedal sunk to the floor. The Buick kept going. Surprised, she pumped the brakes several times. No response. She jerked the steering wheel hard, trying to negotiate the curve, but the car skidded off the pavement and plunged downhill into the woods. The front bumper clipped a tree, showering her with leaves and bark. A low-hanging branch smashed the left headlight. After bouncing off several granite outcroppings, the breezer finally slammed into a huge oak and stopped.

Shaken up and confused, Lizzie eased herself out of the car. Pain bit into her right knee as she picked her way around the car, surveying the damage.

*Jeepers creepers! Sid's going to have my head on a platter.* He treated the Buick like a beloved child. She cringed imagining how he'd react when he saw it with all these dings and scrapes. As she reached to touch a crumpled fender, she noticed blood on her arm. Trying not to let it drip on her frock, she examined the cut and decided it wasn't serious, though it would probably leave a scar. *Damn it all!*

She collected her purse from the car and withdrew a handkerchief. Holding the cloth against her injured arm, she struggled up the hill to the driveway and started walking back toward the Winslows' mansion. *How could this happen?* she asked herself as she limped along the winding road. *Sidney takes meticulous care of his automobile. He wouldn't let the brakes deteriorate.*

A silver Bentley rolled to a stop beside Lizzie. A tall, copper-haired man wearing plus-fours and a tweed jacket got out. Instantly, she recognized his handsome, chiseled features and soulful, dark eyes.

"Good heavens," he said. "Are you all right?"

"Not exactly. I wrecked my auto down the hill a ways."

His expression said he recognized her too. He took her good arm gently and guided her toward the Bentley. "You need a doctor."

"Maybe, but I'd be grateful for a lift back to the house."

He helped her into the car, then hurried around and swung himself up into the driver's seat. "What happened?"

"My brakes gave out on a curve and I ended up skiing down an incline into the woods."

"Are you sure you wouldn't rather I took you to a doctor or hospital?"

Lizzie removed the bloody handkerchief and studied her wound. "I'll be all right. Thank you for stopping and giving me a ride. I admit, I was feeling a bit disconcerted."

The man cleared his throat. "This may not be the proper time to speak of this," he began, rather nervously it seemed to Lizzie. "I'm sorry we've met under such unfortunate circumstances, but I want you to know how very much I've enjoyed your performances this week, Miss Crane. It's been a genuine pleasure to watch your acting, dancing, singing ... well, everything."

"Why, thank you, Mr..."

"Alan Peabody."

"Are you by chance related to the esteemed philanthropist George Peabody?"

"Yes, but let's not discuss that now. The important thing is taking care of your injuries."

"Thank you again, Mr. Peabody. I am indebted to you for your most fortuitous arrival in my time of need."

They pulled into the parking area. Alan Peabody helped Lizzie out of the Bentley, supporting her on his arm and into the mansion.

"Hello, Charles! Mrs. Greely?" he called out with authority. His voice echoed through the entry hall. He shepherded her deeper into the mansion and shouted again.

Lizzie got the impression that he was familiar with Wingate and its operation. But of course, he must be a family friend if Catherine Winslow had invited him to attend this weeklong celebration. She could barely believe she'd been rescued by a relative of the internationally renowned financier for whom the nearby town of Peabody, Massachusetts was named. *What a stroke of luck.*

Charles, the stiff, balding butler, shuffled down the long gallery toward them. He reminded Lizzie of a penguin as his plump, tuxedoed form approached them with a rocking, side-to-side motion.

"Yes, Mr. Peabody? How may I be of service, sir?"

"Miss Crane has had an automobile accident. She's in need of medical attention. Telephone for a doctor."

Lizzie interrupted, "Really, I'm all right—"

"Her motorcar is off in the woods, about a quarter-mile down the road. Have it towed back here and ask Ruben to examine it."

The butler nodded. "Certainly, Mr. Peabody. Right away, sir."

Only moments after Charles disappeared to attend to Alan Peabody's demands, the stork-like housekeeper, Mrs. Greely, appeared. She nodded deferentially to him, but narrowed her eyes at Lizzie. "Mr. Peabody, Miss Crane, may I be of assistance?"

"Charles is tending to Miss Crane's immediate needs, but we would be grateful for a spot of tea and perhaps something to eat on the back terrace."

"Of course, sir." The tall, sharp-boned woman shot a questioning glance at Lizzie, then quickly turned away. "I'll have tea sent to you momentarily."

After Mrs. Greely had departed, he guided Lizzie out onto the back terrace. Although she felt recovered from the emotional upset of the accident, she allowed that she might still be a bit agitated and leaned against him for the pleasure of his closeness, if not necessarily for support. He settled her into an Adirondack chair and took a seat beside her, overlooking the grassy promenade and the sea at its end.

"Thank you again, Mr. Peabody," she said. "I don't know what I would've done without your help."

"I'm sure you would've managed, Miss Crane. You don't impress me as a helpless, shrinking violet. However, I thank Fate for letting me play the knight in shining armor to your damsel in distress. You see, I've wanted to make your acquaintance ever since I first saw you, but didn't know how to go about it."

She laughed at his unabashed admission. The idea that a man of his station might be shy about approaching a showgirl surprised her. "You could've just introduced yourself and said, 'Hello there, Lizzie Crane, I think you're the bees' knees.' "

A serving girl approached them with a tea tray. Lizzie spotted a plate of marinated herring, a wedge of Brie, crackers, and a bunch of purple grapes. Another plate held fresh-baked scones speckled with raspberries. The girl poured steaming tea into two porcelain cups, then stepped back and asked in a thick Irish accent, "Is there anything more you'll be wanting, sir?"

Suddenly, Lizzie remembered her meeting with Anne Cabot Lawrence. The woman would be expecting Lizzie to arrive soon. In her confusion, she had forgotten all about her appointment with Flo's childhood friend. She pulled a calling card from her purse, jotted a brief note on the back of it, and handed it to the girl.

"Would you please give this to Marie O'Hare? She'll know how to get word to Miss Anne Lawrence."

"Yes, ma'am."

As the serving girl retreated, Alan Peabody stirred sugar into his tea. "You know Anne Lawrence?"

"Not yet, alas. We'd planned to have tea this afternoon, but that dastardly accident interfered. I feel dreadful about missing the opportunity. I should have liked to meet her."

"An avid sporting woman, Anne. Excels at tennis, golf, and horseback riding. She even sails her own craft, single-handed no less, down to Newport frequently. Her brother and I were at Harvard together."

Lizzie leaned back in her chair and sipped her tea. Alan sliced a scone in half, then slathered both halves with butter and jam. He placed one half on a china plate and handed it to Lizzie. The gesture struck her as intimate and familiar, as if he'd broken bread with her countless times before.

"Will you be well enough to perform tonight?" he asked, running a fingertip along her injured arm with exquisite delicacy.

She noticed a sprinkling of freckles dotting his wrist, as if someone had peppered him with cayenne. He hadn't any on his face, though, and she caught herself wondering where else they might show up on his body.

"Oh, ab-so-lute-ly. Thanks to you, I'm feeling ever so much better already." She flashed him a seductive smile. "Will you be returning to your home after tonight's performance, Mr. Peabody? Where is 'home' anyway?"

"Boston," he answered.

"Of course, I should have known. Your accent…"

"You mean 'pawk the caw' and all that." But the levity disappeared suddenly and his expression grew serious. "Miss Crane, I apologize for not extending my condolences earlier on account of your friend's death. I must appear quite insensitive."

"Certainly not. The whole situation has been so strange. Sometimes I can't believe it actually happened, that perhaps it was only a bad dream. I haven't had time to come to grips with it yet, what with the demands of this week's performances. And, of course, we've tried not to let the awful affair dampen Miss Winslow's celebration."

"It must have been a strain for you."

"Indeed. But it's also been very rewarding to have the opportunity to entertain so many delightful people."

He raised an eyebrow. "Surely you can't be referring to Ma and Pa Winslow or that gloomy Russian aristocrat they fetched up from the Dark Ages for their daughter."

Despite herself, Lizzie couldn't help laughing. By the time a bespectacled doctor showed up half an hour later, Lizzie had almost forgotten about her injuries. Not wanting to diminish Alan Peabody's concern for her—or to pass up the attention he lavished on her—she allowed the doctor to bandage the cut on her arm and examine her bruised knee. The latter gave her a chance to expose more leg than would have been proper under ordinary circumstances. She slid her skirt to mid-thigh, just above her garter, revealing a sliver of bare skin. When she snuck a peek at her red-haired companion, she noticed he was intently observing the doctor's ministrations—or at least the leg being administered to.

When the doctor had completed his task, he pulled a glass vial from his black leather satchel and handed it to Lizzie. She glanced at the label: "Lydia E. Pinkham's Vegetable Compound." The popular remedy for female complaints had been concocted in the nearby town of Lynn for fifty years. Apparently, the good physician considered her an emotional woman overreacting to a few minor bumps. Knowing that the medicine's success was largely due to its high alcohol content, Lizzie gladly accepted the bottle and tucked it in her purse.

A clanking noise interrupted her contented mood. A truck outfitted with a winch towed Sidney's automobile up the hill to the parking area.

"Oh dear," she cried.

Alan Peabody laid his hand over hers. "What is it?"

"The motorcar. Sid's going to have kittens when he sees it."

"Sid?"

"My business partner, the piano player in our group. That automobile is his pride and joy. I borrowed it to drive to Newburyport to visit Miss Lawrence this afternoon, and now it's ruined."

"It wasn't your fault."

"No, but the result is the same regardless."

"Ruben takes care of the Winslows' vehicles and farm machinery. He's a good mechanic. He'll set your Sid's auto to right."

As if summoned by the noise, Sidney rushed onto the terrace, flapping his arms like a frenetic scarecrow. "Blast it, Lizzie. What have you done to my breezer?"

"I didn't do anything to it. The brakes simply stopped working."

"You could've picked a better time for an accident. We have a show to do in a few hours."

"*Me?* Your silly motorcar could've picked a better time to give out on me." Lizzie held up her injured arm. "I could've been killed."

Sidney waved off her remark. "Stop being so melodramatic."

"Well stop blaming me. Do you think I *liked* crashing through the woods and getting all banged up?"

"Excuse me." Alan stood and introduced himself. "Shouldn't your concern be for Miss Crane's well-being?"

Sidney shook hands with the ginger-haired man. "Of course. My apologies for the interruption, Mr. Peabody. Sorry, Bearcat. Are you badly hurt?"

"Not too. Mr. Peabody has been most kind."

"I'm certain your automobile will be repaired satisfactorily," Alan told him. "I've already sent for a mechanic. If you go out to the parking area, I suspect you'll find him there at this very moment."

Sidney thanked him and hurried off to check on the status of his beloved Buick. Lizzie couldn't help laughing at her friend's overreaction, now that Alan Peabody had handled the problem.

She admired the man's ability to take charge so naturally. Like a wizard waving his magic wand, he commanded and his wish came true. *What might it be like to wield such power?* she wondered. Zachary and Peter Winslow exhibited that self-confidence too. These privileged men were accustomed to giving orders and having people obey them. They didn't question their right to speak their minds or to make decisions that would affect other people—they were born to rule. For a poor girl from the Bronx, the idea seemed incomprehensible. The only power she'd ever known was of a sexual nature, one she'd relied on again and again, but she knew it wouldn't last for long and she could hear the clock ticking.

"I'm afraid I've interrupted your afternoon," she said.

"Not at all, Miss Crane. I consider myself fortunate to have been in the right place at the right time. I've enjoyed our tea, but now I suspect you'd like to rest up before tonight's performance."

Reluctant to take her leave of this man who'd intrigued her from the beginning of her stay at Wingate, Lizzie said, "You're right, of course. I need to gather my strength for this last evening of festivities. Will you be in the audience tonight?"

"Wouldn't miss it."

"May I sing a song for you?" She lowered her chin and gazed up at him through thick, dark lashes.

"I'd like that. How about 'Oh, Lady Be Good'?"

"It will be my pleasure, Mr. Peabody."

He stood, took Lizzie's hand, and kissed it. "Until this evening."

* * *

Sidney found Lizzie still resting on the back terrace. He dropped into the chair vacated by Alan Peabody and filled her in on the Buick's status. "The auto mechanic says the line for the brake fluid was cut."

"What does that mean?"

"Without fluid, the brakes won't function."

"Are you saying someone intentionally damaged the brakes?" Lizzie asked. "Why?"

"Apparently someone has it in for us."

Her mind flashed back to Count Ivanovich's attack on her in the church-yard. Could he have disabled Sidney's car, hoping to intimidate The Troubadours, or worse? He'd said he didn't drive in America—but even if he didn't understand automobile mechanics himself, he could have paid someone to do the job. Or perhaps Zachary Winslow arranged the "accident."

"That's what happens when you stick your nose into places where you shouldn't. Why can't you stop meddling and just let the cops do their job? You're putting yourself and the rest of us in danger with all this sleuthing business." He took her hands in his. "Bearcat, I'm worried about you."

As she considered what he'd said, fear rose in her chest. *I should have taken the count's attack and Zachary Winslow's threat more seriously, instead of thinking they just wanted to scare me.* She hadn't told Sidney about either incident yet, and decided not to bring them up now—that would only upset him further. It seemed that someone really was trying to kill her and she didn't even know who.

"Is everything copacetic for tonight's performance?" she asked, changing the subject as she tried to gain control of her nerves. She didn't want Sidney to feel her hands trembling.

"Unless you throw another monkey wrench into the mix," he groused.

She realized that the shock of the accident had jumbled her thinking. The whole business seemed so surreal. "Can we run through it once again, please?"

"We'll play until eleven, then the kitchen staff will wheel in the pre-wedding cake, so the happy couple can cut it and serve it to their guests. After which someone will invoke the fire god and set off a barrage of fireworks."

"Sounds like fun."

"Hmph. I just want to finish this job and go home. Who knows how long we'll be stuck here waiting for my car to be repaired?"

Lizzie sighed loudly. She chose not to remind him that Sergeant Mulvaney had already told them they couldn't leave anyway, not until he'd nabbed Henry's killer or exonerated The Troubadours.

"Sid, I'm sorry about the breezer. Really and truly sorry, but I can't change that now, so please stop being a pill."

He hmphed again, and Lizzie stood up. A stabbing pain in her knee almost made her cry out, but she didn't want him to chastise her once more for being melodramatic. *Looks like I won't be doing any dancing tonight.* Suddenly, she felt vulnerable and scared and about to break down.

"I'm going up to my room to take a nap before dinner. I'll meet you in the ballroom at 7:30 to go over last-minute details."

# Chapter Twenty-Seven

*"The exhilarating ripple of her voice was a wild tonic in the rain."*

— *F. Scott Fitzgerald, The Great Gatsby*

A lan Peabody was among the first of the Winslows' guests to amble into the ballroom after supper. To Lizzie's disappointment, he escorted a dazzlingly beautiful woman who seemed to be made of pure gold: golden hair, a gold-sequined gown, and an abundance of gold jewelry including an elaborate gold-and-diamond tiara. Even her flawless skin radiated a tawny glow. *Well, at least he shows up with a different lady every evening,* Lizzie consoled herself. *Apparently, he's not serious about any of them.*

Sidney played a medley of tunes as people strolled in and sat down. She studied their exquisite clothing and easy grace, memorizing the details of style, mannerism, and attitude that distinguished them from the *hoi polloi.* For the thousandth time, she tried to imagine what it might be like to enjoy this elevated lifestyle as one's birthright. But even the sparkle of Wingate, she realized, could be dimmed by sadness, fear, and desperation. What good had money and status done Florence Winslow, when the love of her life had been slain and her future consigned to a man she loathed?

As Alan Peabody and his companion took seats at a table near the stage, Lizzie thought she saw him wink and she flashed him her best smile. Before long, Peter Winslow and his debutant entered; they sat with Alan and the golden girl. The two couples chatted for a while, until the rest of the guests had settled themselves and turned their attention to the stage.

When everyone was in place, Mrs. Winslow glided into the ballroom on the arm of her handsome, silver-haired husband. Lizzie couldn't help admiring their elegance—Catherine in a shimmering green gown that conjured up memories of ancient sea goddesses, and Zachary decked out in London's latest and most meticulously tailored tuxedo from Savile Row. As the couple positioned themselves in front of the stage a hush fell over the crowd.

Florence Winslow and Count Ivanovich entered and slowly made their way across the room toward the waiting guests. Flo wore a fluffy white, floor-length gown decorated with tiny embroidered roses. Despite its obvious quality, it accentuated her plumpness. Instead of giving the impression that the bride-to-be was floating in on a gossamer cloud, the dress made her look like a blancmange. *How many people in this room realize the irony of that virginal white dress?* Lizzie wondered. For the occasion, the count had donned a military uniform with an array of medals pinned to his olive-drab jacket. His trousers were tucked into gleaming, knee-high boots and a brimmed hat with a pancake-flat top perched on his head. *I didn't know he'd fought in the war,* Lizzie thought. *Perhaps that helps to explain his aggressive behavior.*

Peter Winslow stood and began clapping. The rest of the audience took his cue and did the same. In response to the attention, the count straightened his shoulders and held his head higher. Flo, however, seemed to recoil, casting her eyes down at the parquet floor as if searching for a trap door through which she could disappear. The pair joined Flo's parents, who stood at the foot of the stage smiling at the applauding gentry.

Zachary Winslow cleared his throat loudly and motioned for everyone to sit down. "My wife and I wish to thank all of you for being with us this week to celebrate the engagement of our daughter Florence to Count Nikolai Ivanovich. We hope you've enjoyed your visit as much as we've enjoyed having you as our guests here at Wingate." He turned to the stage. "We'd also like to thank The Troubadours from New York City for providing such splendid entertainment."

The four performers bowed to the audience and received an enthusiastic round of applause. Sidney stepped forward. "Thank you, Mr. and Mrs.

Winslow. And thank you, ladies and gentlemen. It's been our great pleasure to perform for you this week. My colleagues and I are deeply grateful to the Winslow family for allowing us to share in this joyous occasion. Our very best wishes to Miss Winslow and Count Ivanovich." He bowed to the couple. "And now, we hope you good people will enjoy this last evening of festivities."

For the next hour, The Troubadours played a collection of show tunes, popular hits, and old favorites. Many of the younger couples danced, while the older ones remained in their seats, sometimes tapping their feet and nodding their heads. At one point the count asked the performers to play a Russian folk song, although none of them knew any. Lizzie feared he might come on stage and attempt one himself, but to her relief, he simply shrugged and walked away.

Just before the group took their first break, Lizzie announced, "I'd like to dedicate this next song to Mr. Alan Peabody. This afternoon, Mr. Peabody rescued me after I had an automobile accident, and I am deeply indebted to him for his kindness."

The red-haired man grinned up at her, as all eyes turned toward him. She waved her bandaged arm at him, while searching the faces in the crowd to see if anybody reacted to her statement. If the guilty individual sat among them, however, he or she didn't reveal a thing.

After finishing "Oh, Lady Be Good," Lizzie descended from the stage and slipped through the throng of guests out to the back terrace for some fresh air. She didn't try to talk to Alan Peabody; she didn't want to meet up with his glamorous ladyfriend. She could only attempt to seduce him from the stage. If he wanted to pursue her further after her stint with the Winslows ended, he could find her easily enough.

As she leaned her elbows on the balustrade and gazed out into the gathering dark, Lizzie heard a female voice call her name. She spun around to see a young woman as tall as she, wearing a sleeveless evening dress that exposed broad shoulders and muscular arms. The woman's skin was unfashionably tan and her bobbed hair seemed to have been cut short for convenience rather than style. Yet her large green eyes and Cupid's bow lips lent a feminine note to an otherwise mannish appearance. Lizzie remembered having seen her a few times here at Wingate during the past week.

"I hope I'm not disturbing you," the young lady said. "I'm Anne Lawrence."

"Oh, good heavens, Miss Lawrence. I'm so sorry I couldn't come for tea this afternoon. I hope Marie got word to you about my motorcar accident."

"She did, and I'm glad to see that you aren't injured more seriously."

"I wish I could say the same for the car."

Miss Lawrence forced a smile and asked, "I wonder if you and I might speak frankly?"

"Of course. I understand you and Miss Florence Winslow have been friends for a long time."

"Since we were in diapers. Our parents and grandparents knew one another as well. We're even related through cousins and by marriage and such. That's why you and I have to talk. I was sorry to hear about the death of your friend, Henry Ives."

"Thank you. We're all still shocked and confused. One never expects or quite adjusts to such things."

Anne Lawrence glanced about, watching everybody who came and went on the terrace. When no one was in earshot, she lowered her voice and leaned closer to Lizzie. "About your colleague. I assume you know of Flo's friendship with him?"

Cautiously, Lizzie answered, "I believe she and her brother Peter met Henry through their mutual interest in sailing."

Anne snorted loudly, reminding Lizzie of a horse. "Sailing, my ass. Flo was smitten with Henry and Peter bought hooch from him.

"Peter told me that his father was one of Henry's clients."

"I'm surprised Peter admitted it, but yes, it's true."

Anne paused briefly, drumming her fingers on the balustrade. Lizzie thought this energetic young woman seemed like someone who needed a cigarette to occupy her busy hands, but of course, being an athlete, she probably didn't smoke. Instead of responding, Lizzie remained silent. Waiting, she'd discovered, often led people to speak up and reveal things, simply because they grew uncomfortable with silence.

# CHAPTER TWENTY-SEVEN

After a bit, Anne ventured, "Do you know about the baby?"

Lizzie nodded.

"Flo never told Henry."

"So I gathered. At least, he never let on to us that he knew, but I got the impression he still carried a torch for her. I guessed that Flo had rejected him and he desperately hoped to regain her favor until I found out…"

"Her parents sent her away to have the baby, then quickly engaged her to Count Ivanovich. Flo was devastated," Anne said. "Understandably, they wanted to find a respectable match for her, someone who might take her away from here, so she could put her past behind her. But Flo kept holding on to the possibility of a reunion with Henry. When she learned about his alliance with your troupe, she began searching for possibilities."

An attractive couple passed nearby and Anne stopped speaking. She turned her gaze to the grassy promenade, where people strolled in the moonlight. Lizzie did the same. When the couple had moved farther down the terrace, Anne continued. While she spoke, she ran her hand along the railing as if stroking a pet.

"Flo didn't have a formal coming out, due to her circumstances, so to compensate, mother and daughter arranged this week of entertainment. That way they could formally introduce the betrothed couple into society and ease the awkwardness around Flo's, shall we say, break with tradition."

"And Flo suggested hiring The Troubadours to perform."

"Yes," Anne said. "She wanted to meet with Henry again and see if a spark still burned between them. To see if she had another chance with him before she entered into an unwanted marriage."

*Poor desperate Flo. Poor forlorn Henry,* Lizzie thought. *If only the deck hadn't been stacked against them.* She recalled Flo's reaction while watching The Troubadours practice the crypt scene from *Romeo and Juliet.* The young woman must have made a connection between Shakespeare's star-crossed lovers and her own plight.

"What did Flo hope to accomplish?" Lizzie asked.

"She wanted Henry to run away with her, someplace where her family wouldn't intervene. Canada, maybe, or Europe. She meant to tell Henry everything when she saw him again, but she hasn't confided in me since he died so I don't know if she got the chance. And now she's mixed up in all this mess..."

Sensing Anne's concern for her childhood friend, Lizzie asked, "How can I help?"

"That's just it. I don't know how anyone can help her. I get the feeling she's even trying to distance herself from me because I know the truth." Anne laid a calloused hand on the singer's arm and whispered, "I'm afraid for Flo."

"In what way?"

"I fear she might...hurt herself."

"You mean suicide?"

Anne nodded.

"Shouldn't we discuss this with someone in authority? Someone who's capable of protecting and helping Flo?"

"No! I can't betray her confidence."

"But what if she *does* hurt herself? You'd never forgive yourself."

"I know," Anne sighed. "But who can I trust? Certainly not her parents or the police."

The word "psychiatrist" popped into Lizzie's mind, but all she knew of such things was what she'd read about that sex-obsessed Austrian doctor Sigmund Freud. "Is she religious? A minister maybe?"

"Goodness, no."

Lizzie thought again about Count Ivanovich's piousness and his assault on her in the church cemetery. How might he behave toward Flo if he knew about her past?

"What do you think of Flo's marriage to the count?"

Anne snorted again. "I think it's a travesty. I can't believe she agreed to it. I know her parents can be very persuasive and Flo's never been the independent type. She caved in because she felt guilty and helpless. Still, I wish she'd run off to Canada with Henry, regardless of what the Winslows or anyone else thought about it. Now he's dead and so are her hopes."

Lizzie knew she should be making her way back to the stage, and that Sid would be wondering what had happened to her. However, she had no intention of cutting short the conversation with Anne Lawrence. "I'm sure you've wondered who might have killed Henry," she urged. "Do you think the count could have done it in a misguided attempt to protect or avenge Flo?"

Anne chewed a fingernail. "When you put it that way, yes, I think it's possible. Or perhaps Flo's father was behind it. He was so angry when he learned about her condition. She'd disgraced him and the family—Zachary Winslow's reputation is more important to him than anything. I think he meant to punish Flo by marrying her off to the count."

"If he knew that Flo planned to run away with Henry, do you think—?"

"He'd have gone so far as to have Henry killed? Yes, I do. That's a terrible thing to say, but I've known Zachary Winslow all my life, and I know he always gets his way, no matter what. I can't see him doing the deed himself, but he could've hired someone to take your friend out of the picture."

Anne's answer echoed Lizzie's earlier suspicions. Her meeting with him in the rose garden yesterday afternoon had left her with the same impression: He did what he wanted and no one had better dare to cross him.

"I've thought the same thing. So what do we do now?" Lizzie asked.

"Keep Flo from marrying the count."

# Chapter Twenty-Eight

*"Don't you dare marry him! I won't let you marry him! Do you hear?"*

— *Alice Gerstenberg, Fourteen*

A	t eleven o'clock sharp, two kitchen girls in gray dresses with starched white aprons and white caps rolled a cart made of the new unstainable steel into the ballroom. A multi-tiered cake decorated with icing swags and roses perched on the cart's top tray; underneath it, a lower tray held stacks of china plates. Two more girls followed, pushing another cart that carried a cut-glass punch bowl full of pink liquid and dozens of matching cups. Lizzie wondered if it contained anything stronger than ginger ale.

Following Catherine Winslow's orders, Sidney asked the guests to join Florence and the count for a celebratory dessert. The audience rose and, in pairs and small groups, made their way toward the cake, while Sid, Melody, and Joey played background music. Lizzie thought Flo looked as though she were in a trance as she and the count took their positions beside the cart.

One of the servants handed the bride-to-be a large knife to cut the cake. Flo recoiled and clapped her hands to her chest. Her face blanched nearly as white as her gown. She seemed about to faint. The count caught her arm and held her up, staring at his fiancée with a mix of concern and confusion. Catherine Winslow hurried to her daughter's side and grasped Flo's other arm. She said something to Flo, then nodded to the count, who took the knife from the serving girl. With a quick, precise movement, he sliced into the confection.

Aided by a kitchen girl with a silver cake server, he placed the first piece on a plate and handed it to Flo. Another girl gave Flo a fork. Catherine whispered instructions to her daughter, who obediently ate a bite. *She looks like she's taking bitter medicine,* Lizzie thought as Flo passed the cake plate back to the count. He shoveled a good-sized chunk into his mouth and, while chewing, attempted an awkward smile.

The guests applauded vigorously and then lined up to be served by the kitchen girls. Some stood around in small clusters, chatting. Others meandered outside to the terrace to watch the pyro-technicians preparing for the fireworks display. Lizzie spotted Alan Peabody's red hair among the group on the terrace, but couldn't catch his eye. Glancing around, she noticed Anne Lawrence talking with Peter Winslow and his debutante. Anne, it seemed, had come to the party alone.

"How about some cake, Bearcat?" Sidney asked.

"Flo didn't make it seem very appetizing," she answered. "That young lady looks like she'd rather be anyplace else but here."

"She looks like a lamb being led to slaughter."

"And how."

Behind them, Joey Golick snapped his saxophone case shut. "Well kiddos, it's been swell, but it's time for old Joey to head on down the line."

Sid shook hands with the horn player. "Thanks again for hauling our chestnuts out of the fire, Joey. Seriously, think about joining us permanently, will you?"

"We couldn't have gotten through this week without you," Lizzie said and hugged him. "It's been darb working with you. Remember, we're all getting together for dinner with your cousin Benny in New York."

"We'll talk." Joey patted the top of Melody's head, then hoisted his case and walked away.

"I'm going to get some cake and find Douglas, okay?" Melody said.

"Sure, sure," Sidney replied.

Lizzie sighed with relief and clinked her punch cup to his. "Cheers. Whew, we did it."

"I have to admit, I had my doubts. But we did a good job and I'm proud of us all."

"Now what?"

"That depends on our mulligan pal, Sergeant Mulvaney." He nodded at the detective who'd stood all evening at the edge of the indoor park, trying not to attract attention. "Did you tell him about your accident this afternoon?"

"No, I don't trust him."

"You've got to let the cops in on everything, Bearcat. Melody told me the count bonked you on the noggin with a rock—you should've told me about that. And now someone's engineered a car crash. What's next?"

She still hadn't mentioned her encounter with Winslow in the rose garden. If Sidney noticed the scratch on her throat he'd assume she'd gotten it during the auto accident.

"You don't seem to realize how serious this is. Somebody killed Henry, and I'm not keen on having that somebody bump the rest of us off too—which seems to be the goal. If you don't tell Mulvaney, I will."

She took his arm and pulled him toward the terrace. "C'mon, let's go watch the fireworks."

Before they reached the ballroom's entrance, however, Catherine Winslow cut them off.

"I want you out of here tomorrow morning," she hissed.

Lizzie looked down at her hostess with surprise. The woman had never been more than barely cordial during their stay, but her hostility now, as the week-long event came to a successful end, seemed unwarranted.

"We'd like nothing better," Lizzie said. "But Sergeant Mulvaney made it clear that we're not to leave until he gives his permission."

"I'll handle Sergeant Mulvaney."

"Mrs. Winslow, he's conducting a murder investigation, after all," Sidney reminded her. "I'm sure you want this matter resolved as quickly as we do."

Although previously Sid's obsequious charm had enabled him to manipulate the woman, she showed no signs of backing off now.

192

"My daughter should be happy at this important time in her life and looking forward to her marriage. Instead, she's miserable. All because of this dreadful scandal with your colleague." Catherine Winslow's cheeks flushed with anger. "Furthermore, I won't be recommending you to any of my acquaintances."

Struggling to keep her temper under control, Lizzie pointed out, "We've done everything expected of us and more, even under the most ghastly circumstances. We could have cancelled this whole affair and left you in the lurch after our dear friend was killed *on your property*. And we still don't know by whom. But we persevered, like the professionals we are, despite the terrible loss we've suffered."

"I hope you'll reconsider, Mrs. Winslow," Sidney said, his tone laced with honey. "Your guests appear to have enjoyed our entertainment."

"You brought disgrace to our door," Mrs. Winslow insisted.

Indignant, Lizzie countered, "*We* should be pressing charges against *you*. While under your stewardship, one of our players was murdered. And this very afternoon, someone under your roof engaged in foul play, damaging our motorcar and intentionally injuring me."

"Ladies, please." Zachary Winslow approached them, apparently drawn by their raised voices. He took his wife's arm and steered her away toward the terrace. "The fireworks are about to begin. Shall we all go outside?"

# Chapter Twenty-Nine

*"It is madness in all women to let a secret love kindle within them."*

— *Charlotte Brontë, Jane Eyre*

T he scurrying about of chambermaids in the hallway outside her room woke Lizzie as the sun peeked above Ipswich Bay. Its pink and gold rays bled into the blue-green water, heralding what should have been her last day at Wingate. In the bed next to hers, Melody lay curled in the fetal position, breathing deeply.

Pushing herself up with her good arm, Lizzie tossed off the bedclothes and swung her long legs over the side of her bed. She sat for a moment, getting her bearings. Every inch of her body ached from having bounced around in Sid's Buick on its ill-fated plunge downhill into the woods. She reached for her bottle of Lydia E. Pinkham's Vegetable Compound and downed a good-sized gulp.

It only took a few minutes for the medicine to kick in. As its soothing warmth calmed her discomfort, she stood and stepped to the garret window that overlooked the back lawn. From here, she could observe the activity in the parking area. Even at this early hour, servants assisted guests in loading luggage into automobiles. *Whatever will we do now that they've gone and our raison d'etre has ended?*

After gathering up her personal items, Lizzie padded down the hallway to the bathroom and filled a sink with hot water. She gave herself a quick sponge bath, then brushed her teeth and hair, and dusted her face with powder. *We've only been at Wingate ten days,* she thought, *but it seems like an eternity. How much longer will Sergeant Mulvaney keep us cloistered here?* Although the prospect of spending more time with Peter Winslow appealed to her, she cringed at the idea of dealing with his family without the partygoers to serve as a buffer. *Maybe Catherine Winslow will convince Mulvaney to let us go.*

When she returned to her room, Melody was sitting up in bed, tears running down her rosy cheeks.

"Mel, what's wrong?"

The pretty blond flutist sniffed and dabbed at her eyes with a handkerchief. "Douglas has gone back to Connecticut. His insurance firm needs him."

"You'll see him soon—it's only a hop, skip, and a jump to Hartford."

Melody toyed with her amethyst necklace. "I know, but I'm goofy for him. I've never felt this way before. What if he forgets me once he's back home?"

"Poor little bunny, you've got it bad."

"What if that policeman won't let us go home?"

"He can't hold us here forever," Lizzie reassured her. "Now go wash your face and dust on some fresh powder before we go downstairs for breakfast. Be strong. You're an entertainer. You have an image to uphold."

While she waited for Melody, Lizzie slipped into a yellow low-waisted frock that hugged her shapely hips. She looped a long string of pearls around her neck and slid a few gold bangles on her good wrist. Several times, she returned to the window and watched as the single male guests vacated the gentlemen's quarters. To her relief, Alan Peabody's silver Bentley still sat in the parking area. *Maybe he's decided to extend his visit. Maybe I'll have a chance to see him again, when he doesn't have a lady in tow.*

She looked for him when they entered the sunny breakfast room, but didn't see him. A number of other guests, however, sat at tables, eating and chatting and waving out the windows to their departing friends. As she and Melody took their seats, Sidney ambled in, hands thrust in his trouser pockets.

"I just had a visit from Sergeant Mulvaney," he said, dropping into a chair beside Melody. "He reminded me that we're not to try to sneak away from Wingate during the mass exodus. Of course, the breezer's in no shape to drive anyway."

"Last night Catherine Winslow said she'd handle Mulvaney," Lizzie said. "I figured the dragon lady would tell him to let us go home."

"Hooey. She may think she can sway him, but I get the impression the sergeant is pretty hard-boiled. This is an important case for him and he's not going to take a chance on blowing it."

A serving girl brought coffee and took their breakfast requests, then hurried to refill the remaining guests' cups.

"What's our plan now?" Melody asked.

"Pretend we're tourists on a summer holiday," Lizzie answered. "I, for one, plan to head down to the beach right after we finish eating. After all, we've been through, I'd say we deserve a vacation. Maybe now you'll have time to work on your opera, Sid."

"You're writing an opera?" Melody asked him. "How exciting."

"Pipe down, Mel. Don't spread it around, in case I don't finish it or it's a dud." He lit a cigarette and blew smoke toward the ceiling. "I expect the Winslows will want us to continue playing for them as long as we're under their roof."

"I don't mind. I like playing music more than anything," Melody said.

"Good thing, because you may not have much choice in the matter."

\* \* \*

Dressed in her bathing costume—the same one she'd worn for her infamous bathtub scene—with a filmy gauze shift thrown over it for the sake of modesty, Lizzie walked down the grassy promenade toward the beach. She carried a towel, a parasol to provide shade if the sun got too strong, a copy of Margaret Kennedy's novel *The Constant Nymph,* and a silken pouch in which she'd stashed her seashells and beach glass. By now she'd accumulated quite a collection.

A cool breeze blew in from the ocean, carrying with it the clean, crisp, salty scent she'd come to love. If Mulvaney released them, she'd soon be back in New York breathing the fetid odors of the City in summertime. Despite the difficulties of this engagement, she'd found the sparkling green ocean, white sand beach, and bright blue sky enchanting. Perhaps one day she'd return to this beautiful part of the country under more hospitable circumstances. With any luck, The Troubadours would secure another booking, at the Oceanside or at the home of one of the aristocrats they'd entertained this week. *Maybe Peter Winslow or Alan Peabody will invite me to come for a visit.*

She passed the bronze fountain and nodded to the nymph on the dolphin's back. Before she reached the statues of Apollo and Poseidon, however, she heard a man's voice behind her calling her name.

"Miss Crane? May I have a word with you?"

Turning, she saw Sergeant Mulvaney hurrying toward her. "Of course, Sergeant." She stopped and waited for the overweight policeman to catch up.

"How are you?" he asked, breathing hard from the exertion of chasing after her.

"To tell the truth, Sergeant, I've felt better."

Lizzie started walking again, and Mulvaney fell into step beside her.

"I'm glad to see that you weren't badly hurt in the auto accident."

*Sidney's right*, she decided. *It's time to let the cops in on all that's been going on.* She held up her bandaged arm. "In addition to this, I've got bruises all over—and those aren't the only injuries I've sustained the past couple days. I should've told you earlier, but I was afraid you'd use whatever information I revealed against my friends and me."

"What information?"

"The day before yesterday, I was visiting the ruins of a chapel here on the Winslows' estate. Count Ivanovich attacked me there and threw stones at me. One struck me on the head and knocked me out. I still have the lump to prove it," she said, touching the sore spot on her scalp.

"Why did he do that?"

Lizzie shrugged. "He called me a witch and a whore. He thinks my friends and I have turned his fiancée against him."

"What do you think?"

"I think he's a bad-tempered, deluded lout who might have murdered Henry Ives."

"How did you come to that conclusion?"

They passed a man and woman who were returning from the beach. Both Lizzie and Sergeant Mulvaney greeted them.

"Fine day for a swim," the young man said.

"Indeed," Lizzie replied. When the couple had moved out of hearing range, she continued. "No doubt you've discovered that Flo Winslow and Henry were lovers. I believe that, when Henry showed up here again, the count considered him a rival and killed him."

"Do you have any proof?"

"No, but jealous rage has put many a man in his grave. Besides, the count can't afford to let anyone or anything interfere with this marriage. He lost practically everything during the Revolution, and he needs to get American citizenship so he can stay in this country. If he's deported to Russia, he'll most likely be imprisoned or executed."

Mulvaney nodded slowly, his eyebrows knotting in a frown.

"Then that same evening, after our performance, I was walking in the estate's rose garden when Zachary Winslow assaulted me with a rose."

The beefy policeman burst out laughing. "A *rose*? Miss Crane, is this some kind of joke?"

"Don't laugh. He grasped my arm and dragged the thorns along my throat, drawing blood." She stopped walking and tilted her head back so he could see the scratch on her neck. "Then he threatened me. He said he had spies watching me everywhere I go and that I could be 'removed' for having interfered with his plans."

"So do you also suspect Mr. Winslow of 'removing' your colleague?"

Lizzie shrugged. "I think it's possible. More likely, he hired a hitman to kill Henry. Surely you know that Winslow bought booze from Henry, and I think their association may have been more extensive. I think they might have been partners in the alcohol trafficking business."

Sergeant Mulvaney removed his hat, wiped his forehead on his sleeve, and then replaced the hat on his head. "Miss Crane, you're making some very strong accusations against some very important people—without any facts to back up your suppositions."

"And then yesterday," she continued, "someone cut the brake line of my friend Sidney's motorcar. That's why I had the 'accident,' Sergeant. Not because I'm a bad driver, but because a person here at Wingate tampered with the brakes."

"Can you verify that?"

"Yes. The Winslows' mechanic, a man named Ruben, said that's what caused me to lose control of the automobile."

But even as she said the words, she doubted that Ruben—a Negro man with a good job, employed by a powerful family—would testify to the fact and risk losing his position. How much easier it was to let everyone believe a silly woman driver had simply run off the road and wrecked the Buick. By now he'd probably repaired the damage, doing away with the evidence.

"Sergeant Mulvaney, somebody is trying to kill me. Someone in the Winslow household. I believe that same person murdered my colleague. Surely all this can't be coincidental. Do you really think so?"

"Miss Crane, what I *think* is of little value. All sorts of speculations fly about during a murder case. Occasionally some are valid. I'm not denying what you say, nor making light of the difficulties you've endured. But until I have hard evidence to back up your claims, I can't act on any of it."

Exasperated, Lizzie sighed loudly and threw her hands in the air. "I knew you wouldn't believe me. And now you're going to force me to stay in a place where my life is in danger."

"I appreciate the fact that you are an actress, Miss Crane, but can we dispense with the drama?"

"Sergeant, I'm trying to find out who killed Henry Ives. You told me to report any information I had to you. I've done that, yet you refuse to take me seriously. Sidney insisted I talk to you, but I thought it would be a waste of time. Now I *know* it was a waste of time."

"To the contrary, Miss Crane. I take you very seriously, but so far everything you've told me is circumstantial. Conjecture. Nothing concrete.

Nothing that would stand up in a court of law. That doesn't mean I'm discounting what you've told me. I promise that I will look more deeply into the events you've described and bring all my experience and skills as an investigator to bear in this case. And I ask you to continue to report to me anything you learn that may be relevant to this situation."

"If I agree, will you let my friends and me go back to New York?'

Mulvaney shook his head. "Sorry, I can't allow that. I need you to remain here until we resolve this matter."

"But that could be months. Years, even," she exclaimed. "In the meantime, my life is in danger."

"Miss Crane, are you familiar with the saying 'never try to catch a falling knife'?"

"No, I haven't heard that one."

"It means that if you try to interfere with a trajectory of dangerous events you're going to get hurt. Stick to singing and let me do my job. If you stop poking your nose into places where it doesn't belong, I think you'll be a lot safer." He touched the fingers of his right hand to the brim of his hat. "Good day, Miss Crane."

# Chapter Thirty

*"The liquor is getting low, madam—what with Prohibition and entertaining so much."*

*— Alice Gerstenberg, Fourteen*

Her conversation with Sergeant Mulvaney had left Lizzie feeling frustrated and more than a little fearful about her own safety. *What if we just high-tailed it out of here?* she asked herself. *Would the cops chase after us and arrest us?* Her imagination conjured up images of Mulvaney and his sidekick, Officer Connelly, trying to outrun the breezer as The Troubadours raced toward the state line. But if she bolted now, would the truth ever come to light and the guilty person ever face justice? The police didn't seem to be making much progress.

She took off her shoes and waded into the chilly waters of the Winslows' private cove. *Actually, this part doesn't belong to them.* She remembered reading that according to Massachusetts law, the stretch of land between low and high tide is public property. About fifty yards offshore, Peter Winslow's sloop bobbed on the waves. Perhaps her captain was too busy saying goodbye to friends today to take *Rhiannon* out for a sail. *Does she mind the slight?* Lizzie wondered.

Sloshing her feet in the surf gradually eased her anxiety. The farther she walked, the more relaxed she felt. Here and there she spotted a pretty shell or a bit of beach glass and added it to her bag of treasures. She watched cormorants skimming the sparkling water, searching for a meal. Seagulls shrieked as they flew overhead. Wherever she looked, she saw tiny bubbles in the wet sand, an indication of life buried beneath the beach's surface.

Immersed in nature, away from the tension of the Winslows' mansion, she felt calmer. She inhaled a deep breath of salty air, letting it soothe her mind and body. When she reached the end of the beach, where the sand gave way to rocky coastline, she turned around. With the sun in her face, she started walking back to the place where she'd left her shoes and parasol, intent on sitting quietly for a bit to read her book.

She hadn't gone far when she spotted Peter Winslow.

"Hail, Captain Winslow," she called to him.

He looked in her direction, and she waved. He waved back.

"Hello, Lizzie," he said as she neared him.

"Good morning, Peter. How lovely to see you."

"Likewise." He met her eyes with his, and she sensed something both expectant and sad in them. But before she could pin it down, he sighed and said, "Thank God all that's over! If I ever get married I'm going to elope, or just get the local justice of the peace to preside over a five-minute service. None of this ridiculous hoopla."

She tossed her head and smiled at him. "I've read that a ship's captain can perform a marriage ceremony on board—maybe you could do it yourself. But I hope your sister enjoyed the festivities, and that my friends and I provided some measure of happiness to her and her fiancé."

"My sister…" He turned to stare out at the sea, perhaps at *Rhiannon,* for a few moments before responding. "I doubt anything could make my sister happy. I, however, found your performances nothing short of sensational. I'm not the only one either."

"Thank you. Your opinion means a lot to me. I'm afraid your mother wouldn't agree, though."

"Baloney, don't let my mother's opinion influence you. If God came for supper, she'd find fault with his table manners."

Lizzie laughed, then said, "I don't know if you've heard, but your family might be saddled with my friends and me for a while longer. Sergeant

Mulvaney, the cop who's investigating Henry's murder, has confined us to Wingate for the time being—at least until he nabs the killer or feels confident that none of us is responsible."

"That's swell news," Peter said. "That will give us a chance to get to know each other better."

Lizzie bowed her head to keep him from seeing the enthusiasm sparkling in her eyes.

"Forgive me," he backtracked. "I was only thinking of myself. Of course, you want to return to your home and leave the sadness of your friend's death behind you."

Raising her eyes again to meet his, Lizzie said, "You and your family have opened your arms and your home to my friends and me, and I am grateful for this opportunity to spend time here at Wingate. Yes, I want this matter to be resolved—not only so I can go home, but so your sister can have some peace as she moves into the next phase of her life. But in the meantime, I would like to get to know you better too, Peter Winslow."

He grinned broadly, and for a moment she thought he might take her in his arms. Instead, he pointed to the silken pouch she'd slung over her wrist.

"What have you got there?"

Raising her good arm, she answered, "A collection of seashells."

"May I see them?"

They sat on the beach, side by side, and Lizzie opened the pouch. She shook out the shells and arranged them on the sand according to size and shape.

"I gathered these shells here in this cove. What can you tell me about them?"

He picked up one of the white circles. "This is a sand dollar. Christianity links it with the Crucifixion. See these five slits around the outside? They represent Christ's wounds. The flower design looks like an Easter lily etched into the shell—and if you break it open, you'll find tiny bird-shaped bits inside that are said to be doves of peace."

"What a lovely legend," Lizzie said.

Next, he touched a green shell shaped like a tiny cushion, with a complex pattern of stripes and spots on its surface. "This is a sea urchin's shell. They're related to sand dollars and starfish. When they're alive, they're very pretty, kind of like flowers. They have lots of colorful spines sticking out in all directions, which is why some people call them sea hedgehogs. If you keep searching, you'll probably find more of these shells in various shades of pink and purple."

He pointed at a zigzag scallop shell, a periwinkle, a tiny conch, and a pair of calico clamshells. As he identified each one, he told stories about its habitat, behavior, and peculiarities. When he came to the small, white one she'd found on the grass beside Henry's body on the night of his death, Peter frowned. The pretty, heart-shaped shell was ridged with dozens of concentric lines so delicate they looked as though they'd been engraved with the point of a pin.

Peter ran his fingertip around the top of the shell, then turned it over. "This is what's called a 'sailor's valentine.' It got the name because of its shape. Sailors used to give them to their sweethearts as tokens of love. You didn't find it here on this beach, though—it comes from the Pacific."

*Maybe Henry meant to give it to Flo,* Lizzie thought. Had he brought it with him to Wingate, carried it in his pocket, hoping for an opportunity to present it to her as a sign of his affection? Hoping she might still care for him? But he never got the chance.

"Is it okay if I keep them?" she asked. "I mean, I didn't think to ask permission before I collected them. I wouldn't want to take something that belonged to your family."

"Don't be silly. Of course, you can keep them. Plenty more where these came from."

Lizzie scooped up the shells and gently slid them back into her silky pouch. "Thank you. I like knowing their stories. When I get back to New York, I'll display them on my windowsill to remember my time here at Wingate."

"In the meantime, given that you might be here for a while, would you like to go sailing with me again?"

"I'd love to." She looked at *Rhiannon* anchored in the cove. If a boat could wink, she felt certain the sloop would have done just that. Lady to lady.

"How about tomorrow afternoon? The weather promises to be superb. Meet me here at 3:00—I'll ask Mrs. Appleby to prepare a hamper for us."

"That would be perfect."

"Swell, I'll see you then." He stood and brushed sand off the seat of his trousers. "Sorry, I have to leave you now. I need to see some of my friends off. What will you do for the rest of the day?"

"Read. Then I suppose I should check in with your mother in case she has plans for my friends and me. Sidney thinks she may want us to continue performing for your family while we're in residence."

"I certainly hope so, if you don't mind, that is. I could listen to you sing every evening for the rest of my life and never grow tired of it. 'Til tomorrow then."

She waved as he strode across the sand. When he reached the edge of the grassy promenade, he turned and blew her a kiss.

* * *

Lizzie arrived back at the mansion in time to see Alan Peabody carrying his suitcases out to his silver Bentley.

"Mr. Peabody," she called and waved to him.

He set his bags down on the ground and crossed the parking area toward her. "Miss Crane, I was afraid I might miss you. I didn't want to leave without seeing you again. I sent a maid to look for you, but she couldn't find you or your friends. I thought perhaps you'd already gone back to New York."

"I went to the beach for a bit. I'm so glad I caught up with you, so I could thank you again for your kind assistance yesterday." She smiled coquettishly at him, noticing for the first time the golden flecks in his dark eyes. When he smiled back her heart started dancing.

"Miss Crane—"

"Please, call me Lizzie."

"Lizzie, I wish we could've had more time to get to know one another this week. I wondered...well, I often go to New York on business, and I wondered if perhaps you might honor me by having dinner with me some evening when I'm in your fair city?"

She felt like clapping, or shouting, or throwing her arms around his neck. Instead, she said as calmly as she could, "I'd be ab-so-lute-ly delighted."

"Fantastic." He reached into the pocket of his linen jacket and pulled out an envelope. "I'd planned to leave this for you. A brief note, along with my business card and personal telephone number."

She took the thick, creamy envelope and glanced at her name written on it in a handsome script. His initials were embossed on the back flap.

"Will you promise to contact me when you get home?" he asked. "So at least I know you've arrived safely."

"Yes, I will. But that might be a while. Perhaps you've heard that my friends and I have been ordered to remain here at Wingate until the police finish their investigation of my colleague's death."

He nodded. "Well then, we might have an opportunity to see one another even before you return to New York."

Fantasies of sneaking away on a train into Boston to meet with the illustrious Mr. Peabody spun in her mind. She held out her hand and he took it. For a moment he stroked it lightly with his thumb while he gazed into her eyes, then he bent and brushed his lips against hers.

"We'll talk soon. Take care of yourself, Lizzie."

"You too."

Watching him walk to his motorcar, Lizzie struggled to keep from running after him. She imagined throwing herself into the seat beside him and begging him to whisk her away from Wingate. As he drove off, he waved out the window and she waved back. She waited until his Bentley was out of sight, then hugged the envelope to her chest and jumped up and down a few times, not caring who saw her or what they might think.

# Chapter Thirty-One

*"Truth is so often disconcerting."*

— *Rafael Sabatini, Scaramouche*

As Sidney had predicted, Catherine Winslow asked The Troubadours to play during dinner, for the family and several guests who'd elected to stay on at Wingate after the majority had gone back to their homes and their everyday lives.

"It's not exactly a request," he told Lizzie. "'As long as you're still here you may as well make yourselves useful' is how she put it."

"Okay by me. It'll help us keep our skills sharp and give us something to occupy our time while we're confined to quarters. I'll miss Joey's horn, though."

Actually, Lizzie adored performing. Nothing in the world made her feel so alive, so purposeful, and so in sync with the universe. Since childhood, she'd loved music. Although her family couldn't afford to buy a radio, the barbershop where her father worked had one and she found excuses to visit him there so she could listen to it. She sang lullabies to her younger siblings at bedtime; sang while she helped her mother cook and clean and wash wealthier people's laundry; sang while walking home from school or swinging in the local park or playing hopscotch on the sidewalk in front of the tenement where her family lived. Music was her escape from everyday doldrums, her solace in bad times, and the star to which she'd hitched her cart.

At the appointed hour, the trio positioned themselves in the alcove stage near the dining room and warmed up while their audience socialized. Among the remaining guests, Lizzie recognized Catherine Winslow's brother, a politician in Philadelphia, and his wife. The stout, loquacious matron with the overbite and her horse-faced daughter Evangeline, whom Lizzie had observed on the first evening The Troubadours had entertained at Wingate, were still in attendance, along with the olive-skinned woman whom Lizzie had since learned was a widowed Italian aristocrat. However, she noted with satisfaction that the beautiful debutante who'd accompanied Peter Winslow throughout the previous week's festivities was nowhere to be seen.

As the diners took their seats at the mahogany banquet table, Lizzie caught Zachary Winslow watching her. Dressed in an elegantly tailored midnight-blue suit—a step down from the formal attire he'd worn on previous evenings—he moved among his guests with practiced grace. He held a chair for Mrs. Overbite and shared pleasantries with his brother-in-law's high-strung wife, before taking his seat at the head of the table.

To conceal the scratch he'd etched on her throat Lizzie had donned a five-strand collar of pearls, yet she felt his eyes scrutinizing her like a wild animal who'd inflicted a mark on his quarry and now stalked his prey. She refused to meet his gaze. Beneath his threat lay an undeniable eroticism, the implied juxtaposition of sensuality and cruelty he'd exuded as he trailed the rose's thorns along her delicate flesh. Did he think she was just another woman he could intimidate with his money, power, and good looks? Although Lizzie knew she was no match for him—he held the high cards in this risky game—she refused to let him see he'd managed to frighten her.

Catherine Winslow assumed her place at the foot of the Chippendale dining table, with the count and Florence Winslow on her right. Peter Winslow and the Italian widow sat across from the betrothed couple. To his credit, Peter tried to engage his sister and her Russian fiancé in conversation, but neither responded with anything more than the most perfunctory reactions. Lizzie felt a sense of release when the servants brought the first course, giving the diners something other than each other to focus on.

While the guests partook of their meal, The Troubadours ran through their repertoire of classical and romantic-era music, interspersed with low-key popular tunes that Lizzie gauged would be acceptable to Mrs. Winslow. She only sang half a dozen songs. The rest of the evening Sidney and Melody played "background music" while she struggled to read the minds of Zachary, Catherine, and Peter Winslow, with little success. Florence, for the most part, kept her head bowed as if enthralled by the food on the plate before her.

After the serving girls had cleared away the dessert dishes, Zachary Winslow stood and the others followed. Now, Lizzie knew, the men would repair to the billiard room while the women gathered in the game room to play cards. She turned her attention to Peter Winslow, wondering where he'd go and if she might have a chance to talk with him.

As she cautiously stepped away from the alcove, holding her floor-length gown draped over her arm to avoid tripping on the voluminous fabric, a woman's voice called to her.

"Miss Crane?"

Looking up, she saw Florence Winslow approaching her. The young woman's light brown hair had been swept into an ornate up-do, pinned into place with jewel-studded combs. The oddly outdated style became her and emphasized her pretty eyes.

"Good evening to you, Miss Winslow," Lizzie said. "I hope you enjoyed our performance this evening. We've tried ever so hard to provide you and your fiancé with uplifting entertainment this past week."

"It was fine," she said, but Lizzie sensed Flo hadn't come to offer compliments.

The young heiress remained silent while her relatives and guests filed out of the dining room to amuse themselves elsewhere. Until they'd all vacated the area she stood patiently, barely moving, with her delicate white hands—like those of a porcelain doll—clasped in front of her.

"Is there something you wished to say to me, Miss Winslow?" Lizzie asked.

After casting her gaze about the room one last time to make certain no one might be in a position to overhear what she had to say, the young bride-to-be stepped closer to Lizzie. "My brother tells me you have something that belongs to me."

"Really? What might that be? I can't imagine having anything of yours, Miss Winslow. We hardly know each other."

Florence lowered her voice to a whisper. "My sailor's valentine."

It took a few moments for Lizzie to process the implications of what Flo had said, and a few moments more before she could reply. When she did, she chose ignorance as the safest response.

"Excuse me, but I don't know what you're talking about."

"Oh, I think you do," Flo insisted. "You found a shell shaped like a heart. You showed it to Peter."

Lizzie shook her head, aggravating the ache that still lingered from the impact of Count Ivanovich's stone. As she rearranged the pieces of the puzzle in her mind, something she hadn't realized before fell into place. *Henry didn't bring the sailor's valentine to Wingate, intending to give it to Flo on the night he was murdered. She already had it in her possession.*

Flo fingered a diamond bracelet on her wrist, as if contemplating her next move. "It means nothing to you, Miss Crane, and everything to me. I want it back."

"Sorry, I can't help you, Miss Winslow," Lizzie said, as the truth hit home.

\* \* \*

Too keyed up to sleep, Lizzie drew a bath and sank into the hot water. She reclined in the claw-footed tub, steam rising around her, and turned her thoughts back to the night of Henry's murder. Mentally, she sorted and resorted the information she'd accumulated during the past ten days, along with her memories and impressions, trying to weave a tapestry that would reveal the details of her colleague's murder.

Only minutes before she'd discovered his body, on her way back from the beach, she'd heard voices on the promenade. Upon drawing closer, she'd witnessed someone running away from the scene. Was that person Florence

Winslow?

Ginny Winslow had explained how she and her siblings snuck out of the mansion by climbing down the trellises from their private balconies. Had Flo arranged a clandestine meeting with Henry, then taken her revenge because he'd shamed and abandoned her? Lizzie remembered Flo's shocked reaction when Melody pretended to stab herself onstage during The Troubadours' rehearsal of *Romeo and Juliet,* and how she'd dashed away from the dining room the night she spilled blood-red wine on the front of her gown.

As Lizzie lathered herself with a bar of Ivory soap and sunk up to her neck in the soothing hot water, she wondered if anyone else knew that Flo had murdered her lover. Peter had told his sister that Lizzie possessed the sailor's valentine—did he also know that Henry had given it to Flo? And did he realize how Lizzie came to have the shell in her possession? If so, would he try to relieve her of the valentine, in order to protect his sister?

What about Zachary Winslow? Had he arranged to have the brakes on Sidney's automobile cut, hoping to scare Lizzie off? Maybe Winslow believed he could control the police, but Lizzie was a loose cannon and her repeated probing into his daughter's affair put him and all he held dear at risk. How far would he go to conceal the fact that his daughter had slain her rum-running lover, the father of her child, and a criminal with whom the industrialist had a questionable connection? Lizzie replayed in her mind the words of Flo's friend Anne Lawrence: "Zachary Winslow's reputation is more important to him than anything."

Her thoughts turned to Count Ivanovich next. Ostensibly, he'd attacked her in the chapel cemetery because she offended his religious beliefs. But what if he really meant to protect his fiancée—and his own self-interests as well—by removing Lizzie from the picture?

Finally, she considered Catherine Winslow. Peter had described his mother as utterly devoted to her family. What might she do to protect her child from further harm? An image of the two women walking arm-in-arm in the rose garden flashed in Lizzie's mind. Despite the upset that Flo's relationship with Henry had caused the Winslow family, Catherine appeared to have forgiven the girl and longed to make her daughter happy. After all, she'd orchestrated this entire weeklong extravaganza in an attempt to please Flo—an attempt that seemed to have failed dismally.

Lizzie pulled the bathtub's plug and listened to the water gurgling down the drain while she toweled herself dry. The myriad possibilities—who knew what, who wanted what, who was capable of what—boggled her mind.

Although she suspected that Florence Winslow had killed Henry, she couldn't rule out the possibility that the young woman may have served as a pawn in another person's game. Had someone else with his or her own agenda—the count, Zachary or Catherine Winslow, maybe even Peter—used Flo as bait to lure Henry to his death? Had that person followed Flo to her rendezvous with her lover and stabbed Henry?

One thing was certain, however. They all wanted Lizzie Crane out of the picture—and at least one of them was willing to go to great lengths to accomplish that goal.

\* \* \*

Lizzie woke in a sweat, her heart pounding. In her dream, she was looking down on Catherine and Florence Winslow, who stood in the rose garden that mother and daughter had designed together. Nearby, gardeners dug a hole to add a new rosebush to the collection. While the gardeners and Flo watched, Catherine knelt beside the hole the men had just finished digging. To Lizzie, it seemed the woman might be making an offering of some sort as she laid a tissue-wrapped bundle in the hole. When she'd finished, the gardeners planted the bush and shoveled dirt into the hole.

As Lizzie's pulse and breath slowly returned to normal, she wondered why such a peaceful dream had elicited such a frightening response. She remembered having observed the very same scenario from her bedchamber window, shortly after Henry's death: the two Winslow women overseeing the installation of a new rosebush in their beloved garden. At the time, she'd given little thought to why Catherine Winslow knelt for a few moments beside the freshly dug hole before the gardeners interred the rosebush.

Now she did.

# Chapter Thirty-Two

*"Everywhere was the atmosphere of a long debauch that had to end."*

— *Malcolm Cowley, Exile's Return: A Literary Odyssey of the 1920s*

She had a hard time going back to sleep after her dream, and when she finally did she slept fitfully. The sun's first rays woke her, streaming into her bedchamber. Lizzie buried her face in her pillow, hoping to hide from the light for another hour or two. She tugged her coverlet over her head and curled into a fetal position, trying to push away the mélange of thoughts that had swarmed like busy bees around her during the night.

She heard Melody rise from her bed and leave their bedchamber. At this time of day, all the maids' rooms were empty and a peaceful silence settled over the mansion's usually busy third floor. Downstairs, the girls changed bed linens, scrubbed bathrooms, and Hoovered carpets, trying to restore order after the Winslows' guests had departed. Lizzie adjusted herself on her narrow bed, trying to find a position that didn't exacerbate the pain from her recent injuries. Just as she started to doze off again, the bedroom door creaked open. She turned her head and opened her eyes, expecting to see Melody.

Instead, Catherine Winslow entered.

Fury distorted the woman's lovely face. Sunlight glinted on something at her side. Before Lizzie could ask what her hostess wanted, Catherine raised her hand and Lizzie saw the knife. Lizzie rolled off the bed and onto the floor, as Catherine slashed downward. The knife gouged the mattress.

"What the hell are you doing?" Lizzie shouted.

"I won't let you destroy my daughter!"

Lizzie slid under the bed. With her cheek pressed against the floor, she could see Catherine's feet on the rag rug that lay between the twin beds. Clutching the rug with her good hand, she pulled hard.

Catherine lost her balance and fell. The knife clattered away. Before she could retrieve it, Lizzie seized the woman's ankle and held on tight. Despite her injuries, Lizzie was younger, bigger, and stronger than her assailant. With adrenaline pumping through her veins, she dragged Catherine partway under the bed, trapping the woman long enough to gain the upper hand.

"Bitch! Whore!" Catherine shrieked. She tried to kick Lizzie, but the tight space prevented her from inflicting any injury.

As Lizzie wriggled out the other side and pushed herself up, she spotted the knife on the floor near the bureau. She grabbed it as Catherine clawed her way out from under the bed. Gripping the knife in her shaking hand, Lizzie ordered, "Stay where you are."

Catherine glared up at Lizzie but obeyed.

"*You* murdered Henry because he knocked up your daughter."

Catherine didn't reply.

Footsteps pounded down the bare wooden hallway toward them. Lizzie's mind raced: *A housemaid? Or another enemy?*

Florence Winslow appeared in the doorway. Her eyes grew wide as she stared at Lizzie armed with a kitchen knife, standing over Catherine who lay on her stomach between the twin beds.

"What have you done to my mother?"

"Your mother tried to kill me, just like she killed Henry. She knew you'd arranged to meet him at the bronze fountain and she followed you to make certain he wouldn't convince you to run away with him."

Lizzie held the knife outstretched before her, daring Florence Winslow to come closer or Catherine to try to get up from the floor. Her breath rose and fell in rapid, harsh gasps.

"Mother didn't kill him. I did."

Although she'd suspected since last night that Flo had stabbed Henry, Lizzie needed to hear the young woman admit it. Even so, it took a moment for Flo's admission to sink in.

"But why?" Lizzie asked. "You loved him."

"Don't say anything more," Catherine told her daughter.

Flo dropped her head and stared at the floor. Her shoulders sagged. She rubbed her skirt between her thumb and forefinger, like a frightened little girl rubbing a favorite blanket for comfort.

"I was so happy to see him again. I'd waited so long. I asked him to meet me by the fountain that night. I told him about the baby and my engagement and, well, everything. I asked him to run off with me, so we could get away from all this. Marry and start over."

"Flo, hush!" Catherine ordered.

"Let her talk," Lizzie said. "Why did you bring the knife with you?"

Flo sighed. "If he refused, I was going to kill myself. Without him, I had nothing to live for. I got the idea from that play you rehearsed, *Romeo and Juliet*."

"But you killed him instead."

"I tried to stab myself, but he stopped me and we struggled." Tears slid down Flo's cheeks. "I don't know how it happened…"

"Leave her alone," Catherine demanded.

The girl knelt beside her mother on the bedchamber floor. As she laid her hand on Catherine's back, Flo's face contorted in a tragic mask and she began to sob. "I'm sorry, Mummy. I'm so sorry about everything."

*  *  *

Their shouting caused several housemaids to come running. The girls bunched together in the open doorway, stunned by the scene before them, not knowing what to do. Among them, Lizzie saw Tess O'Hare.

"Tess, find Mrs. Greely," she ordered. "Hurry!"

For what seemed like an interminable amount of time, Lizzie stood with knife in hand, poised to fend off the two Winslow women. She'd expected that Flo might try to wrestle the weapon from her hand, but the weeping girl continued to kneel beside her mother, her head bowed in resignation. When Lizzie felt confident that she wouldn't be attacked again, she edged toward the row of hooks that held her everyday clothes and grabbed a robe to wrap over her nightgown.

Finally, Mrs. Greely pushed her way through the cluster of housemaids. "What's the cause of all this commotion?" the housekeeper asked.

"Mrs. Winslow tried to kill me," Lizzie answered.

"What?"

"It's true," Florence said. "My mother was trying to protect me. But it's no use."

"Mrs. Greely, telephone Sergeant Mulvaney and tell him to come here immediately," Lizzie said.

The matron stared down at Catherine Winslow, lying on her stomach on the floor, then back at Lizzie. "I don't take orders from you."

"Do it," Florence insisted.

Obviously confused, Mrs. Greely turned and hurried away to telephone the police.

"How long are you going to force me to lie here in this indignant position?" Catherine Winslow asked.

"Until Sergeant Mulvaney shows up," Lizzie said.

"Well at least send those nosy maids back to their work. They're not paid to stand around and gawk."

Lizzie waved her empty hand and the girls scattered.

Tears slid down Flo's plump cheeks, but she didn't bother to wipe them away. With her open palm, she rubbed her mother's back in gentle, circular motions and shook her head slowly from side to side. "I'm sorry, I'm sorry," she said again and again.

* * *

It took half an hour for Sergeant Mulvaney and Officer Connelly to arrive at the scene. By now the intensity had drained from the bedchamber. Lizzie's hand ached from gripping the knife. Catherine complained that she needed to go to the bathroom. Flo seemed to withdraw deeper and deeper into herself, though she kept her hand on her mother's back and occasionally rubbed it as if trying to provide a modicum of comfort.

Officer Connelly seemed acutely uncomfortable in the cloistered chambers of the Winslows' female servants, but Sergeant Mulvaney entered Lizzie's bedroom as calmly as if it were his own.

"That will be all, Miss Crane," he said. "Give me the knife."

She relinquished it to him gladly. "Mrs. Winslow tried to kill me."

"So I've heard. Mrs. Winslow, please get up off the floor."

The indignant woman pushed herself up and stood between the twin beds, radiating ire like a cast-iron stove radiates heat. She smoothed her morning frock, glanced at her daughter, then fixed her eyes on the policeman.

"Mrs. Winslow, I've been summoned here in response to a complaint that you attempted to inflict bodily harm on the person of Miss Crane. Is that so?"

"I won't speak without the benefit of legal counsel," Catherine Winslow said.

"By all means, contact your attorney," Mulvaney said, then he turned to Lizzie. "Miss Crane, what is your reason for threatening your hostess with a knife?"

"She entered my room uninvited and tried to stab me. I acted in self-defense."

The policeman frowned, apparently attempting to make sense of the matter. "Why do you believe Mrs. Winslow wanted to stab you?"

"Because I'd discovered that her daughter, Florence Winslow, killed my colleague, Henry Ives."

"And what led you to that conclusion, Miss Crane?"

Now that the adrenaline rush had dissipated, Lizzie suddenly felt very tired. She sat on the edge of her bed, her shoulders slumping, her muscles slowly unwinding from the demands she'd placed upon them earlier. She wished Sidney—or better yet Alan Peabody—were here to offer support. She longed to lay her head on a comforting shoulder and cry until she couldn't cry anymore.

"Please continue, Miss Crane," Mulvaney said.

She took a deep breath, then replied, "The night Henry was murdered, I found a token of affection that he'd given to Miss Winslow lying beside his body. A sailor's valentine."

"What is a sailor's valentine?" he asked.

"A heart-shaped shell that Henry gave to Flo as a way of professing his love for her."

"You say you found this shell at the crime scene. Are you suggesting that Miss Winslow had it in her possession on the night of the murder and that she dropped it there?"

"Yes, sir, I am. It's not native to this area, as her brother will attest. Besides, Miss Winslow told me it belonged to her and she asked me to return it to her."

"Do you have this so-called 'sailor's valentine' in your possession now?"

"I do."

"May I see it?"

Lizzie pushed herself up from her bed and crossed the small bedchamber, which was now so crowded with people that she could barely move about. She withdrew the silky pouch from her cosmetic case and shook out the shell for Sergeant Mulvaney to see. But when he reached to grasp the valentine, she snatched it away and slid it back into the pouch. "I'm not giving it up without a warrant, Sergeant."

Several servants had gathered at the door to Lizzie's room, apparently intrigued by the goings-on. Word of the situation, it seemed, had gotten around.

"Get back to your work," Catherine Winslow ordered, and the girls scattered.

Although the mistress of the manor held her head high, Lizzie noticed she leaned on her daughter as if for support and stood quietly between the two beds as the policeman asked his questions. The commanding authority and haughtiness she'd displayed since The Troubadours' arrival had faded.

"There's something more, Sergeant," Lizzie said.

# CHAPTER THIRTY-TWO

"Oh? And what might that be?"

"I think if you dig in the Wingate rose garden, you'll find the blood-stained frock Miss Winslow wore on the night she killed Henry Ives."

# Chapter Thirty-Three

*"What we play is life."*

— *Louis Armstrong, Louis Armstrong, in His Own Words: Selected Writings*

Lizzie, Sergeant Mulvaney, Officer Connelly, and the Winslows' attorney, along with Florence, Catherine, Zachary, and Peter Winslow, sat in Mr. Winslow's office at Wingate overlooking the tennis court. Lizzie's eyes roamed about the huge and handsomely appointed room. On one wall, floor-to-ceiling bookcases flanked a fireplace with a black marble mantel. Ornately carved walnut paneling covered the opposite wall. Persian carpets lay on the floor and Louis XV furnishings graced the light-filled space.

Lizzie sighed inwardly and rubbed her fingers on the arm of the fauteuil in which she sat. *Such an elegant backdrop to such a sordid affair.*

"Can't you at least remove those handcuffs?" Zachary Winslow asked. "My wife and daughter are not going to run away."

"No, they're not," Mulvaney answered, but he made no move to release Flo and Catherine.

Even to Lizzie, who'd been the target of Catherine Winslow's murderous wrath, the police tactics seemed excessive. She crossed her ankles and stared at the Winslows one by one; they either ignored or glared at her.

In response to Mulvaney's questions, Lizzie recounted everything that had happened, including Flo's admission of guilt. However, she left out her conversation with Anne Lawrence and what Flo's childhood friend had revealed. She also omitted what Peter Winslow had told her about Flo's romance with Henry and Peter's friendship with the saxophonist, hoping to spare the young man from potential criminal charges.

Officer Connelly wrote down everything she said in a spiral notebook. The Winslows' attorney, a thickset man with a double chin and glacier-cold eyes, had instructed Catherine and Florence to remain silent. Flo slumped in her chair, her head bowed, her long brown hair falling down on either side of her face like blinders on a horse. Her limp form reminded Lizzie of a pillow that had lost most of its feathers.

"Has anyone located Count Ivanovich?" Mulvaney asked.

"Not yet," Officer Connelly answered. "I suspect he's on his way back to Europe by now."

Mulvaney tapped the arm of his chair with a thick finger. Although for all purposes his case had been solved, he didn't appear to take any pleasure in his success.

"Miss Winslow, you realize that if you're convicted of murder you could be executed," he cautioned Flo.

"I prefer death to living the rest of my life without Henry."

"Quiet," the attorney ordered.

"You can't prove any of this," Zachary Winslow insisted, pointing at Lizzie. "It's that showgirl's word against ours."

"We'll see," Mulvaney said. "Mrs. Winslow, Miss Winslow, I'm going to take you down to the station now and file formal charges. I expect you'll want to come with us, Counsel. In the morning, a judge will decide whether or not you ladies will be allowed to post bond."

"You mean my daughter and I will have to spend the night in jail?" Catherine Winslow asked indignantly.

Mulvaney raised a bushy eyebrow. "You might spend all the rest of your nights in jail, Mrs. Winslow."

The attorney placed his hand on his client's arm. "Don't make waves, Catherine. I'll have you out in the morning. In the meantime, remember that anything you say can and will be used against you. That goes for you too, Florence." He ran a finger across his lips as if zipping them. "Say nothing."

"Will my friends and I be allowed to go home now, Sergeant?" Lizzie asked.

"I don't see any reason to hold you," Mulvaney answered. "But don't forget, the arm of the law is long and strong. You will be required to return here to testify, of course, if and when a trial is held. If you change your address, you must notify us. Don't attempt to leave the country or become otherwise unavailable. Do not cross me, Miss Crane, or you'll wish you hadn't."

\* \* \*

Maids hauled the musicians' suitcases downstairs, where Sidney loaded them into the breezer. Although the auto's body damage had yet to be repaired, the mechanic had replaced the brake fluid tube and declared the Buick fit to travel. Sid had already arranged for their stage sets and props to travel back to New York by train, though under the circumstances Lizzie didn't trust shipping their personal items by rail unattended. She feared that someone might insinuate false evidence into the mix and complicate the situation further.

Although she'd spent less than two weeks at Wingate, Lizzie felt a sense of camaraderie with the housemaids who'd shared their modest quarters with her and Melody. The young women struggled daily against the odds as they tried to rise above their lowly origins, hoping to find lives that held a modicum of security and dignity and perhaps even happiness. Before leaving, she pressed a silver dollar in each girl's hand and thanked her for her assistance during The Troubadours' stay.

While Sidney packed the Buick, Lizzie stopped by the kitchen to say goodbye to Mrs. Appleby. The plump cook wrapped her in a warm hug and gave her a hamper for the road, with enough food to last a week. Her son, Thomas, stood a few steps behind his mother, shifting his weight awkwardly from one foot to the other, his face contorted with emotions he didn't know how to express.

Lizzie handed him an envelope that contained payment for his assistance. "We appreciate you pitching in when we needed you, Thomas. You've been ever so helpful during our stay here and we can't thank you enough. If your mom will let you take the train to New York, we'll put you up, take you to the theater, and show you around the town."

He grinned and bobbed his head. "Thank you, ma'am. I'd like that."

Next, she passed him a letter for Ginny Winslow and hoped he'd find a way to get it to her. Immediately after Catherine's attack on Lizzie, the girl's parents had shuttled her off to her grandmother's home in Rhode Island. Lizzie's heart ached at the thought of what young Ginny would face in the near future. If only the grandmother could protect her from the worst of it.

Lizzie had tried to locate Florence Winslow's maid Marie before leaving, but without success. Apparently, she and her sister Tess had been dismissed from service and no one seemed to know where they'd gone.

Soon, Anne Lawrence would hear of Flo's arrest, if she hadn't already. When Lizzie got back to New York, she planned to write a letter to Anne, but she wished she had a way to contact her sooner—Flo could use a friend now.

She'd expected that Zachary Winslow might try to withhold payment for The Troubadours' engagement at Wingate, but he gave Sidney cash in full. Maybe he didn't want to cause any more friction, or maybe he was a man who kept his bargains. The industrialist and head of the manor was an enigma, to be sure.

After her meeting with Sergeant Mulvaney and the Winslows, Lizzie had visited the fountain where Henry died. She looked up at the bronze nymph astride the dolphin and recalled the amazing occurrences that had transpired during her stay at Wingate. *So much sadness, so much suffering.* Despite Flo's heinous crime, Lizzie couldn't help feeling sympathy for the brokenhearted and misguided young heiress. And even though Catherine Winslow had tried to kill her, Lizzie understood that the woman wanted desperately to protect her child. Like a mother bear, she was willing to go to any length to achieve that end.

*Let justice be done,* she thought as she snapped shut the latches on her last suitcase and summoned a maid to take the case down to Sidney's Buick. Wincing with pain, Lizzie made her way for the last time down the staircase from the servants' quarters to the main floor of the Winslows' mansion.

She was surprised to see Peter Winslow waiting in the parking area beside the breezer. As she approached him, he held out his hands, palms up, in a gesture of surrender. He looked much younger and much less confident than the man who'd taken her sailing only days before.

Searching her face for a sign of forgiveness, he asked, "What can I say, Lizzie? I'm sorry? It's been a pleasure meeting you and maybe things will be better the next time our paths cross? I'd hoped for something more?" He opened the Buick's door and helped her into the front passenger seat.

He looked so forlorn that she wanted to reach out and tousle his sun-bleached hair, as if reassuring an anxious child. Instead, she smiled and stroked his cheek with the backs of her fingers. "How about fare thee well?"

# A Note from the Author

This is a work of fiction, though it contains real places and events that did happen. Except in the case of historic fact, any resemblance to actual persons, living or dead, is purely coincidental. When real people or situations are presented it is in a fictional context. The Wingate estate, for example, was inspired by Crane's Castle Hill Estate in Ipswich, Massachusetts, although the present-day mansion didn't exist at the time this story takes place and no resemblance is intended between the Crane family and the Winslows in this novel. The Oceanview Hotel in Magnolia, Massachusetts, which also plays a role in this book, was a thriving resort in the summer of 1925 and was far more extraordinary than described here. Again, the characters portrayed have no connection with the real-life owners, staff, or guests of the Oceanview.

I have endeavored to convey all events, people, products, technology, music, literature, social norms, fashion, and other details accurately, in keeping with the period. I hope you'll find this information intriguing and that it will enrich your enjoyment of the story. As we mark the one hundredth anniversary of the Roaring Twenties, I hope you'll have fun reading about this significant decade in our history.

# Acknowledgements

First and foremost, I wish to acknowledge my fellow authors and friends, Kate Flora and Susan Oleksiw, who co-founded Level Best Books with me way back in 2003 to provide a venue for New England's many talented crime writers to share their work. Over the years, LBB's subsequent owners have taken the company to new heights, winning all the important awards in the mystery/thriller field and delighting readers not only in New England, but worldwide. I am grateful to Level Best's current staff, especially Verena Rose, for giving me a chance to reach readers who love historical mysteries and to again become a member of the LBB family.

I also wish to thank all of you who took the time to read early drafts of this book and who offered much-needed guidance, insight, and encouragement: Kate Flora and Susan Oleksiw, naturally, and also Paula Munier – your editorial expertise was crucial in polishing this rough stone and making it shine.

# About the Author

Skye Alexander is the author of more than 40 fiction and nonfiction books. Her stories have appeared in anthologies internationally and her work has been translated into more than a dozen languages. In 2003, Skye co-founded Level Best Books with fellow authors Kate Flora and Susan Oleksiw. After spending thirty-one years in Massachusetts, she now lives in Texas with her black Manx cat Zoe.

Author Website: www.skyealexander.com

# Also by Skye Alexander

Series Title: The Lizzie Crane Series

1. *Never Try to Catch a Falling Knife*

2. *What the Walls Know* (scheduled for publication summer 2022)

3. *The Goddess of Shipwrecked Sailors* (scheduled for publication summer 2023)

www.ingramcontent.com/pod-product-compliance
Lightning Source LLC
Chambersburg PA
CBHW020624110726
47899CB00002B/646